LUCKY KNOT OR NOT

ELIOT GRAYSON

Cover and title typography by Natasha Snow Designs

Published by Smoking Teacup Books
Los Angeles, California
ISBN: 9798340367648

Chapter 1

"It's the glitter, that's why I make more tips," I explained, for the thousandth freaking time, and I couldn't quite keep the snap out of my voice. On another night, the solid stack of cash in my hand would've had me in an unshakeable state of Zen. But not today. "Girls love shiny things," I went on, trying to keep it light. It was that or start snarling. "They're like corvids."

"Cor—what the fuck?" Dominic glared up at me from where he lounged on the old leather couch in the corner.

Gross. Even in my current state of financial panic, I wouldn't have sat on that thing bare-assed in only Dominic's silver lamé jock strap for twice the money in my hand. I might be a stripper myself, and currently liberally dusted with iridescent sparkles that transferred to every surface in the most annoying way, but I knew what some of the guys did on that couch—like rubbing their sweaty naked asses on it, just to start with—and I had some standards, thanks.

We'd retreated to the locker room for a few minutes, both done with our first sets for the night. I'd wanted to stash my take so far, and Dominic had declared that he needed a break from entertaining the clientele on the floor, because it wasn't worth his time. While he was being more of a dick about it than necessary, it had actually been a pretty slow evening. We'd had one super enthusiastic bachelorette party, the source of my pile of tips, but they'd moved on to other venues. Besides that, none of our regulars had come in, and on a Tuesday in mid-January there weren't many conventions or tourists in town.

Nothing to write home about, in short.

If I'd been inclined to write home about my job at all. But my parents had a short list of occupations they considered respectable enough for a member of our family, and coating myself in body glitter to get groped by screaming drunk girls didn't qualify. As far as they knew, I'd moved to Vegas to work in the accounting department of the Morrigan casino.

Of course, they also thought, in no particular order, that I'd finished the bachelor's degree in economics that would've qualified me for such a job, that I'd paid off the wasted college loans they'd cosigned for with money earned from gainful employment and not borrowed from a loan shark, and that I would never in a million years have taken out a high-interest credit card so that my now-ex-girlfriend could get a boob job.

I mean, fuck, I didn't even particularly *like* huge breasts.

If my mom found out the truth…it'd start with her tail twitching, something she could somehow pull off even in her human form. Her green eyes would get that feral gleam. A hint of fang—and then the storm would break, and she'd bite my head off. Not literally, if I was lucky, but then my dad would start in on what was left of me.

No, I had to avoid that at all costs. Being a fully grown thirty-one-year-old man and an alpha gave me no edge at all in that scenario. Neither of my parents had alpha magic, and they'd still kick my ass. Worse, they'd be so disappointed, and it'd break my heart. Even worse than worse, they didn't have any assets except their house…

"What's a cor-thing?" Dominic went on, startling me into blinking back to reality, the glare of the ceiling lights and the crumpled texture of the damp bills I held, the bass pumping through the walls and vibrating the floor. They had it cranked up to a level that seemed exciting for humans who'd been pounding shots, which meant more than loud enough for alpha shifter ears to be ringing.

But that was what I'd signed up for. What I had to do to pay my ever-mounting debts in a way that waiting tables and construction work and a brief stint as a delivery driver hadn't accomplished. I ignored him and started to count again, the music and my edginess making it hard to focus.

He didn't take the hint. "Tony? Hey, Earth to Tony! Is that slang for like, a drunk bridesmaid?"

Okay, what? That was enough to have me looking up after all. Over three hundred so far, and he'd made me fucking lose count *again*.

"Slang for a drunk bridesmaid? Corvid? Does that sound like—why would I say 'girls are like drunk bridesmaids,' Dominic? Drunk bridesmaids *are* girls. It's a whatchamacallit, there's a logical fallacy in there somewhere."

He glared at me, eyes glowing faintly golden, but it didn't impress me much. See above: the silver lamé jock strap that had one of his perfectly shaven balls sort of sliding out the side in a goofy-looking way, not to mention how he was sprawled across that disgusting body-oil-and-spunk-tainted couch in a smelly locker room.

Plus, Dominic was only a werewolf. An alpha werewolf, sure, but anyone who said shifters didn't have an interspecies hierarchy was trying to make our culture sound a whole lot more egalitarian than it really was. They should try walking into a werewolf bar and saying, *Hi, I'm an alpha gerbil*, see how that worked out.

Aside from the jock strap, Dominic might've been more intimidating than your average, or even above-average, gerbil.

But nah.

"We're all alphas here, that's kind of the point," I gritted out. My claws itched at my fingertips, but I kept it under control. A year and change of working at Lucky or Knot had kind of burned out my *other alphas need to be put in their place* instincts. "Don't waste your time."

Dominic made a sound somewhere between a grunt and a scoff and then pointedly held eye contact with me while he pushed his errant testicle back into its shiny hammock.

I couldn't help it; despite everything, I started to laugh. Dominic's face went red and his eyes glowed brighter, and I gave up on getting a few minutes of relative peace and quiet. Back to the floor it was, where at least the bachelorettes wouldn't stick their hands in their underwear while they stared at me in a pathetic attempt at displaying dominance—and would get kicked out if they did.

Anyway, I needed to make some bank this week, or that nightmare of my parents finding out about my situation would come true. Louie had called me earlier in the day, threatening to start calling them and harassing them for the money if I didn't start paying up. He knew damn well that breaking my kneecaps wouldn't accomplish anything, because I'd heal quickly enough to chase down his goons and beat the shit out of them before they could even get back in the car.

But if he got my family involved...

They'd sell the house to pay my debts. They'd feel like they had to. Which meant Louie had me by the balls.

Stashing the money in my magically secured locker only took a few seconds, and then I adjusted myself in my own faux-leather pants and headed out, ignoring Dominic grumbling behind me.

I had to brace myself before I opened the door from the back hallway to the main floor, and even so, the wall of sound that smacked into me nearly knocked the pleasant smile I'd plastered onto my face right back off of it.

In my absence, a few more patrons had trickled in. Like most all-male clubs, we kept the main floor female-only except when we had a pre-booked male group to fill it up, but the upper level had a few more men sitting there than before. One previously empty table held a wide-eyed, clean-cut trio in polo shirts, none of whom looked old enough to drink. But they must've been, because they'd gotten in, and our bouncers were good about checking ID.

Fuck, I really didn't want to go flex my muscles and leer at kids. No matter how much I desperately needed the money, I'd feel dirtier than that couch. But the other guys besides me and Dominic who were on the floor were already pouring champagne and strutting their stuff and flirting. No one was performing on the smaller stage upstairs at the moment, either, so the guys up there only had their more distant view of Cassidy on the main stage to keep them entertained.

As I hesitated by the hallway door, trying to work up the willpower to go up the stairs and do my job, Dominic pushed past me and took the steps two at a time, muttering something about easy money and how he'd show me.

Jesus Christ, what a douchebag. The bouncer stationed on the landing pulled a face at me as Dominic passed him, and I shook my head in answer.

As I watched Dominic saunter over to their table, the three young guys went from wide-eyed to bug-eyed. Fair enough. Dominic might be nothing like my type, but I could see the objective appeal, at least before he opened his mouth and started talking: he was over six feet of tanned alpha muscle, and the silver really stood out against his skin. I tended to stick to darker colors, myself. My natural tone glowed in the dark, unless you counted the freckles, and the one time I'd tried the fake tanning thing…well, red hair, golden-orange eyes, and orangey-bronze skin didn't go together.

To say the least.

When I'd come into the club the day after the spray tan, the bartender had screamed like a little girl when he saw me. That seemed like a hint to take the week off and buy some exfoliant.

The song playing ended with a final flurry of drumbeats, quickly drowned out by hooting and applause. I glanced over at the stage. Cassidy had been performing, and he grinned and bowed and scooped up money and the discarded bits of his firefighter costume, his bare buttocks glistening.

Dammit. We'd told him so many freaking times not to use that much oil on the stage. The next guy was going to slip and fall down on his own shiny ass one of these days. Since we were all alpha shifters, none of us would get seriously hurt, but no one wanted to look like a fucking idiot in the middle of a dance.

A bit of motion in my peripheral vision caught my eye: Scott beckoning me over to his DJ booth against the wall. I headed his way, pausing only to flex my arm muscles and smile flirtatiously at a couple of women at a nearby table. One of the other guys was already hanging out, but hey, two of them, two of us, maybe? And they had a bottle of the expensive bubbly in an ice bucket. They might be good tippers.

Louie's remembered laughter rang in my ears. Fucker enjoyed twisting the knife, maybe even more than he enjoyed getting his money back with interest.

I should've gone upstairs and milked it with those pretty little probably-college boys, damn it all. They were probably going to get sucked in by Dominic's smarmy charm and lured back to a VIP room.

Hopefully no one would get sucked *off* in the process, but I wouldn't put it past him. Dominic claimed to prefer women, but he had a few regulars who sucked his cock and paid generously for the privilege, and he was always open for new opportunities.

And while I liked blowjobs—in both directions, in fact—as much as the next sexually omnivorous alpha, and had been told more than once that the raspy texture of my tongue could send a sensitive recipient into the stratosphere, I never got that physical with customers. Just not a line I was willing to cross.

Whatever. Dominic wasn't my problem, thank every deity above and below, because I had enough of my own—and I wouldn't have wanted to be responsible for him even if I was bored.

The booth didn't have a ton of space in it, but I managed to wedge myself inside and push the door closed behind me, shutting out a lot of the noise with it.

Scott looked up from adjusting some kind of switch on the board in front of him, and a club favorite with a catchy beat started playing out on the floor. He had his headphones on one ear and off the other, and his sweaty black hair stood up in spiky tufts. One of the only humans in the place, and he looked more like a hedgehog than anything else.

"I know you just got off stage less than an hour ago," he said, "but Morgan's supposed to go on, and he's in the back. Actually, peek into room three if you walk by. Kind of an odd couple. Married, I think? I'm not sure which one of them wanted to come here, they both seemed weird about it. Whatever, they were tipping a lot."

Scott's gossip washed over me, but I nodded, actually kind of relieved. Going around and making nice with people at tables, or trying to get them to do a private session, sounded exhausting. Dominic's irritating conversation had been the cherry on top of my stressed-out sundae.

"I don't mind dancing again," I said. "I'll be ready in like two minutes."

"You gonna change?" he asked, looking me up and down. In addition to the pleather pants, which still showed the thick bulge between my legs just fine, I had heavy boots, and also a sparkly black G-string under the pants, although he couldn't see that. My chest was bare, except for the glitter. "Or you want to just do Closer?"

My usual persona was a lot goofier and more fun than that, and people loved it. My Nicki Minaj routine got a lot of cheers, especially the getting on the floor—and sometimes I even got everyone to do the hands up to touch the sky part, if I really worked the crowd. Once they waved their money in the air, they felt stupid not tossing it on the stage afterward.

But yeah. Tonight, Closer would fit my mood a lot better. Besides, I really didn't feel like getting dressed up in anything fun. For this song, I could rip the pants off during the song's first chorus, right on "closer to God"—they had Velcro down the inseams, because I liked the quick, hard reveal—and then use my boots, G-string, and my very own claws, fangs, and glowing eyes for the rest of the "costume." After all, that was why people came to Lucky or Knot in the first place. We were the only all-alpha strip club in the world, as far as I knew. And people went pretty nuts for it. When Vegas wasn't in a slump like it was now, we always packed the house.

Declan MacKenna, who owned the Morrigan casino on the Strip and this place and who knew what else, was a fucking visionary. If I had half his intellect and acumen, I wouldn't have been about to lose my parents' house because of a college loan I'd wasted by not graduating and a 28 percent APR on a pair of fake tits for a girl who'd cheated on me.

Fuck. Deep breaths.

"Tony? You okay?" Scott said, and I shook my head to clear it a bit and forced another smile. "I can have Dom go on if you're not. It's cool, dude. You look out of it."

"I'm good. No, really." I punched him on the shoulder—

lightly, because human. "Seriously. Thank you. Closer's perfect. Give me a minute, okay?"

I slipped out of the booth before he could keep questioning me and headed for the same door I'd come out of a few minutes ago, on my way to the locker room and then backstage.

It only took me the promised minute to get myself ready: a little more glitter, silver and black this time to fit the song's darker fantasy, and some leather armbands, because why the fuck not.

Scott announced me as I jogged up the short flight of backstage stairs, and then I was under the lights and center stage, the distinctive staticky opening beat of the song accompanying me.

Fluid movements, getting them enticed, prowling…I'd started stripping simply because it paid the best out of the jobs that depended mostly on my having muscles for days.

But when the audience stopped their conversations mid-sentence, their drinks held poised in the air as they forgot to take a sip, their eyes fixed on me with complete focus…well, that gave me a certain amount of satisfaction. Not an erotic type of satisfaction— luckily, because Nevada law wouldn't let me take everything off on the stage in a club that served alcohol, and some genius in a bureaucratic hellhole somewhere had decided that erections, even clothed, counted as nudity.

So since attention didn't really turn me on, it didn't take me too much effort to keep my cock under control, and honestly, not to brag or anything, but even totally flaccid it made itself known under any type of fabric.

But the crowd's reaction did give me a bit of a frisson, a charge of energy that fed my alpha shifter magic. My eyes started to glow, and my claws were a millimeter from sliding out. My gums tingled where my fangs wanted to drop.

My hips gyrated, Trent Reznor rasped his way through those X-rated lyrics, and I reached down, groping my groin, really massaging my balls, getting more than a few gasps and little screams from the audience. Someone right up front had already thrown a handful of fives, fucking sweet.

And even sweeter, those guys up above were hanging over the railing with their mouths wide open, a scowling and ignored

Dominic standing behind them with his hands on his hips. Ha! I resisted the urge to blow him a kiss.

I turned my back to the audience right as the first chorus started and spread my legs wider, ready for the reveal, getting my fingers in position to yank off the pants...

...And then, as if Scott had flipped one of his switches, Trent's voice faded into a meaningless hum, the noise of the crowd became a murmur, and the lights on me seemed to dim. My body froze, fingers rigidly digging into my thigh.

Jesus fucking Christ, that was...

The scent of love, of home, of desire and want. It washed over me, teasing me, wrapping around all my alpha senses: wild, fresh, tantalizing, a sweet-tart aroma, lemon blossoms and honeysuckle and oxalis flowers, like my parents had in their garden.

It stirred a hopeless craving in a part of me that I usually suppressed in order to get along in society: my instinct to hunt and capture and claim and possess, to have something that was *mine*. Some*one*, actually. Someone as beautiful and alluring and sweet as that scent...

All the hair on the back of my neck stood up, and my cock was trying to get hard, pushing insistently against the G-string, throbbing as if in response to a physical touch. My claws pushed out, my fangs dropping. My heart pounded.

Fuck. This wasn't natural or normal.

It had to be magic. Literally. Someone was using magic on me. But fucking why? I didn't have any enemies that I knew of. Or stalkers, either.

A prank? Had Dominic hired a warlock or someone to hide out in the audience and screw with me and ruin my dance, or worse, make me flip out and get fired? Or even arrested?

No. Hell no. Damn it, I'd been doing this and doing it well for three years, and I could do it now, no matter how tantalizing that scent might be.

I forced my brain and body to reboot almost instantly, barely missing a beat of the song, quickly enough that no one probably even noticed. But as the music blared into full volume again, and the lights flashed in my eyes, and I tore my pants off in one go to a shrieking wave of applause—seriously, fuck you, Dominic—and spun around to show off the front of my G-string and its alpha bulge, the combo of being angry, off-kilter, and drenched in that magical scent slammed into me all at once.

More critically, my foot found the body oil residue on the floor at the same instant.

My leg flew out from underneath me as I flung my pants aside, and I went straight down and landed on my alpha ass with a thud that shook the whole stage.

A tiger. Tripping on his own feet and falling over.

I'd never live this down.

The hate that it brings, Trent wailed.

Truer words. I was going to stuff Cassidy's body oil bottle down his throat, or maybe up his ass, and then I'd fucking kill him.

Right after I got up off my own ass and figured out who'd brought that incredibly distracting magic into the club, and fucking killed *them*.

Damn it.

Chapter 2

Scrambling to my knees only took a moment, but that was long enough to catch a glimpse of Dominic going all red and doubling over laughing amidst a sea of open mouths and wide eyes.

Oh, I'd be killing him too, whether or not he had any hand in this. Bastard.

I rolled to my feet and pulled a funny face, hoping to convince the audience, at least, to laugh with me instead of at me.

Dominic would be laughing at me until the heat death of the universe. Or until I killed him.

At least my embarrassment and annoyance kept me from popping the world's most prominent and illegal erection as I focused on circling my hips and strutting my stuff again. It wasn't easy. That magical scent had tensed all my muscles and set my heart racing, my whole body ready for action. Shifters, alphas especially, had a lot of strengths. Literal strength, for one, and sharp senses, not to mention the even sharper claws and fangs.

But we had a secret we tried to hide from the world at large: our instincts enslaved us in a way no other beings had to cope with. If I lost my cool, I'd do it spectacularly.

On the other hand, I was an adult, and a professional, and I forced myself to channel my body's reaction into displaying my claws and fangs and glowing eyes, giving my mostly human audience the thrilling edge of erotic danger they'd come to Lucky or Knot to experience.

Right below, a cluster of women threw bills at the stage, and I gyrated my hips in their direction, flexing my muscles and my claws. More money rained down.

The part of the song with lyrics was almost over, which meant Scott would be fading it out soon, thank the gods. My hip-thrusting bump-and-grind, aimed at the women paying me for my time, was taking a lot more effort than it should, and I desperately needed a few minutes of quiet to simmer down and get myself under control.

I gathered up my money, bowed and waved, and smiled and flexed some more, bulging my biceps and rippling my eight-pack.

When I sucked in a deep breath, that scent hit me again, a thread of almost unbearable freshness in the sweat-and-booze-and-sex reek that always pervaded the club, no matter how powerful the air conditioning system might be.

My cock stiffened again. Shit, I had to get off stage before I got myself fired after all. With a last flourishing bow, and a waggle of my ass at the particularly appreciative group down in front, I scooped up my pants and booked it down the stairs.

I slumped against the wall in the little hallway, breathing deep, grateful for once for the stale reek of concrete permeated with decades of cigarette smoke that characterized the area backstage. It almost completely drowned out the mysterious scent. One breath, two, and I let my head fall back as some of the tension drained out of me and common sense flowed back in to take its place.

Someone trying to sabotage my dance seemed ridiculously unlikely.

So a prank, probably. Jesus. Why couldn't people just act their ages?

Prank or not, though, I had to head out to the floor. Immediately after a dance was the best time to mingle in the crowd and hopefully capitalize on their enthusiasm, turn on the charm and get a few private or semi-private dances, make the real money.

Louie's deadline…

Of course, thinking about that wouldn't help me bring my blood pressure down.

Another deep breath, a flex of my claws to stretch my ligaments before I retracted them, and I pushed off the wall and went to toss my pants and my stage money into my locker.

As I slammed it shut, footsteps came down the hall, and one of the bouncers stuck his head in.

"Guy's in room four hoping you'll come and join him," he said. "He put half an hour totally private with a bottle of champagne on his card already, so maybe he'll be good for more. You up for it?"

A guy in a room who'd already paid even though he didn't know if I'd want to do a private dance—or anything else. Yeah, not suspicious at all after what had just happened. Too good to be true, actually.

Noah might be big, built, and not a total idiot, but he was also human, with a human's limited sense of smell and insensitivity to magic. He wouldn't be able to tell me anything useful about whoever had asked for me, so I'd be going in clueless.

Fuck it. Curiosity and the possibility of a good night's pay won out over my reluctance to give whoever was screwing with me what he wanted. I could practically hear my father's voice in my head: "Don't argue with morons, Tuncay. It only makes you stupid, but it doesn't make them any smarter." When he had some serious wisdom to impart to me, Dad used my traditional Turkish name instead of the American alternative he and Mom had given me as a middle name. I always kind of wished they'd been more familiar with their new home's pop culture before they named me, but too late now.

Anyway, engaging with someone who pulled childish pranks was the definition of getting stupider, but I'd never claimed to be a genius in the first place.

"Be right there."

Noah nodded and left, and I took a second to put my pants back on before I followed him. After all, you never knew. This guy might be totally legit, and he'd pay more to get me to take them back off again.

But the second I pushed open the door to the private room, I *knew*. That perfect scent wafted out as if blown on a sweet spring breeze, and for an instant, I was standing in an orchard, surrounded by fresh grass and bees and apple blossoms.

I blinked away the madness, strode through the door, and shoved it closed behind me with way too much force, irritation eroding my usual self-control.

This room was the smallest one, designed to hold one or two customers and one stripper, max—one large stripper, given the club's theme. But even though the guy who jumped up, startled, from the L-shaped padded bench as I came in barely qualified as normal-sized, the room felt even smaller than usual. His mouth-watering scent surrounded me, along with the faint tingling skin-prickle of his magic.

Long, glossy black hair, sheened faintly pink by the room's low red lighting, pale skin tinted rosy, and jet-black eyes gone wide and glossy. Slim, dressed all in black from the high collar of his shirt down to the tight fit of his capri pants and...

And...

I should've done my job and seduced money out of him, or subtly asked him about his scent, or tried to work out if he and Dominic were in cahoots.

Instead: "Who the fuck comes to a strip club in stripper heels?" I demanded, totally and uncontrollably nonplussed.

Also, horribly aroused.

His nails sported some subtle pastel color where they peeked out of his open-toe pumps, and I'd never once in my entire freaking life been a foot guy, but his toes were so slim and delicate and his ankles looked breakable, and let's be honest here. Anyone who smelled like he did? I'd have sucked any part of their bodies, including toes. Maybe starting with toes and working my way up. I wouldn't mind being on my knees.

How did he not topple over in heels like that, let alone leap up from a seat without wobbling even a little bit? And how gods-damned short would he be without them, when he only came up to my chin wearing the things?

On my knees, I'd still have sucking access to at least three quarters of his body.

"Maybe I'm here to audition," he said, his voice as light and sweet-tart as his scent, laced with a thread of...amusement? "I wouldn't even fall over. You're wearing combat boots. What's your excuse?"

That snapped my gaze back up to his face. My fists clenched at my sides, my claws poking out enough to prick my skin.

"What's my…" I trailed off into something like a snarl. My excuse. My excuse! Another step forward, and now the room really felt claustrophobic. Probably more so for him, because no one could loom like a pissed-off alpha. I had to be twice as wide as him. Maybe more.

A flash of something like *oh, shit* passed over his pointy little face, and his eyes went slightly, impossibly wider, arched brows rising.

But he stood his ground, maybe because even someone with extraordinary balance couldn't back up in those shoes without doing an unintentional somersault into the champagne on the table behind him.

At this distance, I could smell the actual warmth of his skin underlying that magical scent. And I could feel him against my own skin, the energy of him, the frisson of another body's pulse and electricity.

He bit his lip, a very pearly tooth digging into a flower-petal lower lip.

Jesus, he had to be using some kind of illusion on top of whatever seduction magic he had going on. Didn't he? For one thing, he might be disguising the scent of his magic. Usually I could distinguish types of magic by their top notes, like perfumes, but his had me confused. He could be a human warlock, or something not human at all.

But seriously, no one looked or smelled like this naturally, right? If Dominic was responsible for setting me up for this nonsense, there'd be nowhere on Earth he could hide.

By the way my mystery man's eyes were darting to the side, he'd realized he had nowhere to hide, either, and a tendon stood out in his slender neck.

Damn it.

"I'm not going to hurt you," I said, and forced myself to take that step back that he couldn't. I'd almost lost my temper, and that hadn't happened in years, even working with Dominic. For an alpha, I was almost stolid. "You're a paying customer, after all."

My little attempt at humor fell so flat I could almost hear it thud into the floor. His eyes narrowed slightly. The pink lighting nearly drowned out the flush on his face, but I could smell the heat of his skin increasing, a fresh waft of his sweetness in the stale air.

"So far only for the bartender," he said. "But I, ah. I. Ah."

His shifty gaze lingered on something off in the corner of the room rather than on me. Huh. You had to be really nervous about making eye contact not to keep your attention fixed on the enormous predator confronting you in an extremely enclosed space.

Also, he had to have noticed the rampant, straining erection that no Nevada law could possibly have kept in check at this point. That likely added to the threatening quality of my presence, even though I didn't mean it that way. I liked to think of my big alpha cock and knot as more of a promise.

"A E I O U," I suggested, a bit breathless myself. "You? Ah? Sometimes Y?"

That earned me a sharp flick of his gaze and a twist of his lips that could've been meant as a sneer, but ended up looking more like a soft, kissable pout.

"You don't need to make fun of me," he said softly, with a flutter of his very long, feathery eyelashes.

Oh, for—Christ. My mouth opened, with something like, *Will you knock it off, I work here, not you, so stop it with the magical seduction routine* ready to come out.

But for a miracle, my brain managed to hang on to a tiny bit of the blood flow that'd mostly rushed south to make me stupid. He might be using magic on me, but he had paid up. I needed the money more than I needed to vent my irritation.

So I could play along, right? That would be the potentially profitable thing to do, wouldn't it?

Somewhere in the back of my lust-clouded mind, a voice whispered that I never crossed the line with clients. And that while a bit of playing along was part of the job, I was always the one in control...and I'd never felt less in control of a situation than I did now. If this pretty little magical whoever-he-was followed through on any of the suggestions his gleaming eyes and softly parted lips were silently making to me, I ran the risk of knotting my tear-away pleather pants.

Okay, I'd be playing along, at least for now, and pretending otherwise would only be lying to myself. Fine. But was I playing along with some fantasy of his, a prank like I still half thought, or with my own magically stimulated libido?

Only one way to find out, I guessed.

I shifted my weight forward again, leaning, not quite moving yet—but finding a middle ground.

"I'm only teasing," I said, letting my voice drop to its lowest, raspiest register. "Maybe I like that you're flustered. It's flattering."

His blush deepened, spreading down his neck, a scarlet stain on his white skin. I didn't know the name for the type of collar his shirt had, but it had a sort of rim that stuck up to the middle of his slim throat. Not a turtleneck, but more like what you'd see on one of those embroidered silk outfits Chinese aristocrats wore in old photos. It had a button at the front that my fingers itched to undo, to see how far down the blush went.

"I'm not flustered," he protested unconvincingly. Hmm. Humans could lie, while some nonhumans could and others couldn't. But this bit of untruth didn't prove anything either way. As long as you believed what you said, technically you were telling the truth. Did he honestly think he was fooling himself, let alone me? His gaze snapped up to meet mine at last, eyes all wide. "I'm perfectly calm!"

He so wasn't. Odd, because he'd seemed calm enough when I walked in. It was when we'd talked about him being a paying customer that he'd started to get ruffled, now that I thought about it.

Huh. Jesus. Maybe his credit card was going to decline and this would be a big fat waste of time.

I took that step forward again after all, because why not? And I wanted him to really lose his cool, if only because he seemed likelier to start stammering out some explanation for what the hell he'd been doing to me.

"Oh yeah? I can see your pulse in the side of your neck. Pounding away." Another small step put me right in his personal space, enough that he had to tip his head back to keep looking at me. "Maybe you want me to do some things to get you even more worked up, huh? Or maybe you want to get me worked up? I can sit down and let you do that audition. You want to show me how you can dance in those heels?" As an experiment, I added, "Put your money where your mouth is."

His whole body tensed, and his eyes flitted away from mine again.

Bingo, and the satisfaction of being right gave me a momentary sense of smugness.

But figuring out his problem somehow revolved around money didn't help me much. And anyway...like, join the club, dude.

Whatever, no matter how attractive this guy might be, and no matter how much magic he'd used on me to make himself appear that way, I had a loan shark to pay. If he hoped that seducing me would get me to give him perks for free, I had to shut that shit down.

Playing along stopped as soon as he didn't pay. No exceptions.

"I can dance instead," I suggested—reluctantly, because now that I had the image of him writhing in my lap, all covered up in his ridiculously modest clothes but wearing those even more ridiculous shoes, flushed and flustered, neither of my heads were letting go of it easily. "Since we're back here where it's nice and private, I can do a little more than I did on stage. Forty for the first song, but if you want to keep going, that can be thirty each for the next couple of dances."

I gave him my smirkiest, most suggestive smile, and his eyes flicked up. His chest visibly rose and fell now, and his pulse had gone wild. Was he hard? If I stepped back and took a good look I'd be able to tell, but from this angle I couldn't be sure.

His tongue flicked out to moisten his lower lip, and...no, I had to have imagined the slight fork at the tip, right?

Christ, what had I gotten myself into?

"Do you want a dance or not?" The words came out a lot more harshly than I'd intended, and definitely not in a customer-friendly tone. I should've taken the night off. Had a couple of beers. Watched some hockey. Simple, dammit. I liked my life *simple*.

Not infested with forked-tongued magic stripper-wannabes who made me fall down on my ass on stage and then got me all hot and bothered.

He pressed his lips together and cocked his head, and then nodded once, like a man—almost man-shaped being?—who'd made up his mind.

"No," he said at last, and then, "No, I don't," more firmly. "I don't want a dance. Not because you fell down!" he added hurriedly, in what appeared to be an attempt at tact, and then even more hurriedly, probably because I couldn't help the low growl that curled out from between my teeth: "Not that it was, um, it was a great dance. Very seductive. That's why I'm here, in this private room with you," he finished triumphantly, and pasted on an obviously forced smile.

"Okay," I said, with all the patience I could muster. Beer. Hockey. Or, failing that, a normal paying client. Fuck. Fine, forget patience. And forget customer service. "If you don't want a dance, why are you back here? You wanna talk or something? Or just drink the overpriced champagne? I don't have any drugs, but I don't care if you want to do some, but I charge the same to watch you do lines as I do to dance, FYI. Double if you want to do it off my abs."

That was a request I'd gotten surprisingly often. Or maybe not so surprisingly, considering that more than half the people who came in here, no matter what sex or species, had gotten all their ideas of what you did in a strip club from watching shitty movies.

He blinked at me, his mouth falling open. "Ugh! Seriously?" he asked, his voice going up a startled octave. "By the time you scraped it together, it'd be half glitter!"

That startled a laugh out of me, because...agreed, it would be, and it was indeed ugh. On my side of the equation, too.

But then my laugh turned into a choke as he reached in his pocket, whipped out a shimmering gold coin, and said, "I want you to give in to your instincts and knot me thoroughly, and I can offer you this in exchange."

Chapter 3

"The fuck you do," I wheezed, and then sucked in a deep breath, only to immediately double over coughing again as I got a whiff of the coin between his fingers.

It absolutely reeked of magic. Strong magic.

Fae magic, in fact, of the most wild and inhuman kind.

"Christ," I tried again, and then hacked, sniffed, and pushed off my knees to stand upright again.

Blinking to clear my watering eyes, I examined him through this new lens. Yeah. Fairy absolutely fit. Short, slim, unearthly beauty, the too-wide eyes and the glossy black hair color that I'd assumed came from an expensive salon and instead had actually grown that way. Plus, super fucking weird. Fairies always were.

Like any shifter with a functioning nose, I could usually pick one out of a crowd, but his scent wasn't like anything I'd ever encountered. At least this explained the tongue.

The coin gleamed a rich, pure yellow-gold even in the pink lighting, taking on no hue whatsoever. My fairy would-be john's thumb partially obscured the side facing me, but an intricate raised design peeked out, maybe outspread wings.

"Well?" he said, and I tore my eyes away from the glittering thing and back to his face. "What do you think of my offer?"

His offer. Right.

At least now I knew I didn't need to blame Dominic for this.

This little fairy asshole had been using magic to entice me so that I'd want to accept his "offer" of fucking for money. The fall on stage must've been an accidental side effect—which meant I'd still need to kill Cassidy for the body oil thing. But that hadn't been malicious on his part, I didn't think.

Besides, I was pretty sure he'd put on his apparent bravado like his clothes. The arm holding the coin upraised had the very slightest tremor. Had he used his magic in order to boost his own confidence? Could he be incredibly ugly underneath an illusion of beauty, and self-conscious about it? Unable to get laid any other way?

Maybe if I'd been new to my profession I'd have been surprised, shocked, or more pissed off. But aside from the fairy magic thing, which was a new one in the annals of club clients trying to pay for sex…yeah, I'd been here before. Many, many times.

So my tone was more resigned than anything as I said, "What do you think I think of your offer? I'm a stripper, not a prostitute, dude. I don't do that."

His lips tightened, and his chin jutted out stubbornly. "You sell your body every day. How is this different?"

"I'm looking at your face right now. If I rubbed my hand all over it, how would that be any different? Right? Come on. Don't be an asshole. I'll dance for you, or let you dance for me, or some other stuff you can probably think of, but that's not in my repertoire."

"*Repertoire*'s a fancy word for someone who tripped and fell on his behind while performing a Nine Inch Nails song," he snapped, lifting that small chin another couple of degrees.

Oh, for—and here I'd been making excuses for him in my head, trying to give him the benefit of the doubt!

"Okay," I snarled, stepping forward again, hands on my hips and totally done with the Mr. Nice Guy routine. "Yeah, maybe it is. But *behind*'s a pretty fucking prissy euphemism for someone who's trying to trade shitty fairy trash for getting knotted by a glittery stripper!"

"Oh!" he gasped. "Shitty fairy—how dare you!"

"How dare *I*?" I demanded back. "You're trying to pay me to knot you. One of us is being crass, and it isn't me. You could at least offer actual cash, not whatever the fuck that is. I mean, that's doubly insulting."

"This," he said with as much dignity as a fairy trying to pay a weretiger for sex in the seedy back room of a strip club could muster—surprisingly, more than zero, "is pure gold, worth thousands of human dollars. That means nothing to me, of course, as I can get as much gold as I like." He shrugged. "I gather you've figured out what I am?"

"Yes, and I also know that your kind aren't exactly honest when you make bargains, and your 'gold' tends to not stay that way."

As the words left my lips, it dawned on me that what I'd said sounded a lot less like absolute refusal on any terms, and a lot more like negotiating.

Damn. It really did. His magic had gotten to me, because my body definitely liked the idea of his offer, even if my mind had more sense.

Maybe he wouldn't notice.

He sighed heavily and shook his head. "There's no need for rude stereotypes," he said chidingly, "and I give you my word that this coin is truly made of gold. I don't have access to any cash that's not traceable in ways I don't want it to be, and I'm assuming you don't want to use any other method that's traceable to you, either? Since we're discussing price now, aren't we?"

Well, double damn. He might be weird, but he didn't seem to be stupid. And for a fairy, giving his word meant something. The coin was really gold, and even though I didn't know a lot about precious metals, yeah, that had to be an ounce or two, and I'd lived in Vegas for long enough to have the contacts to sell it for close to what it was actually worth. The workmanship and its fairy provenance might drive the price up, too.

Fairy provenance.

And the beautiful, tempting little fairy offering it to me. Tempting, because he'd made himself that way. I might not even want him naturally, and I had no idea how much of what I was seeing, smelling, and feeling was real.

Oh, this coin and its owner were bad news. Very, very bad

news, that'd pay Louie off for the time being and buy me another couple of months of breathing room. During that couple of months of grace, I could work double shifts and shake my ass like I'd never shaken it before.

It didn't really matter if I wanted him of my own free will, did it? As long as I knew it might not be real and made the conscious choice not to care?

Thousands of dollars. And the chance to satisfy this ache, this gnawing physical craving that had been building, naturally or not, since the moment I first scented him.

A good fuck. Paying off Louie. A turn in my luck, maybe, and all because of a weird fairy's weird whim.

But that didn't mean I had to be completely stupid about it.

"Yeah," I admitted after a second. "Yeah, I guess we are. But it's not just the price. I don't trust you. Why me?"

"Honestly?"

"No, please lie to me."

"There's no need to be sarcastic," he sniffed, and tossed his head, his glossy hair rippling like something out of a vaguely R-rated shampoo commercial.

It hit me all of a sudden that when—if, dammit, if—I took his offer, which I couldn't really believe I'd basically committed to doing, I'd be able to wrap my hand in that smooth shiny waterfall of hair. Around and around. Tug his head back with it. Unbutton his collar.

Bite my way down his throat while I...

"Mmmph," I said, biting back a real groan. Knot my pants. That's what I would do.

Christ, I needed to fuck him and get this magic out of my system.

His brows furrowed. "Are you quite well? Did you hurt yourself when you fell down? You're an alpha, aren't you? Don't you heal?"

The knee-jerk response came out before I could stop it. "I'll show you how much of an alpha I am."

"Good," he said sweetly. "Then let's get out of here."

Get out of here. Go to...not my apartment, I knew better than to take a fairy home with me. Somehow I also knew he wouldn't be taking me to wherever he called home, either. A hotel, maybe? He'd better be paying for it. The club was plenty staffed for the night, and it was getting late anyway. We could head out to wherever he had in mind once I had a quick word with Scott and let him know I wouldn't be on stage anymore.

But I'd asked him...my head spun. A question. I blinked, and he faded in and out. Magic sucked so hard.

"Why me?" I dug my claws into my palms a bit, and the sting cleared my head. "Straight answer, or no deal."

"I lost a bet with a friend," he said after a noticeable hesitation, his eyes darting away again. Hopefully he never played poker, because he had more tells than a drunk frat boy on his first trip to Vegas. This one, in my limited experience, seemed to indicate discomfort and embarrassment. "I'm not sure if you know what happens to my kind when we fail to carry out an obligation, but it's deeply unplea—anyway, that doesn't matter to you. All that matters is that this seemed like a more or less safe place to find a suitable alpha. And you were the first one who caught my eye. It was difficult to overlook your performance."

Right. He probably figured I'd be the most desperate, since I couldn't even get through a dance without slipping on a banana peel—although that had been his fault in the first place, for having the most distracting scent on Earth.

Not that I'd be telling him that. He didn't seem like a guy whose ego needed a whole lot of stroking, especially since he didn't seem inclined to stroke mine in return.

Because rephrasing his fairy weaseling as bluntly as possible, he'd picked me to fuck him because he'd probably die horribly if he didn't, and he thought I might be enough of a sad sack to take whatever he paid me.

How fucking flattering.

That said, however much it stung, he wasn't completely wrong.

"Fine," I said shortly. "Wait for me in the parking lot out back. You drive here?"

"We can walk to the hotel." I suppressed a growl. The details of his transportation didn't matter, particularly, but I'd started getting annoyed by the way he tended to answer a different question than the one I'd asked. "I booked a room at that place with the big palm trees around the corner. It didn't look like we'd get lice from walking in the door, but otherwise, I can't make any promises."

Meh. I worked in a strip club with people like Dominic, so my standards were already a little iffy. His were guaranteed to be much higher.

Besides, he hadn't made the obvious joke about fleas that most people did when talking about shifters and potential vermin in the same sentence, and I had to give him points for that.

"I'll meet you out back in ten minutes," I said, and headed out of the room without waiting for a reply, shutting the door behind me.

I gave it fifty-fifty that he'd actually follow through after ten minutes to think better of it, and he was probably giving me the same odds.

But when I emerged from the discreet employees-only door at the corner of the building, there he was, leaning against the low cinderblock wall that divided our parking lot from the strip mall next door. Moonlight glinted blue on his hair and snowy white on his face and seemed to be absorbed into his outfit like it would into a black hole. Another slight gleam picked out his painted toenails. The whole effect unsettled me, and I actually jumped a bit when he started moving, walking toward me like something out of a particularly surreal dream.

It had all my hackles up as he fell into step with me without a word, crossing through the strip mall's parking lot and around the corner to the cheap hotel on the other side of the block.

Hopefully that was really where he meant to go, anyway. If he tried to lead me out of the mundane world, I'd be out of here, debts or no debts, painfully hard erection or not.

Past midnight in this far off-Strip area, only a few cars went by, and all the other businesses had closed. My footsteps echoed loud in the relative silence, and his high heels clicked on the pavement, a reassuringly normal sound. A chill desert wind brushed by us, and my breath came out in huge puffs of steam. Even more reassuringly, so did his.

That faint, nagging sensation of prickling wrongness didn't vanish, though.

But a quick glance around, and a deep breath to parse any scents in the air, gave me nothing at all to concern me.

By the time he pulled a key card out of his pocket and beeped open the door to a ground floor room at the back of the hotel, I'd pushed it out of my mind. Fuck it. Of course I'd feel weird about the whole situation; I was being paid to knot a fairy who'd gotten me hard with magic.

He flipped the switch by the door and bathed the drab room in equally drab yellow light: a maroon bedspread with the faint sheen of cheap polyester, chipped particle board furniture, and a dark blue carpet that, surprisingly, bore the faint imprints of an actual vacuum cleaner.

Whatever. It didn't smell any mustier than the back of the club, and shifters didn't really get human diseases. It'd take a worse breeding ground than this place to produce a fungus that could overcome my inborn healing magic.

The room had no personal touches at all except for the expensive-looking glass bottle of lube on one of the nightstands. I had to choke back a laugh. This guy really had planned ahead. How incredibly presumptuous—except that he'd had a solid gold coin and magic to back up his confidence.

Speaking of which.

The fairy stepped aside, and I followed him in and closed the door behind us with a click.

"Let's see that coin again," I said.

He nodded and fished in his pocket, and when he held out his hand the coin glittered in his palm. It looked bigger lying flat like that, and now I could see that the wings belonged to a dragon, stylized and outspread, with its tail curling around the edge of the coin and traceries filling in the rest of the design.

I reached out and took it, and he didn't stop me, though he whipped his hand away and rubbed his fingers together as I did. Huh. Well, if I worried about every weird thing he did, I'd need a therapist. It had more heft to it than I'd expected, and the warmth of it heated my hand. It'd been in his pocket this whole time absorbing his body heat, but…fuck it. Put that in the same category of things I shouldn't worry about. It felt like gold, and he'd promised me it was real in a way that would bind a fae, and more questions would be useless, anyway, I had no doubt.

I slipped the coin into my own pocket, pay rendered for expected services, no more denial possible. And there we were. Closing the door had shut out the wind and the groan of the ice machine compressor along the walkway and the idling car a few doors down. Silence fell. Near silence, anyway, since my alpha shifter ears picked up everything. But now I could hear him breathing, short, sharp little inhales and exhales, as if his apparent calm poise was nothing more than the thinnest façade.

On the walk I'd been more focused on my surroundings and my sensation of unease than on his physical presence. But now that we were alone in a private place, with the bed right there…he might not want me, particularly, but I had nothing here to distract me from how fucking badly I wanted *him*.

Would his scent intensify if I rubbed my face against the curve of his throat? Or wrapped my hands around his waist, his hips, his thighs? Maybe his breath would come even faster as I slid my palm over his cock, teasing out an erection I could fondle to full hardness as I pressed into him from behind, my own cock digging into his lower back…

"You might as well do whatever it is you're thinking about that's getting you so worked up," he said irritably, and I snapped out of it with a jolt, biting my lip to keep in the…yeah, I'd been fucking growling. Well, at least he couldn't claim he wasn't getting the alpha experience. He'd done that chin-lifting thing again, that made me want to bite his neck, and his black eyes blazed. "I'm paying you to do it, and we're here, so get it over with. Please don't trip and fall on me and mess up my clothes."

Everything around me—the faint hushing of water through the hotel's pipes, a distant siren, the turning of the gods-damned Earth—came to a halt so grinding I could feel it in my teeth.

Get it the fuck *over with?*

Don't *fall on him and mess up his clothes?*

Okay, this was some bullshit. And I'd had enough. Dominic and his metallic jock strap and his dangling hairless testicles. Cassidy and his miserable body oil addiction. Motherfucking Louie planning to call my parents, reveal that their only son was a hopeless screw-up, and break their hearts.

More than anything, me, and my own feckless habit of kicking the can down the road and hoping it'd all work out somehow.

And now…this. This mysterious, condescending little magical jerk who'd used magic to make himself more appealing to me on the one hand, and then had the nerve to snark at me for getting "all worked up" on the other!

"Okay then," I said, and I moved at last, prowling like the tiger I was, circling him, not closing the distance between us until I'd forced him to twist around to face me, off-balance and flushed. I leaned down until our faces were only inches apart, until I could feel the quick, uneven brush of his breath and see myself reflected in his pupils. "Let's get this straight. You are requesting, and in fact demanding, that I earn my pay by doing whatever I'm thinking about doing. I have to knot you, and other than that, it's up to me. Yes?"

That quick, not-quite-human tongue darted out again, flickering over his lower lip and leaving it glistening. His pulse pounded in the side of his neck.

"You're not allowed to hurt me. I could defend myself effectively, I warn you, but I don't want to have to. I don't want to be concerned that I'll need to."

"No hurting you," I said, and meant it down to my bones. He might be annoying as hell, but—no. "I don't want to, and I'll be careful not to. You can relax."

The fae could detect lies most of the time, I thought. I'd heard it somewhere, probably from the same dubious source that had claimed they couldn't lie themselves. Maybe he could tell if I told him the truth, maybe not, but either way, he believed me; he nodded slowly, and some of his tension seemed to ease.

"Fine. Then yes, do whatever you need to do to get the job done. You have carte blanche." He paused. "No ruining my shoes, either. I'm not sure how you would, but it's worth mentioning."

He thought I was a graceless, crude knothead with more glitter than brains, and he obviously expected me to flip him over, pull down his pants, trip, and possibly only manage to fuck him because my cock went in when I fell over on top of him.

No. Screw that. I had carte blanche, and I was going to give him the absolute best fuck of his life.

Whether he liked it or not.

Chapter 4

As an opening salvo, I grinned down at him, wicked, teasing, letting my fangs—long and sharp even compared to other tigers—drop all the way. When we were teenagers, my big sister had nicknamed me Smilodon. Being a dumbass, I'd thought she meant I looked friendly until I'd accidentally learned what it was on a class field trip to a natural history museum.

Sisters were more monstrous than any prehistoric beast you could name.

But my unusually large canines came in handy sometimes, and watching the fairy's pretty mouth fall open in shock made my sister's howls of laughter worthwhile. My eyes glowed alpha gold, too, now that I'd stopped making an effort to prevent it.

"What are you going to do with those teeth? And don't make a Little Red Riding Hood joke," he added. "I'm not in the mood."

"Whatever I want. Also," and I dipped my head down even lower, finally, *finally* nuzzling under his pointy chin, with my nose behind his ear…and the scent of him, fuck, "I'm not a stupid werewolf."

"No?" He'd gone high and breathy. Mmm. Satisfying. I smiled against his neck, probably looking a lot like an actual Smilodon, if he'd been able to see it. "What are—oh—you, then?"

My lips barely brushed the soft skin below his ear, the first time our bodies had touched. And damn him, but it was more than enough for an electric heat to bloom in my mouth, travel down my spine, raise all the hair on the back of my neck. The wild impulse to bite, to savage him, rose up and nearly choked me. I forced it down, sweat beading on my hairline.

"None of your business," I said, my voice a low growl, and closed the last millimeter of distance between my lips and his tender throat.

He let out a startled sound halfway between a cry and a whimper, and when I swiped his skin with my tongue, letting him feel its rough texture, he trailed off in a moan.

The lemon-sugar taste of him nearly had my eyes rolling back in my head. If all fairies were this delicious, no wonder they kept themselves secluded away from the rougher, more predatory species. Not even magic would be enough to keep them safe from a powerful alpha with no scruples.

But *I* had scruples, even if my instincts didn't.

Some. Not many.

Anyway, ravaging him would only get me a pissy fairy, not his surrender. After his bullshit and his attitude, I wasn't going to be satisfied with anything less.

At last he swayed against me, and I caught him with one hand splayed against the middle of his spine and the other sliding down over the curve of his hip and ass. Scruples didn't have to include not copping a feel, after all. And he felt as lush as I'd hoped, slim but with rounded, firm muscle where it counted.

I pinned him there, not quite pressed against me, and licked and sucked at his throat, savoring every bit of his sweetness, moving to the front and nipping him right above that high collar, making stinging marks on his perfect fae skin.

He started to squirm, muttering little protests. I slid my hand up and indulged myself, collecting a fistful of that shiny fall of hair and tugging his head back.

Not painfully. Not enough to break my promise. But it threw him off balance, and his hands flew up to grab my shoulders and steady himself. His fingers dug in like claws. I wished they were. He could scratch the hell out of me if he wanted to, hiss like a wildcat. But he'd probably be horribly offended if I suggested it.

He arched, wriggled, and then gasped, eyes going wide, as I

gave in to temptation and used my hand on his hip to shove us flush together.

The fairy froze, mouth open. My cock dug into his stomach, fully erect, and by that expression of shock, he could feel every gods-damned inch. I rubbed against him, slowly, using the same bump and grind of my hips that I would have on stage. And I didn't waver from staring him right in the eyes, either, letting him see and feel and really understand what I was going to do to him.

Fuck him so hard and deep I'd run the risk of breaking his ribs, for one thing. For another, make him come so many damn times he'd be sobbing out apologies for doubting me.

The long, bent-back curve of his throat showed it clearly when he swallowed hard, and I was pleased to see the blush on his cheeks had spread all the way down to his collar.

"What's your name?" I smiled, showing the fangs again. "I need something to call you by when I'm telling you how to take my cock."

His grip on my shoulders tightened almost painfully. Christ, but he was a lot stronger than he looked.

Good.

His eyes glinted with something akin to an alpha's glow, giving a window into his inner magic. He couldn't lift his chin, because I had it at a sharp angle already, but he somehow managed to give the impression of doing so anyway.

"You are *not* going to tell me how to take your—mmph!"

Nope, not putting up with that kind of talk. I swooped down and kissed that absurdity off of his parted lips, biting the lower one, sweeping into his mouth, a full-body shiver coursing down my back and lodging in my balls as he responded, the forked tip of his tongue flickering. I'd never been tickled while I kissed someone, never tasted a mouth even more inhuman than my own, with its flavor of hot sugar and lemony tartness and spring wildflowers.

I crushed him against me and bent him back, devouring him, and if I'd already had the foresight to strip him out of those ridiculous clothes, I'd have spread his legs and shoved inside without further ado.

Luckily for his ability to walk tomorrow, I hadn't even gotten around to that maddening button yet.

So instead, I lifted him mostly off the ground, stripper heels dragging on the carpet and kicking me in the shins, and carried him the few steps to the bed. He'd stopped trying to do anything but kiss me back, soft lips pliant but tongue wickedly teasing, and I could do that for hours, but that way lay madness, so I broke the kiss and tossed him onto the bed, his mouth forming an O of shock and his arms and long hair flying in all directions.

He landed with a thump and creak from the worn-out mattress, splayed out like a starfish. Long legs for his height, perfect for getting between in any way I could manage, and his shirt had ridden up a couple of inches, giving me a glimpse of a sliver of pale skin above the waist of his pants.

Did fairies even have navels? I'd never thought to wonder, but now I had to know.

Well, I'd wanted to get on my knees for him, hadn't I? And he wouldn't be expecting it.

So I got down on the floor—gracefully, this time, thank you and fuck you very much—and caught his knees with my hands as he reflexively tried to bring his legs together. He pushed up on his elbows and gazed down at me, all wild eyes and tangled hair and heaving chest and kiss-reddened lips.

Oh, he looked perfect like this, all mussed up. Before this I'd never understood the appeal of smearing my partner's makeup during sex, or of tearing someone's clothes. Now I got it.

"You didn't tell me your name," I said, sliding my hands up his thighs excruciatingly slowly and pushing his legs wider as I did. The front of his pants had a visible bulge, pointing right at me. Ha! He could pretend all he liked that this wasn't about anything but a bet for him. "You don't like answering questions with a straight answer, do you?"

To my surprise, he smiled at that, and it looked genuine. He really couldn't be much prettier if he tried—although it might already be all effort and no reality, and I had no way of knowing. Fairies. Dammit.

"You can't really expect me to answer that, can you?"

"You just did," I pointed out. "Your name, if you please?"

"Touché," he said. "And no. Names have power. You should know that. Don't you use a stage name? Surely your parents didn't choose The Hammer for their newborn?"

So he'd heard Scott introducing me before I went on stage, then. I grinned at him. "My—"

"—penis is the hammer, yes, thank you, I get it," he cut in, with a dramatic roll of his eyes.

"No," I corrected him. "You haven't gotten it *yet.*"

"Oh my dear lords," he muttered, collapsing back down with another thump of the mattress.

"You're the one paying me for my hammer," I said helpfully, earning a loud huff and enough time to throw him even further off balance.

Instead of going for that tempting ridge of his cock in those tight black pants, I went the other way, moving over to his left leg and running my hands down all the way to his ankle. That delicate little joint looked ridiculously fragile in my huge hands.

"What are you doing?" he demanded.

"Making sure your shoes don't get ruined when I have your legs over my shoulders. I promised, right?"

This time, he didn't bother trying to contradict me. Good, he was learning.

Thank the gods his shoes didn't have any tiny buckles or laces or anything fiddly, although they did have perfectly smooth bright-red leather soles. I tugged at this one, sliding it off his foot and setting it aside on the floor. I didn't *actually* want to suck his gleaming-tipped toes the way I'd thought about in the club, but…

I shook my head, trying to clear the haze, but yeah, I still wanted to put every part of him in my mouth. My cock hadn't slacked off in the slightest, pressing persistently against the fly of my jeans.

Fairy magic really ought to be regulated. Or abolished.

The other shoe came off just as easily, and I put it next to the first, lining them up neatly in a way I never would have bothered with at any other time. I'd promised to treat his clothes gently, and the thought of valeting him with care and then stuffing him full of my knot gave me a perverse, anticipatory thrill.

By now all the fooling around had had the desired effect. His whole body vibrated slightly with the force of his heartbeat; I could feel it in his ankle, even.

"What are you doing?" he complained.

"What's your name?" I countered.

No, I wouldn't suck on his toes, but his second ankle proved irresistible. I kissed it, pushing his pant leg up a bit to nibble my way along the back of his calf. He made a soft sound that went straight to my cock.

He didn't answer—not that I'd expected him to.

When I lifted my head and took a peek, he'd lain back and closed his eyes, long eyelashes a dark shadow on his pink cheeks, hair fanned out all around his head and his hands clenching fistfuls of the bedspread.

Did he think he could pretend to be uninterested in the proceedings? Fine, let him try.

He stayed almost perfectly still while I unbuttoned his pants, only lifting his hips slightly as I tugged them out from under his ass to peel them down and then set them on the nearby chair. The black silk boxer briefs I revealed were way more brief than boxer. They probably had less fabric in them than the G-string I'd worn on stage earlier. His cock and balls filled them out nicely, especially in proportion to his stature.

But what really took me off guard, probably because the Lucky or Knot guys all shaved, waxed, and tanned within an inch of their lives (and I did the first two myself), was the contrast between his snow-white magically perfect skin and the silky dusting of jet-black hair on his calves. I hadn't imagined that a fae would have any body hair at all, somehow.

It only made him more delicious, that contrast between his willowy delicacy and feminine grooming, and the clear masculinity hidden away beneath his odd, androgynous clothing.

But it really didn't matter either way. If he'd been bright purple and covered with scales under his pants I might've been into it, because at this point, I'd gone so far past arousal that I'd turned the corner and entered another realm. My cock had settled into a resigned holding pattern, and the world had closed down to my immediate sensory inputs: the fairy's quick shallow breaths, the hard floor beneath my knees, not padded at all by the room's cheap carpeting, the way the low-watt light bulbs cast murky shadows on the man spread out half-naked in front of me. Even the bad lighting couldn't dim his radiance, though.

His looks *had* to be an illusion. Right? And this stabbing, desperate sensation in my lower belly when I focused on him, the result of magic?

Well, fuck it, I'd enjoy it while it lasted. And get paid for the privilege. I'd chosen this with my eyes open, after all.

He lifted his hips to let me get his underwear down, too, and then pulled out his feet one at a time, knees bending up toward his ears.

Oh, and that was—I tossed the boxer briefs vaguely in the direction of the chair, unable to give a fuck about taking care of his clothes anymore.

He tried to put his legs back down, but my hands landed on the backs of his thighs, and I wrenched him open again, his knees framing his indignant face. Not that I was looking at his face, gorgeous as it might be. My eyes had been riveted a lot lower, where plump balls hung down and almost obscured his pretty pink hole, and his straight, slim cock stood up at a sharp angle, the head thick and juicy and a slightly darker shade of rose than his lips.

My own blood throbbed in my ears, a whooshing that eclipsed anything else. My mouth watered. I had to taste—

"No!" A sharp pain bloomed in the side of my head, and I jumped and looked up, assisted along by the fairy's punishing grip on my ear.

Everything flashed back into focus. He was panting, and I'd gotten about a breath away from swallowing his cock. The scent of him rose up around me, heady and musky and sweet, almost overwhelming. Pure sex and desire, but still with that achingly familiar, comforting overtone that had short-circuited my brain back at the club.

"No," he said again, more gently, as I blinked at him. His fingers didn't relax their grip, though, and my ear had gone numb. "Don't do that."

"You," I tried, and had to swallow. My mouth had gone so dry, and my voice came out husky. "I'm not expecting you to reciprocate."

"Don't. I mean it. It's not about that. Fuck and knot me. You shouldn't even have kissed me, but that'll wear off, I think." He shook his head. "Keep your mouth to yourself and do what I hired you to do."

That'd *wear off*? He *thought*? The fuck did that even mean? Even if I really wanted to know, I for sure knew he wouldn't answer me if I wasted my time asking. Fairy magic. I couldn't even. No names, no kissing, no cock sucking, no fucking him with my tongue, no guarantee that I wouldn't wake up in the morning in the body of a diseased frog. Don't worry, it'll wear off! Fuck me.

"Fine," I said, declining to argue about it. Now that I'd snapped out of it—and to be fair, he'd been the one to do it—my single-minded focus on getting him in my mouth had been a bit unsettling, hadn't it? "I'll fuck you and knot you. No more kissing." He stared at me, unmoving. "You can let go of my ear before you rip it off, if you don't mind."

At last he released my stinging ear and lay back down, something wary and cloudy in the depths of those dark eyes.

In my turn, I let go of his legs and allowed his feet to thump down to the bed.

When I stood up and started to get my clothes off, he lay still, his eyes gleaming from under half-lowered lids with his long eyelashes shadowing their expression. Being watched like this was completely different from being watched on stage, and even different from doing a private dance. Loud music set a certain type of mood, and—well, his attention simply felt different. I hadn't been self-conscious about taking my clothes off ever, really, and certainly not since I started at Lucky or Knot.

But I almost started to blush under his steady gaze, and my skin was almost as pale as his. It'd show. Hopefully he'd think I was turned on and overheated instead of embarrassed and weirdly shy.

My shirt landed on the heap on the chair with his stuff, and I crouched down to untie my boots.

"Take your shirt off," I said.

I'd have preferred to slowly strip it off myself, but I knew without asking that wouldn't be welcome.

What had changed? Something had changed between when I started taking his clothes off and now. His mood had shifted, from that odd bravado he'd had at first into this pensive silence. My intention of putting him in his place a bit didn't feel appropriate anymore—if that word could've been applied at all.

He hesitated, but then he pushed up, unbuttoned his collar, and whipped the shirt over his head, keeping a perfect angle with his torso in an impressive display of core strength that would've had any yoga teacher drooling.

It had me drooling, too, only probably not for the same reasons. Christ, I wished we were here for fun and not for a transaction. I'd put him on top and make him work for it.

He lay back, completely bare. No hair on his chest, but a silky thatch peeked out under his arms. Maybe I'd get a chance to lick him there, at least, if not between his legs. And fairies did indeed have navels. Also nipples, small and pointed and nearly as pale as the rest of his skin.

"Do you want me to get myself ready?" he said. "Or do you prefer to—oh, lords of the air," he choked, gratifyingly wide-eyed, as I shoved my jeans and that G-string I hadn't bothered to change out of down to the floor.

Of course I wanted to get him ready. Fuck him slowly with my fingers, kiss him until he writhed underneath me, all red-cheeked and needy...

Yeah, no. "You'd better do it," I said, with great regret.

He paused, this time chewing on his lip. Another tell. I probably wouldn't have time to learn them all, and that realization hit me shockingly hard.

"How do you, ah. I, ah." His voice went soft and thin and high. "Want me?"

Fucking hell. My cock gave an almost painful pulse. How did I want him? Sprawled out in front of me, long, silky limbs akimbo and glowing white against the crappy bedspread, a diamond set in nickel, his hair tumbling over his slim, muscular shoulders. And he asked me how I wanted him.

My breath came in short little bursts, too shallow and too fast. Magic. It had to be more magic. Otherwise I was just fucked.

Chapter 5

Stepping out of my jeans and toeing off my socks gave me a way to stall for a second. *How do you want me?* Fuck. Let me count the ways.

But I could cross one of them off the list. If I took him on his back, the temptation to kiss him wouldn't be something I could resist.

"On your hands and knees," I growled, and had to grab the base of my cock and throttle it back at the thought.

He rolled up, snatched the lube off the nightstand, and flipped over again in one smooth motion, all with the grace of an acrobat. Yeah, if he'd auditioned at a strip club, they'd have given him top billing.

The way he was making me watch him reach behind his round, firm globe of an ass and slide the tip of one slender, lube-slick finger into his hole—without my being able to touch or lick any of it—had to be against the Geneva Conventions. Every muscle in my body went taut with the effort of not participating. A soft-looking brush of black hair surrounded his cock and balls, but it didn't reach as far as his hole, which glistened rose-pink as it swallowed up two of his fingers. And then three, and gods, but he was flexible, and the wet squelching of his hole and his soft gasps as he took his own hand...

At last I couldn't stand it anymore. My cock pointed straight at him like a dowsing rod, knowing exactly where it wanted, needed, to go before I exploded. The bed dipped and groaned in protest as I knelt down behind him, my knees nudging his calves.

Two points of contact, and the heat of him burned through me and set me alight. He pulled his fingers out and braced himself, his head hanging down.

My big hand wrapped around his hip looked obscene, a violation of perfection. Graffiti on a Renaissance painting. I leaned in. The head of my cock brushed between his cheeks.

Now *that* was obscene. Thick and purplish-red and shiny and so much bigger than its target, even though he'd done a good job working himself open. Sliding my hand over to spread his cheek made him moan, the line of his back bowing down and his ass pushing up in the air. With the other hand, I picked up the bottle and drizzled lube along my shaft, letting it drip down and pool at the head, trickling onto and into him.

I'd gotten us both so wet that my cock nearly slipped off of him when I tried to thrust in, but I steadied him and pushed—so tight, my eyes rolled back—and then my cockhead popped inside and wedged there, stretching him open to fit.

The quality of his vibrating silence suggested a suppressed moan. No, fuck that. I deserved to hear it.

And maybe I wanted a lot of things I wasn't going to get, but this I could have. Besides, I was practically vibrating myself with the urge to bury my cock deep, feel his wet heat clenching around every inch of me.

So I satisfied both desires, splaying my hands over his cheeks to hold him open and leaning forward, letting my weight sink my cock into him inch by inch. Slowly. One inch, and his fingers clenched convulsively in the bedspread. Two, and his legs shook where they pressed against mine. A little deeper, fuck, and I might break before he did, with sweat starting to prickle at my shoulders and my balls tight, pressure beginning to build.

He whimpered, low and soft.

There.

I pulled back slightly, letting him feel the drag of my thick cock on his sensitive inner walls...and then thrust forward, deeper, drawing out a helpless, breathy murmur.

Again. A sharper cry as I angled down, almost fully in, the thickest part of the base of my cock pressing on everything inside him.

Muffled sounds suggested he'd tried to bite his lip or the bedding to keep himself silent, but he didn't stand a chance. I tilted up his hips and pounded down into him, holding him up so that his knees didn't even touch the bed, ignoring his half-protesting cries that trailed off into rhythmic gasps and moans. The bed thudded and creaked, with one of my knees now noticeably lower than the other as the mattress gave way.

Fuck it. I adjusted my angle to compensate and swiveled my hips, testing out how deep I could go, wondering how he felt with the thick length of my cock buried so far inside him. Holding him up with one hand, I reached the other underneath his hips.

By the way he whined and moaned and kicked at my calves, trying desperately to get some leverage, and rutted his rock-hard cock into my palm, he thought being impaled on my alpha cock felt incredible.

I'd already noticed he was a lot stronger than he looked. He could take it.

Both hands on his hips again, I stopped restraining myself. My fangs dropped, my claws pushed out, and I lifted my fingers to keep them from piercing his skin and fucked him harder. I wouldn't be able to keep myself from coming for much longer. That tingling had started in the base of my cock, and another sensation that only an alpha would experience: a throbbing pressure that meant my knot was ready to fill my lover's soft hole, wrench him open, lock us together.

Sweat trickled down my spine and my legs, and a sheen of it dampened his back, too, catching strands of his silky hair and sticking them to his skin. My whole body had gone so tense I shook with it. The air around us crackled with magic, his wild fae strain and my own alpha power blending and folding over and over on top of each other.

The way he moved against me, like water, yielding but endlessly resilient…

Except that his cries had risen to an almost pained timbre, and

I forced myself to stop.

Everything in the world seemed to freeze for a moment as I bent down over him, lungs laboring, blinking the sweat out of my eyes. His body quivered under my hands, around my cock, which was still buried to the hilt. His sharp sit bones dug into my groin.

"Oh," he gasped. "Why are you—what's wrong?"

I stared down at him, the delicate lines of his torso, one outflung arm, the curve of his cheek where the curtain of his hair had parted to give me a glimpse. Something in my chest caught and twanged. Gods, I hoped it wasn't tenderness. That way lay madness.

But my voice came out a lot gentler, and a lot more breathless, than I wanted as I said, "You know, I don't have to knot you. I can control it." If I used every bit of willpower I had, and then some. "We can...*not* knot, and say we did." But that wouldn't work for a fae promise, would it? In a burst of selfless, unwilling inspiration, I added, "You can finish me off with a hand job. If I knot your hand, I've still knotted you, right? You can win your bet."

His shaky little laugh vibrated through my cock, and I had to choke back a groan. The sound of it lodged in that same place in my chest that I'd been trying to ignore. Damn it.

"No," he said, and then, in a strange reversal of his usual M.O., answered a question I hadn't asked rather than dodging one I had. "You won't hurt me. Don't—worry about me."

I wanted to believe him, except that he almost sounded like he might be about to cry.

Shit. But people had all kinds of odd reactions during sex, right? And not-quite-people had them, too. Exhibit A: that twinging, twisting not-quite-guilt-or-something under my breastbone.

Nah, you couldn't ask another dude if he was crying, not even if you were balls-deep in him. Maybe *especially* not if you were balls-deep in him.

"Okay," I said. "Then heads up."

At this point, coming wasn't going to take me any effort at all. I didn't need to fuck him hard to get there. Instead, I rocked into him, gazing down, letting the slow, easy friction get me buzzing, the sight of his shiny wet rim stretching and swallowing me up mesmerizing and unbelievably hot, the hottest thing I'd ever seen.

And then there was no turning back, with the pressure forcing its way up my cock, my knot swelling, the spasms that whited out my vision and bowed my spine as I spilled into him in pulse after pulse. Over the sound of my own wildly thudding heartbeat, I could barely hear his cries, and my knot grew more, forcing me to thrust deeper to get it all the way in. The pressure of his insides against the hardness of it wrenched another aftershock out of me.

Knotting had never taken me like this, an irresistible force that blurred my senses, leaving me with nothing but static and the need to collapse down, close my eyes, and get a breath. At the last second, I managed to tip us sideways and tuck him into the cradle of my hips so I didn't crush him, and then I closed my eyes and tried to drift.

But the panting of his breath hadn't let up in the slightest, and he kept squirming, the motion massaging my cock and knot, almost too much and too intense. His wriggling brought me back to reality after a moment, and the world rushed back in: the cool air in the room drying the sweat on my skin, the pipes clanking in the wall, a car outside.

Wait a minute, had he...

I closed my eyes, swallowed hard, and focused, forcing my claws back in, and then reached around him.

My hand closed around his cock and balls. They weren't small, but my broad palm and long fingers encompassed most of what he had.

He'd said no kissing, but the peak of that slim shoulder, skin gleaming with perspiration like dewy flower petals, drew me in like a magnet.

"Come on," I whispered, and pressed my lips to his skin. My tongue flicked out, and one drop of his sweat beaded on it, heady and delicious. "Come on my knot, sweetness."

The endearment came out of fucking nowhere, fuck, and I overcompensated, giving his cock and balls a firm squeeze. He convulsed in my arms, legs scissoring, clenched around me hard enough to make me reel dizzily, and spilled all over my hand. With a drawn-out—dammit, a sob, I really couldn't mistake it for anything else—he slumped and went limp. The scents of tart citrus and honeysuckle rose up around us, mingled with my own sweat and the salty musk of my come.

If his come tasted the way it smelled, no wonder he had to warn guys not to blow him.

With an effort of will that deserved way more credit than anyone was ever going to give me, I resisted lifting my hand to my mouth and sucking it clean. Instead, I massaged his limp cock and his spent balls, because he kept shuddering and clamping down around my knot and making me crazy, and—overstimulated sauce for the goose, thank you very much.

His breath hitched, and I squeezed him again, and his little shiver had me curling around him, all my instincts screaming at me to keep him warm, enclose him, stuff him full, hold him, taste that tempting curve of his neck…

"Stop licking me," he said, and I froze mid-lick, caught like a kid with my hand in the cookie jar. "It's for your own good."

Okay, now I was going to fucking well ask, because he was taking a little bit of nuzzling way too seriously. I hadn't eaten out his pretty ass, so what the hell more did he want from me?

"What's the worst that could happen?"

His long, long pause didn't reassure me in the slightest. If I hadn't still been deeply knotted in his delicious body, every inch of mine tingling with endorphins and with the pleasure of having his sleek curves and angles pressed up against me, I might've been some variety of concerned.

"I don't like hypotheticals," he said at last.

His voice still had the slightly thick quality of someone who'd been crying. Yeah, he really had been. Fuck, had I hurt him after all? And the fact that the possibility of having done him harm worried me way more than whatever "hypothetical" he didn't like, well…that worried me the most.

"I don't either," I replied, wishing I could get angrier. But with him in my arms, and the taste of him on my tongue, and the music of his heartbeat and his breath in my ears, nothing else really seemed to matter. Gods, I could lie here forever. Knot him again and again. Fuck, I had to focus. Hypotheticals. Right. "I especially don't like imaginary, unknown hypotheticals that you won't even tell me about."

His scent kept getting stronger, sweeter, more soothing. My eyes drifted shut. I tried to force them open, but my lids were so heavy. I tucked my arm around him more tightly, my come-sticky hand pressing against his sternum, and laughed as he made a disgusted little noise.

Still no answer. Mmm, whatever. Hardly shocking that he was being cagey, and anyway, we could nap before we discussed the worst that could happen. Surely it wouldn't be before we woke up.

His heart had an odd rhythm to it, fast and a bit thready, vibrating against my chest. I petted him, nuzzling his shoulder, wrapping myself around him as best I could to shelter him from anything and everything. Nothing would get through a weretiger. Even without my ego involved, there really were very few beings on Earth that could.

Between one breath and the next, I dozed off, my arm pinning him safely in place, my knot keeping him tied to me.

***

What seemed like one more breath later, my eyes popped open, my whole body coming tense and alert instantaneously. I rolled onto my back and out of bed, claws out, mouth open in a silent snarl.

Heart racing, I whipped my head around.

The hotel room lay in a gloomy murk, with all the lights off but with threads of sunlight leaking in around the edges of the drawn curtains. But that was more than enough to show me no fairy—and no all-black clothes or stripper heels. My own clothes still lay scattered on the chair and the floor where I'd left them.

Sunlight. Fucking daylight, and by the down-slanting angle of the sun, at least mid-morning. That meant I'd been asleep for a minimum of seven hours or so, a ridiculously long time by my usual standards. I straightened up from my automatic defensive crouch, sniffing the air and figuratively cocking my ears. Cars went by on the street outside, someone yelled and laughed in another room of the hotel, a distant phone rang. Tart sweetness lingered in the air, along with a hint of soap. I'd have been able to hear any movement anywhere in the room, but I went around the bed and pushed the bathroom door open anyway. Nothing.

Although not quite nothing. One towel had been used and tossed on the floor, and a couple of the complimentary toiletries had been opened and scattered on the counter. All the steam of the fairy's presumed shower had already evaporated, though, so it hadn't been the sound of him using the bathroom that had woken me.

The outer door closing?

Two seconds later I'd flung it open and stuck my head out.

No fairy. No one at all in either direction along the length of the hotel, and no one in the parking lot except...shit, a woman in a housekeeping uniform, standing by the palm trees, who'd looked up from her phone and cigarette to gape at me.

Naked. I was naked. Fuck.

I dashed back in the door like a reverse Jack-in-the-box and slammed it shut.

Double, triple fuck.

Another wild look around the room showed me nothing new. No sign of where he'd gone, or when, though unless he could vanish into thin air as well as everything else, he'd left a while ago.

Usually I slept lightly, half-attuned to what went on around me even while unconscious, like the giant cat I was. And yet he'd slipped off my cock, climbed out of my arms and the loudly creaky bed, and then gone into the bathroom and taken a shower. Gotten dressed. For all I knew, he'd watched some TV and called a friend and repainted his gods-damned toenails.

And I'd been dead to the world through all of it. Lying there with my mouth open snoring, probably.

Drooling.

Fuck me.

The way I'd fallen asleep hadn't been natural. That had been magic. The intensity of his scent. The warmth and comfort. All of it. And I hadn't noticed the enchantment creeping over me, of course I hadn't, because it'd made me too mentally pliant to notice anything at all.

Rage rose up and nearly choked me, rage and offense and something I absolutely did not want to recognize as betrayed hurt.

My claws popped, and the roar that tore out of my throat rattled the lamps and echoed in the small room, probably sending any small animals for a mile around running for cover with their ears back. I subsided, panting, as little bits pattered down from the popcorn ceiling, sprinkled over the carpet like snow and dusting the rumpled bedding where I'd kissed and licked and knotted that sneaky little fucking magical prick.

Christ. Well, I hadn't paid for the room, which meant I wouldn't be liable for the ceiling or the suspiciously tilted and crooked-looking bed, but after that roar—and flashing the housekeeper—I should probably clear the hell out of here.

A shower could wait. My nose and a cursory visual inspection informed me that the only residue the little bastard had left on me had the consistency and scent of the kind of fancy wildflower honey I couldn't afford to buy at the bougie grocery store.

Ironic, that. He'd paid me, and I wouldn't be able to afford him.

After I ducked into the bathroom to piss, I pulled on my jeans and T-shirt, skipping the sweaty G-string in favor of freeballing it. Socks and boots were next, and I sat there for a second after I'd finished lacing them up, elbows on my knees, massaging my temples.

What a fucking clusterfuck. A slight throbbing had set up residence in the edges of my head, probably a reaction to magic.

Or to one of those unknown "hypotheticals" the fairy had said he didn't like to think about. Great.

The G-string caught a stray shaft of sunlight from around the curtain, and its glittery accents winked sadly at me from the dingy carpet. Ugh. Well, I wanted to wear it again even less now that it'd been on the floor of the hotel room, but on the other hand, I couldn't afford to keep replacing my stage outfits if they could be salvaged. Even with whatever I could get for that coin, I had to put every penny toward my debt. I snatched up the G-string, stood, and stuffed it into my pocket...

And then froze. My pocket was empty. I scrabbled into the other front pocket of my jeans, and then the two back pockets, just in case.

Nothing.

The coin hadn't gotten stuck in my jeans somewhere, that was absurd. I'd feel it, or it'd have fallen out when I got dressed.

But I still took every scrap of clothing off and checked in my boots before I got dressed again.

Then I got down on the floor and looked under the bed. Another pair of flimsy, tacky underwear appeared to be wedged at the head of it, halfway behind the headboard. Fucking gross. But no coin, and no corners where it could've rolled to.

Besides, I absolutely knew I'd put it into my pocket! And when I'd undressed and dropped my jeans the night before, I hadn't seen it fall out.

Frustration almost had me roaring again. But I forced myself to keep it together, to be methodical, because the moment I admitted that searching would be completely fruitless, I'd have to face the truth.

I went through that fucking hotel room like a forensic analyst, every second expecting a knock on the door from one of the hotel staff demanding I get out before they called the cops. By the time I'd finished, I was sweating and dusty and desperately in need of a shower after all. I stopped short of taking apart the built-in air conditioner under the window, but I came close.

Finally, standing there in the middle of the room, all the furniture pulled out and at odd angles, I didn't have any choice but to acknowledge that the coin had disappeared just like the fairy.

With the fairy, in fact.

He'd enchanted me, lied to me, cheated me, and then enchanted me again so that he could steal from me. I'd been made a fool of in every possible way, and the humiliation of it burned like acid in my gut.

No. No one did that to me and got away with it.

I was going to find that motherfucker and get what was mine if it was the last thing I ever did.

Chapter 6

My first stop for information, the club, yielded exactly fucking nothing. When I finally slammed the hotel door behind me and headed back around the corner, no one I needed to talk to was at work yet. Coffee and a bite to eat at a diner didn't take nearly long enough, but after a couple of hours of seething and pacing, I finally managed to buttonhole one of the bartenders who'd been on shift the night before.

She rolled her eyes, shrugged, and agreed to look at the credit card info from last night—only to inform me that he'd used a pre-paid card.

Plan B, trying to get a look at the security camera feed from the parking lot the night before, also hit a dead end. If the fairy had parked there and I'd been able to get his license plate, I'd thought I could probably find someone able to pull his info for me. If nothing else, Louie would have a contact, although trying to convince him that doing me a favor would lead to him getting his cut of a magical coin sounded...exhausting.

But the club's head of security, a werewolf who didn't appreciate how much bigger my shifted form was than his, absolutely refused to show me any of the footage or even check it for me. He explained, in excruciating and condescending detail, his ethical standards for overseeing the privacy and safety of our customers.

His implication, unstated but obvious, had been that I wanted to stalk one of said customers for my own creepy purposes.

He really didn't like cats in general. Or me in specific.

I struck out with Scott, too, tracking him down in his booth where he'd gone with the largest paper cup of coffee I'd ever seen. He didn't look like his night had been a whole lot better than mine.

"C'mon, Scott," I complained. I wasn't whining. Tigers didn't whine. "Jeremy has a soft spot for you. He'll show you the footage if you ask him nicely."

"No can do," Scott said, and chugged from his cup. He wiped a drop off his chin onto his sleeve. Yeah. Rough night. "Jeremy doesn't make exceptions to his policy, and anyway, he'd know I was asking on your behalf. You shouldn't have talked to him first."

It wasn't Scott's fault, so I did my best not to growl at him as I told him not to expect me that night and headed out to try my last play.

Bothering the owner of the club I worked in with a petty, personal issue that involved me breaking the law had been my very last choice. But since Scott wouldn't help me, that left Declan MacKenna as the only person who could go over Jeremy's head.

Before going to the Morrigan to hunt Declan down, I went home, showered thoroughly, and dressed in clean dark jeans and a blue button-down, making myself look almost like the accountant my parents thought I'd become. In fact, if I hadn't been lying to them, I'd have been in this very office five days a week, wearing clothes similar to this, fitting right in.

But the staid, gray-and-navy reception area of the Morrigan casino's business office couldn't have been more different from my usual little hedonistic corner of Declan MacKenna's Vegas empire, and I had to force myself not to fidget self-consciously as I waited.

And I had the uncomfortable suspicion that the receptionist had only pretended to let Declan know I was here and intended to let me rot in this comfortable chair until I gave up. Had I missed some glitter in my hair? Damn it. She glanced up from her computer and shot me the world's fakest smile. Great.

I cooled my heels there for over an hour, with the clock ticking past five and office workers starting to leave for the day, with every passing moment totally failing to blunt my anger.

Last night kept replaying in my mind. *I want you to give in to your instincts and knot me thoroughly, and I can offer you this in exchange,* he'd said. Offer it to me. Not pay me, not give it to me, nothing that necessarily had to be construed as me keeping it after I'd fucked him. Of course he'd felt comfortable giving me his word that the coin was worth a lot of money, because he'd intended to take it back from me all along!

Oh, he had no idea which of my instincts I'd be giving into when I tracked him down. My instinct to wring his scrawny neck, for one. Or my instinct to put him over my knee.

More than anything, my instinct not to be cheated and stolen from. Maybe if we'd been actually dating that would've been par for the course, but no way would I allow that from someone I spent one night with in a cheap hotel. I had standards.

The clock had almost hit six. Scrolling on my phone couldn't keep my attention.

He'd cried when I knotted him. Why? Guilt? Pain? Some bizarre fae emotion I couldn't even comprehend? But my stomach tightened and twisted with something between helpless desire and rage every time a visceral memory assaulted me.

His soft, broken sounds. The clench of his heat. The sweetness of his skin. The way I'd called him that, *sweetness,* in my stupid, enchanted daze.

"Mr. Kaplan? Mr. Kaplan?" When I glanced up from frowning down unseeingly at the floor, I found the receptionist frowning too, standing up from behind her desk as if she thought she'd need to tap me on the shoulder to get my attention. She had her purse over her shoulder, clearly about to leave. "Mr. MacKenna can see you now," she said, sounding both surprised and disapproving. "His assistant's coming to get you."

Well, fuck her, anyway.

I still thanked her politely as the double door opened, and I nodded and followed a much more pleasant older lady down a long and bland hallway. My whole unlived life seemed to flash before my eyes, and I shuddered. No, I really didn't regret not answering phones and staring at a computer screen in one of the offices we passed on our walk to Declan's.

Much better to gyrate on a stage and occasionally get not-paid for sex by gorgeous, lying fairies.

Fuck my life.

We reached the end of the corridor, where a huge glass-walled office occupied the corner of the building. It'd still been full daylight when I arrived, and I blinked at the disorienting view of black sky and Vegas lights.

The assistant put her head in, said, "Tony Kaplan, Mr. MacKenna, let me know if you want coffee," and went back to her desk.

Declan MacKenna rose from behind his own, coming around to shake my hand. He wouldn't have been out of place on stage at Lucky or Knot himself, to be honest, being an alpha werewolf with dark-haired good looks and quite a few tattoos peeking out of his rolled-up shirt sleeves. Not my type, but he'd make great tips if he wanted to moonlight away from his fancy executive suite.

"Sorry to keep you waiting," he said, the faint tinge of an Irish accent seeping into his voice. "I had a meeting that ran long. And I've another one coming up, so I'll have to make this quick. Is there a problem at the club?"

Declan tended to a more friendly, down-to-earth style of management despite how many calls he had on his time, and he made a point of knowing everyone who worked at Lucky or Knot, dropping in now and again to have a drink with us after closing. So I'd spent a fair amount of time with him, though he hadn't come by for a while.

The way his scent had changed since I saw him last—mingled with someone else's and with overtones of sex and contentment—confirmed the rumors I'd heard about his reasons for spending more time at home.

"No, more a personal problem, and don't apologize, I didn't have an appointment," I said as I took the seat he waved me to next to a coffee table at the end of the room. He dropped into a matching one and sprawled his legs out. "Speaking of personal. Congratulations. Heard you mated?"

I'd actually heard he kidnapped another alpha, turned him into a sex slave, and then went feral and staged some kind of shootout in the desert—and *then* mated, but I figured only the last part would be polite to ask about.

Declan's flashing grin had me smiling in return, despite my mood. "That I did. And maybe you'll meet him one day, and maybe not. I'm keeping him the hell away from Lucky or Knot. No matter how often he asks me to take him there."

"Looking forward to it, or maybe not," I said, laughing, and he laughed with me.

Pretty sure he wasn't joking, not that he had much to worry about. Even if he hadn't been a hot, rich, intelligent alpha, I could smell how happy they both were by the way their scents had almost fused into one. My nose always knew when mates weren't devoted to one another. And Declan and his mate were, without a doubt.

"Sorry to bring you this bullshit when you have better ways to be spending your time," I went on, and he sat back and nodded, giving me his full attention. "But I'm here to ask for a favor. Last night…"

I left out most of the more prurient details, but I had to confess that I'd agreed to fuck a club customer for money—not something you wanted to tell your employer. But he didn't even blink, not being naïve or stupid. He knew what went on at literally every strip club anywhere, and as long as we were discreet and exercised a bit of judgment, he didn't give a fuck.

On this occasion, well. At least I'd been discreet.

When I finished my story, Declan shook his head, sighed, and grinned. "Sorry, but it sounds like you really did get rolled by a fairy," he said. "I'd be furious too, if I were you. But I'm also never going to let you live this down. You know that, right?"

Yeah. I'd known it going in. "Fuck you, Declan."

He laughed again. "Fair enough. And you want me to pull the security footage for you? I'll do it. Jeremy is doing the job I pay him to do, but in this case I'll overrule him."

"Thanks. I wasn't super eager to tell him I got—you know."

"Rolled by a fairy in stripper heels?" Declan stood and headed for his desk. "Don't blame you. And I know Jeremy has an ego," he threw over his shoulder. "He's good at his job, but believe me, I know. I don't think I need to even involve him, anyway. I can log in from here. Come on over."

He sat down and started tapping away on his laptop, and I came around behind him to look over his shoulder. A moment later, a tiled screen full of live camera feeds popped up, and he moved it over to the big monitor set up next to his laptop. Cassidy danced onstage in one of the feeds, and there was the semi-private champagne room, the door to Scott's booth, a dozen other angles.

A moment later, the screen went to a shot of the parking lot, and then Declan had a drop-down menu open. My heart started pounding. I might be able to see *him* on the screen, and it pissed me off beyond anything to realize my excitement stemmed as much from the idea of seeing his face as from the possibility of getting his car's license plate.

"Try about midnight," I said. "His credit card transaction went through at twelve-twenty, so he probably arrived around then."

Declan chose the right time window and turned up the speed a bit, letting the footage run. And— "There!" I said, tapping the screen.

Even on the grainy black and white feed, my keen alpha eyes picked out his long hair and slim body. But it was the thud my heart gave against my ribs that tipped me off a second before I consciously recognized him.

Declan stopped it and ran it back, slowing it down to a normal speed. A dark-colored luxury coupe pulled in and parked near the back of the lot, the license plate way too far from the camera to be legible. After a moment, the fairy got out and walked to the building, glancing up toward the camera when he was halfway across the parking lot.

The sight of his face stopped my breath and dizzied me for a frozen instant. My vision blurred, and I had to catch myself as I swayed toward the monitor.

I clenched my fists and breathed through it. *That'll wear off, I think.* Yeah. Not so much. When I found that little fucker, I really couldn't be answerable for my actions.

"Shit," Declan said, sounding startled. "Hang on." He started running the recording back again.

"I don't think we'll be able to get the plate number from this angle, even if you replay it." Keeping my voice somewhat even took a serious effort, and I knew I wouldn't be fooling another alpha. He earned my extreme gratitude by not commenting. "Maybe you could try looking at the recording from this morning, see if it was daylight by the time he—"

"No, I will if you like, but it's not necessary," Declan said, and his tone had gone grim. He paused the video at the precise instant that the fairy tilted his face up, giving us both the best possible view. "I recognize him. I know exactly who this is. And you're not going to like it any more than I do. Here, I'm just going to show you."

All the hair rose on the back of my neck, right where my tiger's hackles would've been. Would it have been too gods-damned much to ask that another high-heeled peep-toe pump wasn't waiting to drop?

Of course it would. Because nothing could be simple.

I waited with my jaw clenched for whatever Declan wanted to show me. I already didn't like it.

He minimized the camera feed and pulled up an internet browser, typing in a name that rang a bell. Arnold Cunningham. And when he clicked over to images, I realized why: the hard-jawed, harder-eyed guy in the photos had a finger in half the real estate pies in Vegas, and I'd seen him in the local news more than once, usually shaking hands at a ribbon cutting or standing next to a state representative. His last name appeared on so many of the construction signs in the city that I'd tuned it out like background noise and forgotten where I knew it from.

Also, I vaguely remembered that...

"Didn't he have a stake in this place before you bought it back?" I asked. My arrival in Vegas had coincided with Declan taking over the Morrigan, which I was pretty sure his grandparents had originally built, way back when. The details of his family's ups and downs hadn't interested me enough for me to bother learning all of them, but I knew that much. "And I hear he's a total prick."

"He didn't want to sell, and he got outmaneuvered." Declan turned in his chair to look up at me. "He hates me for it. And he is a total prick. He's an alpha were, did you know that?" I shook my head, and he quirked an eyebrow at me. "Right, most people out-side of his immediate contacts don't, because he doesn't publicize it. You want to know why?"

"I want to know where the fuck you're going with this," I said bluntly, because I was starting to get some ideas of where he could be going. And I hated all of them. "Who is this asshole to the guy I was with last night?"

"I'm getting there. He's an alpha, but he's a coyote. And he resents it, and everyone who's something a bit better, as it were."

I nodded, because while I didn't particularly care what people were, the smaller, less elegant predators definitely caught a lot of mockery and flack from the flashier species—like mine. Or even the werewolves. In a way, it was harder than being "prey." Of course, tell that to a gerbil.

"He has a real chip on his shoulder about being the big man and the alpha in the room," Declan went on. "And he's an art col-lector. A wine snob. And so on and so forth. Makes a big fuss out of his taste and his possessions and having the very best of every single thing you can own. And compensates for being less-than among shifters by only associating with the right sort of rich peo-ple, and I," Declan bared his teeth at me, "am far from the right sort, and I bought this place out from under him."

A collector of the best and the most beautiful, obsessed with his status. That kind of man would have a certain type of taste in lovers, too, wouldn't he?

My stomach had turned to lead, my hands and feet tingling with the urge to transform, to claw, my throat raw with a roar I had to suppress. Not that Declan would hold it against me, I didn't think, but it'd be beyond rude.

"Yeah?" I said roughly. "All right. Give me the punchline."

"I think you already know. Your fairy's his—" Declan's steady dark gaze had been fixed on me, and he stopped abruptly, his jaw tightening, as my reaction passed across my face. "Beg your par-don," he rumbled. "Companion, let's say. The last few times I've seen Cunningham somewhere, he's been with him. I wasn't intro-duced, but my assessment was that the fellow's one of Cunning-ham's ruinously expensive *objets d'art*. I'm sure you take my meaning."

"Yes," I managed, swallowing to get some moisture into my dry mouth. "I appreciate you trying to put a finer point on it, but yeah, I get it. Except that what the fuck—Christ, Declan, what the fuck happened last night? The fuck!"

I couldn't stand still anymore. I'd explode. So I spun on my heel and paced, rubbing at my forehead where that headache had come roaring back like an angry tiger, a low growl I couldn't control rolling out of my chest. The spacious, frigidly air-conditioned office felt like an oven with the walls closing in, constricting around my throat, broiling me alive.

"I'm sorry." Declan's voice came from behind me, echoing as if he spoke to me through a tunnel whose walls were closing and opening and pushing the sound through at odd angles. "This isn't what you wanted to hear. And you need to be careful. Tony. Focus."

I stopped, vibrating down to my toes, and closed my eyes. One rasping breath in, then out, then another, until my blood pressure dropped and my urge to rend and destroy and maim simmered down to a low-level pounding in my veins, my alpha magic ebbing enough that I could see more than the golden haze of my own fury.

Magic. He'd enchanted me and made me want him, then enchanted me to knock me out. My rage had to be at least half due to that, and the same with my headache. Shifters didn't fucking get headaches unless someone hit us over the head with a steel beam— or magicked us.

I had to get it together. None of what I felt was real, which meant I could push it aside.

But it sure seemed real. Turning around to face Declan took effort. Controlled motion was so much harder than simply remaining still. But I gritted my teeth, tasting blood as my lowered fangs pierced my lip, and managed it.

He'd taken up a position between me and the office door, poised and wary, his own eyes glowing and a couple of inches of claw gleaming at the tips of his fingers.

Guilt hit me hard enough to almost drown out the rest of my churning emotion.

"I won't lose it," I rasped out. "I apologize for the—I'm sorry. You don't need to protect your staff from me."

Declan nodded, and the tension slowly eased out of his big body, his hands flexing as his claws whispered back in.

"All right. You're paying attention?" he said, taking a step towards me and lowering his voice, even though the office's glass door was shut. I nodded. "Good. Because Cunningham's a prick and a right bastard, and he's at least as possessive as the average alpha. More so. And vindictive. And he'd hate you on principle simply for what you are, but if he found out what his pretty boy had been up to last night, he'd hate you more than he hates me. You understand?"

Oh, I understood. Vegas had always had a vicious, violent undertone to it, because huge sums of money made people crazy and ruthless. The mob was bad enough. Add magic and alpha weres to the mix…

Christ. My head spun, from the magic and from literally fucking everything.

Hockey and beer. Why the ever-loving fuck hadn't I taken the night off for hockey and beer?

And then I'd never have looked into his glossy black eyes, seen him pout with those flower-petal lips. Never have kissed his sweet, hot, forked-tongued mouth, licked his satin skin, filled him with my come and my knot and made him cry while he took what I gave him.

I rubbed at my temples. "I need a fucking drink."

Declan sighed and shook his head. "That you do," he said heavily. "I'm—look, I can't skip this meeting. I wish I could. But I'm out of time for this tonight, much as I hate to send you off with this shite hanging over you. You want my advice?"

The quirk of his lips suggested he knew damn well what I'd think of that.

"You mean your advice to drop it, let it go, and walk away? The advice you'd never take in a million years if you were in my shoes?"

"Precisely," he replied. "That advice. It was one night, Tony. You got a good fuck out of it, that coin was probably worthless anyway, and the fairy's not worth it, either. It's a funny story you can tell when you're drinking in a few years."

"And if you were me?" I pressed. "Don't bullshit me. I know you can get more information for me about him, if you want to."

After a long, reluctant pause, he said, "I'll text you later once I have someone look into it. But you're going to get yourself killed."

That didn't seem worth arguing about. It didn't actually matter, because I wouldn't, and couldn't, walk away, and we both knew it. So I thanked him, shook his hand, and showed myself out.

Chapter 7

Thrifty budgeting be damned, I picked up a mid-shelf bottle of Scotch on my way home, parked myself on my dilapidated couch, and settled in to brood. From my sprawled position, I had a view through the living room window of the tall sign for the gas station next door, with its blue glare illuminating the top of a scraggly palm tree.

Somewhere out there, through that window and a few miles across town to the more expensive parts of Vegas's environs, Cunningham had his own no-doubt luxurious lair. A view of the whole Strip. Much better Scotch. A hundred comfortable rooms. And in one of them, a beautiful, deceitful little fairy, who probably took all of the opulent trappings of his lifestyle for granted.

The hotel room last night had been more of a slumming-it experience for him than I'd realized at the time, I guessed.

Maybe so had I.

He might be spreading his legs for Cunningham in a plush, silk-sheeted, king-sized bed right at that moment.

The Scotch went down pretty quick. I poured another.

One drink became maybe-six-or-more, and at last I slumped all the way into the corner of the couch, some of the tension in my body draining away. It took a lot of alcohol to get an alpha relaxed, what with our incredibly fast metabolisms and high muscle mass, but it felt fucking incredible when I could afford enough booze to accomplish it.

Especially right now, when every time I closed my eyes I pictured my lover from the night before, either under me—or under Cunningham.

At least this way my blood pressure didn't spike every single damn time.

My cock had perked up, though. I ignored it, because sitting there half-drunk and getting myself off thinking about the guy who'd tricked and lied to me was simply too pathetic, even if no one would ever know about it but me.

Why had he tricked and lied to me, though? It didn't make any sense. Half of me wished Declan had been available to talk it over, but I was mostly glad he'd been too busy to keep plumbing the depths of my humiliation with me, useful as his perspective might have been.

Arnold Cunningham had all the money in the world, probably even more than Declan, but at that point only super rich guys showing off for other super rich guys cared about the difference. I certainly didn't. And that car the fairy had been driving cost over a hundred grand, so apparently Cunningham extended his showing-off-his-wealth to showering it on his…companion. If Declan had seen them together at events, that meant Cunningham didn't keep him hidden away as a dirty little secret, either.

Which meant…well, it meant the fairy hadn't needed to cheat me. The bit about not wanting to use any traceable form of payment made sense, if he had a jealous sugar daddy, but why take back the coin when money had to be the least of his problems?

And of course, his explanation about the bet had obviously been total bullshit. Now that I thought about it, he hadn't been very specific about the terms, had he? And his unstated and therefore not-an-actual-lie implication, that he'd lost a bet with a friend about taking an alpha knot, didn't make any sense, either. He hadn't needed my knot; his boyfriend had one, which he probably put in him on the regular.

I took a shot of Scotch, but it didn't quite banish that image. Fuck me.

All right, so what, then? No matter how I turned it around in my mind, I couldn't come up with any theory that fit.

Declan might be right that trying to get to the bottom of the mystery, get what I was owed, and get revenge would end in disaster—because all of those would require seeing the fairy again.

Seeing him again. And possibly more than seeing him.

No, dammit. That would be too stupid even for me.

I poured another drink and tried to convince myself that I was smarter than that, and hoped I'd manage it before I passed out.

***

Declan delivered on his promise. I woke up on the couch the next morning to several texts from him. He'd sent me three addresses: Cunningham's main office downtown, his mansion in the hills, and info about a penthouse he maintained at one of the Strip's most upscale casino hotels, in which he apparently owned the majority stake.

While I scrolled through those, I rolled off the couch, wincing at the excessive amount of sunlight pouring through the blinds I'd forgotten to close the night before, and wandered into the tiny kitchen to start some coffee.

Shifters didn't get hangovers, so I couldn't understand why I had this heavy, not-quite-right feeling. Coffee would help. It might be mostly psychosomatic, given that caffeine didn't affect me much more than liquor did, but the smell always reminded me of my father in the kitchen in the morning, brewing his little pot of tar on the stove in his copper *cezve*. The aroma and the bitter flavor always helped me focus and prepare for whatever came next.

Although I used a coffeemaker instead of doing it the old-fashioned way, much to my dad's disgust.

As I clicked the machine on, my screen lit up again. Declan had sent an attachment, and it had only started downloading onto my crappy outdated phone when I opened up the message thread.

The attachment popped up. The mug I'd been pulling out of the cabinet slipped from my hand, and I cursed and flailed and fumbled, barely catching it.

That was the fairy's face looking up at me from the screen in a photo very obviously taken for his driver's license, and even with the gruesome lighting and the DMV's best attempt at making him look drunk, dead, and angry, his skin glowed and his eyes and hair gleamed and his lips pouted kissably…and my cock twitched.

All of a sudden I was all the way awake, even though the coffee machine had barely begun to hiss and spit.

Declan hadn't only sent me the fairy's photo. He'd somehow gotten hold of the entire driver's license application, photo included. A lot of the little boxes had been filled in with a code the State of Nevada used on paperwork when the answer to a question didn't apply to a supernatural or non-human entity. The fairy hadn't provided a birthdate, place of birth, or his mother's maiden name, just for example. He'd also declined to register to vote and to be an organ donor, probably luckily for democracy and also the health of anyone in need of a kidney.

But he had put down a name, because apparently even fae skittishness about the magical power inherent in names wasn't enough to defeat the Nevada bureaucracy.

Despite everything, I couldn't help starting to laugh.

Tyler Tania. Really? I mean…*really?*

Of course, the same clerk who hadn't quibbled over Ty Tania the fairy also hadn't disputed his absurd claim to be five foot six, so maybe it'd been a don't-give-a-fuck kind of day at the DMV.

Tyler. All right. I'd call him Tyler. I'd call him whatever, but mostly, I'd just call him.

Because right below an address that I was pretty sure matched that hotel Declan had texted me about was a phone number.

And fuck it. Seriously, fuck it. Maybe Cunningham would answer. Maybe it'd be the concierge of the Audacity Casino and Hotel. Maybe my number would be tracked and recorded and a hit squad of pissed-off werecoyote goons would be breaking down my door before I'd finished my pot of coffee.

Whatever. I had a phone number, and my gums itched as my fangs descended, my blood pumping faster in my veins.

Mine. He was—he owed me.

The coin, damn it. The coin was mine.

I punched in the number, hit send, and waited, holding my breath.

One ring. Two. Three. And right as my heart sank, and I'd braced myself for an impersonal recorded voice telling me to leave a voicemail that I obviously wouldn't, the call connected.

"Hello?" His voice, clear and sweet despite the tone of annoyance. It struck into my chest like a knife and rang in my ribs like a bell. "Hello? Yes?"

He sounded a bit distracted, too, maybe by whatever was making all that background noise. Not a casino, though I did hear something electronic. A store's cash register? He'd picked me up at the club, spread his legs, cried, and stolen that coin, sneaking out like the thief he was. And then shrugged and gone shopping. I swallowed hard. I really hadn't expected him to pick up the phone at all, but somehow the shopping pushed me over the edge.

I bared my teeth at the phone, wishing he could see. "It's me."

The horrified pause that followed, half-filled with a soft, startled gasp that my alpha ears couldn't miss, thrilled me all the way down to the tips of my…claws, which had started to come out without my even noticing.

His voice shook a little, probably imperceptibly to anyone else who might be listening, as he said, "I'm sorry, I think you must have the—"

"You know exactly who I am and if you hang up my next call's to Cunningham," I snarled, cutting him off.

Because yeah, no. Fuck that. Rage welled up, rage so sudden and violent that my phone creaked in my grip. He thought he'd what, simply hang up? And then disappear again?

He sucked in another quick, hissing breath. I could picture him, his cheeks reddening, his long lashes fluttering, that sharp, pearly canine tooth digging into his lip in frustration.

"That would be worse for you than for me," he said, and—he was lying again.

Shifters couldn't necessarily hear a lie, unless we were close enough to detect the skipping of a heartbeat. But I knew. He was afraid. And not for me, because he didn't give a fuck about me.

Another fae half-truth, then. He wanted to believe it, and so he was able to say it with a straight face.

"Maybe it would, but I don't really give a flying fuck," I shot back. And I had the advantage of telling the real, unvarnished truth. "At this point, it's scorched earth, *Tyler*. You'll—"

Fuck, fuck, shit, what would he what? I should've taken the time to think it through before I called. Drunk a cup of that coffee. Every second that I talked to him on the phone, more of my brain cells seemed to commit some kind of ritual suicide, and all I could think about was seeing him, touching him, breathing the same air as him, or I was going to crawl out of my own skin.

That was it.

"—meet me tonight," I finished, barely missing a beat.

Not the same hotel, we were probably on wanted posters behind the desk after the way I'd left the room all pulled apart and with half the ceiling on the floor. But my buddy worked night audit at a way, way off-Strip casino hotel where no one would ever expect to find Arnold Cunningham's pretty boy. And he could get me a room and make sure no names or credit cards were necessary.

"At the Silver Lode. Midnight. I'll text you the room number, and you'd better fucking show. At twelve-oh-one, I'm making another phone call."

"I can't," he protested, and his voice had lowered to a frantic whisper. "I *can't*. This is absurd. You don't want to—"

"Midnight," I repeated ruthlessly. Good. He should be squirming. A thief and a manipulator who magically whammied people without warning. He deserved it, and more. "The Silver Lode. Don't fuck with me." *Again* remained unspoken.

I gave myself the satisfaction of pulling the phone away from my ear and ending the call before he could say another word. And then, of course, I immediately regretted it, staring down at the flashing screen and wondering if I should've let him, what, argue with me? Make excuses? Could he enchant me again over the phone somehow? I couldn't imagine that he'd be able to hit me with his fae magic at a distance, but giving him the opportunity to prove me wrong would probably have been a terrible idea.

Still. Even though I'd cut him off, I couldn't seem to resettle in my own skin. And now I had, fuck, fourteen hours until the time I'd set.

Why had I chosen midnight? Because it sounded cool? Yeah,

basically. Jesus Christ alive, I needed help.

Instead, I poured the coffee and texted the scheduler at the club, letting her know I'd be coming in for a mid shift if that worked. I got an enthusiastic thumbs up before I'd even drunk half my cup. No one really wanted to work the less lucrative afternoon and early evening on a January Thursday. No one who didn't desperately need a distraction, anyway.

Not that any of it worked. I spent the rest of the day unable to focus on anything but counting down the minutes until midnight. Showering, getting my stage clothes together, packing my gym bag, driving to the club…all of it faded into a background for my obsessive speculations about what I'd say to him, what he might say to me, what possible explanation he could give, what he might be doing in the meantime while I danced and smiled and rubbed glitter all over my pecs.

On one of my breaks, I texted my friend at the Silver Lode and got confirmation that I'd have a room waiting for me.

And other than that, I didn't have anything to do but pretend to give a shit about the people staring at me. My lack of interest showed in my measly tips, and by the time I finally called it quits a little before ten, I only had a couple of hundred dollars, and that headache had trickled back into my skull, pulsing in my temples and setting my teeth on edge.

That still left me with too much time to kill. I could go home, get really clean, make sure not a trace of sweat and glitter and oil remained. Put on some nicer clothes.

But no, fuck that. A quick stop in the locker room shower, and my usual old jeans and hoodie, would be good enough for the purpose. This wasn't a date, dammit. And I didn't need to impress him. Who cared what he thought of me? It already wasn't much, anyway, judging by how he'd treated me. And I'd still be cleaner tonight than I had been when we'd gone to that hotel two nights ago. He'd been willing to get fucked by a sweaty, glitter-dusted stripper *then*, so I'd be damned if I'd try to make myself appealing to him *now*.

The drive from the club to the Silver Lode wouldn't be nearly long enough to fill the time, since I hadn't lingered over getting dressed, so I found myself pulling over halfway there—strangely enough, into a strip mall with a 24-hour sex shop. Maybe they had the same brand of lube the fairy had brought to our rendezvous the other night.

I'd parked and shut off the engine before it hit me what I'd been doing.

Fuck. I leaned my forehead against the steering wheel, struggling to get a breath to go all the way down to the bottom of my lungs. My head still hurt, throbbing in time with the weird itching under my skin, a craving that I couldn't seem to satisfy.

I had a really horrible suspicion that only one thing would satisfy that craving, and that it might or might not be turning up at the Silver Lode at midnight.

That'll wear off, I think.

Well, it fucking hadn't. My anger grew along with the pain in my head, both throbbing in time with the matching sensations in my hardening cock.

No. I would not buy lube. I would not give in to this. The second he appeared, I'd wrap my hand around his throat and I'd squeeze, pricking him with my claws, watching his eyes go round and terrified, and I'd force him to fix whatever the fuck he'd done to me.

And pay me.

Then I'd leave him there and I'd never want to see his lying face ever again in my life.

With that all sorted out and clear in my mind, I started the car again and pulled out of the lot, heading for the Silver Lode. And if I drove a little over the speed limit, well, no one could blame me for wanting to use my time efficiently.

Chapter 8

At exactly 11:56, not that I'd been checking my phone obsessively every three seconds or anything, he knocked on the door of the hotel room. And I knew it was him, because I could sense his magic in every cell of my body, scent him even through the door.

Relief washed over me and weakened my knees. If he'd called my bluff and blown me off, I didn't know what I'd have done.

Actually, I did. Because calling Cunningham, satisfying as it might have been in one way…well, I knew I couldn't and wouldn't do it. The half hour I'd had to wear a track in the hotel room's carpet, pacing and waiting, had been enough to let me think that through.

The fairy—and I simply couldn't bring myself to think of him as Tyler, of all the bullshit—had sounded genuinely afraid on the phone. Not of me, except insofar as I represented a blackmail threat, but of Cunningham. Maybe I'd have been offended by the fairy's lack of respect for the more concrete threat I represented, except that it occurred to me that I'd promised not to hurt him, and he probably considered me still bound by that, fae logic being what it was.

Honestly, it offended me more that he thought I needed a promise to keep me in check. Choking fantasies aside, I'd never be able to bring myself to beat up on someone so much smaller than me, even if he had powerful magic.

Spank him, maybe. My cock twitched. Yeah, I could spank

him, possibly even mark up all that perfect white skin by nipping and sucking on him until he squirmed.

But not beat him.

Cunningham might beat him. Or worse. That asshole's reputation didn't give me any confidence in his having a gentlemanly reluctance to abuse his lover.

So *my* gentlemanly reluctance to land the fairy in the kind of hot water that could get him bruised, battered, or even dead would've meant he got away scot-free.

Thank the gods he'd shown up, and I didn't need to choose between my morals and my pride. I rubbed my hands over my face to scrub away my worry and weakness before I stepped forward to answer the door.

When I wrenched it open, the sight of him standing there froze me in place for a long, suspended moment. And the scent of him, my gods. Light and tart and somehow green like the beginning of spring, soft like a breeze off a warm sea. He'd worn his hair in a ponytail tonight, sleekly pulled back from his face to show off those cut-glass cheekbones and the delicate line of his jaw. He'd worn all black again. His long tunic had another high collar, this one more of a wrapped scarf sort of affair. Tight, shimmery black pants led down into knee-high leather boots.

He blinked at me, long eyelashes sweeping down and then up again, feathery soft, his eyes wide and deep and dark, more enchanting than his magic. If he ever wore eyeliner he'd give me a fucking heart attack. My heart galloped anyway, trying to force its way out of my ribs.

His lips were pressed together in a tight, anxious line, and he raised his eyebrows at me.

Right. I'd been standing here gaping at him like a teenager catching his first glimpse of porn, and with much the same effect below the waist. Hopefully my jeans would camouflage my reaction a little bit.

"Nice of you to show up, *Tyler*," I ground out, trying to regain a bit of the upper hand, and stood back to let him in.

Moving farther away from him took conscious effort, as if I had a solid object behind my legs that I had to push through.

He slipped inside like a beam of moonlight, and I shoved the door and let it click itself shut. The fairy stood facing me, biting his lip, hands balled into fists at his sides. The air between us thickened, buzzed, drew me in like quicksand. The hotel room blurred into a halo of cheap lighting and unimportance, a meaningless background to his shining beauty.

I leaned in, my body straining toward his, my breath fast and rough.

"You shouldn't," he whispered. "You'll only make it worse." But he didn't move away from me, and his chest rose and fell as quickly as mine.

Make it worse. That'll wear off, I think.

The buzz faded enough to let me shake my head, shake it off, at least a little bit.

Fuck. I'd been about to—gods dammit. Everything about this was already worse, including my growing suspicion that kissing him had been like the first hit of heroin, and that my longing and my headaches and my mental strain and fog had all been symptoms of withdrawal from his particular brand of heady, intoxicatingly deadly magic.

"That's why you stopped me from sucking you off or eating you out," I said, and it wasn't a question. "Trying to make yourself feel less like a son of a bitch for enchanting me to get me to take your deal, and then again so you could sneak out and steal that coin you supposedly paid me with. And you didn't stop me from kissing you last time. So I'm not that impressed."

"It's not my fault that you kissed me without asking permission!" He spoke too quickly and too breathlessly to be convincing, and I started rethinking the choking thing. I could choke him a tiny bit, couldn't I? Shake some honesty out of him like a stubborn bottle of ketchup? "And licked my neck and my—"

"*You* told me to do anything I needed to do to get it over with, and *you* told me it'd probably but not definitely wear off, without even explaining what 'it' was, and *you*—"

"—shoulder and my ankle and—"

"—cheated me, stole from me, and lied to me!" I finished in almost a shout, drowning out his list of body parts that I'd supposedly licked. I didn't remember licking his ankle, but whatever.

He crossed his arms over his chest, mouth tightening, and lifted his chin. "I did not lie to you," he said loftily. "I don't directly lie about factual, objective things, although I do occasionally exaggerate when it's a subjective matter that's open to interpretation." Subjective…open to…the sheer, jaw-dropping chutzpah bullshit of that statement had me, well, standing there gaping at him like an idiot. He took advantage of my total gobsmackedness to keep talking. "I can pay you another way, since you seem to have lost the coin. You can do anything you want with me, as long as it doesn't involve your mouth, and if it does, that's your lookout. I've warned you."

It took a moment for all of that to sink in, but…was this what it felt like to be the only sane person in an asylum?

"Lost the coin," I repeated flatly. "Lost. The coin. And so you propose to pay me another way? Let me get this straight, pay me. For fucking you. Which you offered to pay me for. By letting me fuck you?"

My hands flexed at my sides, claws sliding out and all the muscles in my arms going hard and rigid. Everything in the room had taken on a gilded tinge as my alpha glow intensified.

"Ah," he said. "I, ah." He glanced shiftily from side to side, feet shuffling, as if he sought an escape route that he already knew didn't exist. "Ah? Yes? You seemed to enjoy it the first time?"

Enjoy it the first—the golden glow went crimson around the edges as my chest tightened with pure, incandescent rage.

I was going to fucking *kill* him.

Kill him, or—I lunged, and he cried out and twisted like an acrobat to dodge me, but I seized him inexorably around the waist, jerked him against me, and fused my mouth to his, hard and brutal. My head went light and spinny as the whole world narrowed down to the sweet softness of his lips, the flick of his tongue, my own forcing its way into him. He writhed in my arms and I clamped him tighter, and maybe I'd have come to my senses and let him go.

Except that between one instant and the next, his arms wrapped around my neck and he clung to me, his helpless moan swallowed in my kiss, his body arching up to melt into mine.

If I hadn't needed my mouth to ravage him, I'd have let out a roar of triumph deep and wild enough to bring the whole building's roof down. Instead I yanked him even closer, bending my body over his, shoving a thigh between his legs and half lifting him off the ground.

He squirmed on my knee, riding me, spreading his legs, and that forked tongue curled around mine, and that was it.

We crashed down onto the bed, his hands clawing at my back. One of mine wrapped in his long tail of hair, with the other working under the hem of his shirt and splaying over the softness of his skin.

I tore my mouth away from his and nipped him under his chin. His scarf-like collar was in my way, concealing that throat I needed to bite and lick—

"Don't rip it," he gasped, and shoved at my shoulders. "Don't!"

The frantic note in his voice shocked me out of my single-minded focus on stripping him bare and splitting him open on my cock, reminding me that I was…

Angry. I was also furiously angry, in addition to the surge of pure, bone-searing lust.

"Why not?" I growled, and lifted my head to stare down into his eyes, baring my teeth. "Why the fuck should I care about your fucking clothes? Hmm? Why shouldn't I claw every stitch you're wearing to shreds and leave you here to find your way home in a fucking hotel bedsheet?"

His cheeks, already pink, went cherry-red. They'd be burning hot if I pressed my lips to his skin, and my cock pushed violently against his thigh, seeking his tight wet hole—

And the look in those beautiful eyes was pure, unadulterated terror.

My cock ached with the need to force him open, take him, knot him. But slowly, reluctantly, I pushed up and off of him, bracing myself on my hands to either side of his shoulders, giving him room to breathe.

That was something I needed as much as he did, and I sucked

in air, trying to get my heartbeat to slow, grounding myself in mundane sensation: my knees digging into the too-soft mattress, the faint shush of the fan high up in the wall, the cool air on my sweaty skin.

"Explain it to me," I said, as gently as I could manage with my laboring lungs and around my dropped fangs. Smilodons weren't known for their reassuring affects for a reason. "Why shouldn't I?"

His lips pressed together in as flat a line as a mouth that plush could manage. "It doesn't matter. Simply respect my—"

"Absolutely fucking not." If I didn't stay firm, those big, glossy eyes gazing pleadingly up at me would have me caving in seconds. Usually I didn't lean on my alpha magic to get my way. But this time I didn't feel bad about it. "No," I said, and my voice resonated with command. "Answer the question *now*."

I'd expected him to react. Possibly with instant obedience, although I hadn't been counting on it, and more likely with annoyance or a few words reluctantly dragged out of him.

Instead, his whole body jerked as he gasped and flinched away from me, his eyelids fluttering, his hands flying off my shoulders to come up in—yeah.

A defensive position, like someone would take when trying to deflect a blow to the face.

If someone had offered to bet me a million dollars at a hundred to one that my desperate lust and offended fury could vanish like magic within the space of a single heartbeat, I'd have taken that bet.

…And I'd have lost.

I stared down at him, both of us frozen in place.

He had an alpha—no, I couldn't think of Cunningham as his lover. Nothing that neutral or benign. Abuser probably fit a whole lot better. And I'd dominated him. Threatened him. Used my alpha magic to try to command and control him. Probably the exact same way Cunningham did before he…

My gut churned and bile stabbed at my esophagus, and I rolled to the side, coming to sit on the edge of the bed next to his dangling legs, scrubbing my hands over my face and breathing through the nausea.

Suspecting that Cunningham might be the kind of man to mistreat someone in his power had been one thing.

Seeing the absolute confirmation of it was something else.

"Jesus motherfucking fuck," I choked out, as my determination to have my revenge and make him pay came crashing down around me and crushed me under the rubble, "fucking Christ."

Had I ever felt this guilty? No, and that included living with the knowledge that a Vegas loan shark might force my parents to lose their home.

A soft rustle to my left suggested the fairy had moved, and then the bed dipped slightly as he sat up, the motion a flicker in my peripheral vision. I didn't turn my head. Meeting his eyes would be more than I could stand; I'd have to see my own behavior reflected in their panicked brightness.

His silence had a breathless, wary weight to it.

As if he were afraid that the wrong word would bring on a burst of violence, maybe.

My working assumption, based on my preexisting experience with and opinions of the fae (generally justified, to be fair), had been that this particular fairy had been wreaking mischief and mayhem on me simply for his own amusement, or possibly for some malicious reason no human-adjacent species could comprehend.

Now...

Well, now it simply didn't matter. There were a few things about him I'd been missing. And those far, far outweighed any damage done to me, even if he had been messing with me for fun.

"I'm not going to call him," I said at last, and dropped my hands to my knees. Looking at him still felt impossible, but I could at least give him a view of my expression. He might trust me more if he could gauge my sincerity. "You have my word. It doesn't bind me the way a promise does you, but I'll keep it. You can get up right now and walk out of here, or do anything you want, and I swear to you, that fucking son of a bitch is never going to hear about any of this from me."

Although I might go and kill the aforementioned fucking son of a bitch, obviously without breaking my promise and telling him why, as soon as the fairy had walked out the door—but that didn't seem like something he needed to hear.

His minute twitch was more than enough to tell me how much I'd surprised him. I half expected that he'd simply get up and leave as I'd offered, but except for that involuntary reaction, he didn't move a muscle. My consciousness of his body next to mine had changed, from pure desire to something more awkward and strained, but it hadn't diminished. All the cells in my body seemed to have oriented themselves in his direction, iron filings chasing a magnet.

His breath came too fast and too shallow, but he still didn't move.

"How did I—how did you—you didn't seem to, to know anything. When I arrived." He paused to suck in an audible breath, blowing it out slowly. "What do you think you know?"

Translation: How had he given himself away?

At last, I gave into temptation and twisted around, shifting my weight and looking him right in the eyes. Those eyes, gods.

I'd grown up in central Washington, with a view of Mount Rainier framed perfectly in my bedroom window. And every damn morning—or about half of them, anyway, given the typical weather—I'd looked outside and had to do a double-take, because the mountain was just so incredibly *big* that you never got used to it.

His eyes were the same. Every time they caught and held me, every time I really looked at him, it startled me all over again that anyone could be so incredibly beautiful.

"I'll be honest," I said—with a bit of irony, because I knew I was pulling the same bullshit he usually did, answering a question he hadn't asked while ignoring the one he had. "I thought about throttling you, and possibly turning you upside down and shaking you to see if that fucking coin fell out of one of your pockets." That earned me the faintest, palest glimmer of a smile, and my breath caught as I forced myself not to lean in and kiss it off his mouth. "But I really don't understand how anyone, especially anyone like me, someone who's stronger than most—like, where does that even come from, looking at you and wanting to hurt you?"

Those unbelievable eyelashes swept down as he stared at his

hands twisting together in his lap, biting his lip. Rosy heat spread over his cheeks again. Shame, probably. Figured. I knew a lot of strippers, and people in our profession didn't tend to attract the nicest guys, so I'd seen this before. Somehow, it was never the assholes who knocked their lovers around who were ashamed of themselves, but the opposite.

The wall heating unit chugged into life, humming and clicking, highlighting the bubble of silence between us.

Not surprisingly, I cracked first, because the suspense of waiting for him to speak had started to build up into a crawling sensation in the back of my neck and a twitching in my fingers, and if I didn't do *something*, I'd have him flat on his back again.

"I know because you have more tells than a ten-dollar-tournament player, and because I'm smarter than I look."

The fairy glanced up, and all the traces of fear in his face had faded away at last, thank the gods. A small amused smile played around the corners of his mouth.

Shit. I'd really walked into that one.

"Go ahead. Say it," I told him. "It's because—"

"—you couldn't possibly be stupider than you look," he finished for me, his smile widening and mischief starting to spark again in his eyes. "But you know, within the first minute that I saw you, you fell down on stage. My first impression didn't indicate, um, how do I put this?"

"Don't put it at all," I growled. The impulse to place the blame for that fall where it belonged, on the incredibly distracting fairy who'd caused it, rose up strong. Except that no, I didn't want to admit that his scent had been enough to short-circuit my brain and motor functions, right? Instead, I chose to ask him something else I'd been mulling over. "And I know you were fudging the truth when you told me you picked me because I was the first one you noticed. You knew I used The Hammer on stage, which meant you'd already been in the club looking around before I came out, if you heard me get introduced. There were other guys out there and visible before that."

A minute twitch of an eyebrow told me that hit had landed. Not a big tell, that one, but still enough to get him fleeced at a card table. He really didn't belong in Vegas.

"So you chose me while I was dancing," I went on. "Which means you wanted a fucking idiot. So you could cheat me and get away with it. And I really want to know why. What were you doing? What was the point, why me, why this bullshit? I'm not going to go to that motherfucker, and I won't hurt you. So why not just tell me? Since you welshed on our deal. Pay me by telling me the truth."

"The truth?" His smile faded away, and I could've sworn the light in the room dimmed. "You know, according to my own people's rules, I really don't owe you anything. I paid you. And whether or not you believe it, I didn't steal from you."

What? That coin hadn't walked off by itself, that would be...

...That would be...

Part and parcel of an artifact that stank of magic and had been given to me by a fairy.

"It's the coin, isn't it?" I said, as realization finally dawned. "This is all about the coin."

Chapter 9

The ensuing silence told me more than one of his evasive answers would have. He simply gazed up at me, eyes all limpid and wide, plush lips pursed.

"Well?" I prompted him, knowing as I did that I had no leverage at all. I'd already abandoned my blackmail plan. Given that he didn't seem to experience guilt in any meaningful way, I'd be dependent on his sense of fair play to give me answers.

Ha.

But to my shock, the next words out of his mouth, whispered so quietly that a human wouldn't have been able to distinguish them, were, "I'm so sorry."

"You're what? I mean, yes, you fucking well should be!"

That won me another faint ghost of his pretty smile. "I know. By your morality, I'm a terrible person. Even by my own…" He trailed off, gesturing with one hand as if to say, *I really have no fucking idea.* As if he was as surprised as I was that he had morality in the first place. Freaking fae. "I wish I'd chosen the very bronzed one in the ridiculous silver underwear. *He* probably isn't any smarter than he looks. And I might not have regretted involving him in my problems the way I regret doing it to you." He swallowed hard, the motion of his throat incredibly distracting. "You should go. Stand up, leave, and never think of me again. Take my apology, and go."

Of all the absurdities that had come out of his mouth.

My laughter rang too loud in the quiet room, and his

indignantly raised eyebrows only made me laugh more.

"Sorry," I managed. "But look. Your thing about your friend you lost a bet with. That was total bullshit, I'm guessing. But I'm also guessing your sample size of alpha shifters is kind of small?"

"There was a bet, a long time ago, but it wasn't binding. More of a...humans play a game called truth or dare? Something like that." Truth or dare, only with young fae? The mind boggled. My teenage parties had obviously been a lot tamer. "And yes, it's limited to—limited," he bit off, and I winced. Limited to Cunningham. "How did you know?"

"Because you don't seem to know a lot about how we work. Once we get the idea that something belongs to us? We never let it go. Not ever. So you offered to pay me, and—what's wrong?"

All the color had drained out of his face, leaving him a horrible chalky color, like a lime-flavored antacid tablet, but his eyes blazed, with an actual flicker in their depths, I was pretty sure, a glint of pale purple in his black irises.

"Do you think I don't know that?" he choked out. He went on, his voice rising with anger. "I know he's never going to let me go! I *know* that, and that's why I was trying to—and now you're telling me I'm also stuck with *you*? You fucked me once! One time! Surely you weren't a virgin, you can't possibly stalk everyone you've ever fucked!"

He broke off in a howl of pure rage, panting, fists clenched on his thighs, leaning in to yell in my face in a way that had my blood pumping and my body straining toward his again. Tigers didn't mate gently, and everything about him screamed *mate who wants to snarl at me and fight me while I own him.*

It took me a moment to force that instinct down and control my burgeoning partial shift, and my voice still came out low and raspy, harsher than I intended.

"I was referring to the coin or its value in actual money, not you," I said, and he jerked back slightly, lip curling, as if I'd upset him or something? What the hell, he was pissed at me for refusing to leave him alone a second ago! Anyway, that wasn't the main point here. "And you were trying to what, exactly?"

"Get free of him, obviously. What else?" he snapped without

hesitation. I filed it away for later, if I needed the information: he stopped choosing his words so carefully when he got angry. "I might as well—damn it. He gave me the coin. Paid me with it, for a night with him. Or I thought it was for only one night. It's beautiful and it's magical, and yes, I was a fool, but I coveted it in a way that—you wouldn't understand. It's in my nature. He wanted to knot me, and he told me that the coin would be mine and I would be his, and I accepted. And now as long as I have the coin, my magic won't work against him and I can't leave him. I hoped if I paid another alpha to knot me, the symmetry of the two bargains, being paid to be knotted and then paying to be knotted by someone else, would satisfy the coin. But apparently not, because it won't leave me, and when I paid you with it, it was on my dresser when I got back. There. Are you happy now? Will you go away," his voice broke slightly, "and leave me alone?"

"No," I replied without hesitation, even though I hadn't thought it through. Two seconds of thinking it through allowed me to add, with a high degree of confidence, "And you don't want me to."

Through his own fae lust for magical gold, he'd managed to trap himself, and now he couldn't escape. Not the most sympathy-inspiring story compared to all the people out there who were in trouble through no fault of their own, although maybe I should cut him some slack, given my own saga of fake tits and loan sharks. And while the fairy's captor might not be a match for me one-on-one, he had all the money and resources and security to make sure it never came to that.

Yeah, I should walk away.

But this beautiful, lying, desperate man in front of me needed…someone, anyone. If he'd had any other options, he surely wouldn't have been looking for a way out in Lucky or Knot.

He only had me.

Walk away? Not a chance.

Besides, he still hadn't paid me. Until he did, I didn't have much choice but to stick around, right?

"I do want you to go," he protested unconvincingly.

The way his head tilted back to offer me his lips and his soft throat, the slight spread to his legs, his hand sliding onto my thigh—and I'd have been willing to bet he didn't even realize he'd touched me, even though sparking heat radiated out from that one, delicate point of contact, sweat prickling behind my knees and along my spine. All of it suggested that he very much didn't want me to go anywhere.

"I should never have brought you into this mess. Besides," he added much more sincerely, "it didn't work."

Laughing despite myself, I leaned closer too, unable to resist his pull any longer. My body ran much hotter than his, but I could still feel his presence, a tingling awareness. It grew stronger as I edged nearer, the bed dipping and creaking as my weight shifted toward him.

"I have two more questions," I said. His warm breath brushed softly over my chin, and every moment of it killed more of my brain cells. "Your name. Even a fake one. I mean, another fake one. Something better than Ty fucking Tania." His sly little laugh shut down my remaining higher cognitive functions, hopefully not permanently, and it took effort to add, "And I need to know why you were crying when I fucked you last time."

Context was everything, and now that I knew more about him…well, in the moment, I'd been able to dismiss his reaction as one of those weird things that happened sometimes, but I couldn't anymore. My cock had risen insistently against my fly again, trapped there and painfully hard, but I could wrench myself away and keep my hands to myself, if I had to. So I needed to know.

"You have an active imagination." I rolled my eyes at that ridiculous dodge, and his lips quirked up. "But if I had been crying…" His voice dropped to a sultry, low timbre that sent a shiver along all my nerve endings. "If I had been, it'd have been because I'd been so afraid, and you—didn't give me any reason to be."

Oh, thank all the gods.

Slowly enough that he could push me away or dodge if I'd misunderstood him, I bent down the last few inches and tilted my head, at last getting my mouth on his skin. A brush along the line of his jaw, an inhale of his sweetness and the pheromones of his desire, my arm snaking around his waist, every inch of me trembling with anticipation…

"You can call me Raven," he whispered.

"Tony," I said against his throat, and pushed him down onto the bed, biting at the side of his neck where his high collar left a sliver exposed.

The feel of his slim body under mine hit me like a freight train, every muscle going rigid, every nerve on fire, my cock straining.

"He checks my clothes for damage to make sure I'm not wasting his money," Raven gasped. "Careful."

Cunningham checked his…my vision washed crimson and my claws popped, too close to ripping his clothes to shreds after all.

"Then you need to get them off," I growled.

Mine. Not Cunningham's. *Mine*, to fuck and knot and protect, and shit, I hadn't meant to say any of that out loud.

The bed gave an almighty creak and jounce as Raven suddenly writhed, legs wrapping around me, pushing us up off the bed with shocking strength. We flipped and rolled, my head slamming down on the pillow and Raven straddling my hips, hands pinning my shoulders.

Well, not pinning, exactly. In a pinning position, more like, without enough force behind it to hold me.

If I'd had the slightest interest in fighting him off.

Sprawled out spread-eagled with Raven breathing hard above me, leaning down with wild eyes gazing at me, and his peach of an ass resting on my massively erect cock…no, I wouldn't be resisting.

"Don't move," he said, and licked his lips in a way that riveted my attention and accomplished his goal of freezing me in place, paralyzed with lust. "You're right, I should take care of my own clothes. You're too clumsy, and I don't trust you. You couldn't even take off stripper pants without falling down."

Apparently I'd be getting that private dance I'd teased myself by imagining the other night at the club.

My eyes nearly rolled back in my head.

"Are you going to show me how it's done?" I asked breathlessly, in lieu of something more likely to make him change his mind, like defending myself or pointing out that he was going to dance for me after all. Smugness would make him dig in his heels.

Arguing would derail his intention to strip. But a challenge. This was, after all, the guy who'd used to play fairy truth or dare. In other words, an easy mark, once you knew what buttons to press. "I've been stripping for years. That was a fluke. I doubt you can do better."

His eyes narrowed. "You're not very subtle," he said. "But of course I can do better. And if you touch me, I'll stop."

Before I could ask for some clarification on the no touching, he let go of my shoulders and shifted his weight, pressing down on my cock.

He reached up and whipped the hair tie out of his ponytail, dropping it carelessly and tilting his head back and forth to shake out his shiny black mane. Crossing his arms over his front, he started tugging up the hem of his shirt, simultaneously gyrating his ass on my cock and continuing with more of those hair-tossing motions.

It should've been cheesy or ridiculous.

It so, so fucking wasn't.

Raven didn't need music or a beat, and he didn't need colored spotlights, and he didn't need body oil or glitter. His body rippled like water, his skin and hair gleamed rose and white and as glossy black as his namesake, and the mundane background of dim hotel room lamps and the rattle of the heater just made his otherworldly beauty stand out even more. My breath's rhythm grew harsher and deeper, his lighter and faster, and the two wound around each other and made their own music, punctuated by the faint creak of the bed as Raven twisted, putting his weight on one knee and then the other.

Keeping my hands to myself didn't take as much effort as I'd expected. Of course, my claws embedded five or six inches into the mattress helped. I'd need another high-interest loan to pay off the damages to the hotel room, but I didn't care, couldn't care about anything except the way Raven had pulled the shirt up enough to expose the dip of his waist, the line of his ribs, so that he could trace a circle around one pale-pink nipple with the tip of his finger.

And then across, trailing his hand over his chest and flicking the other nipple, raising it to a tiny, pebbled peak.

Even mostly clothed, with only his stomach and chest exposed, he was more erotic than any fully naked stripper I'd ever watched perform.

From my angle, the ridge in the front of my jeans looked like Mount Everest—and felt like it, my eyes starting to water from the discomfort of having my cock trapped for so long. Raven swayed, flexed, and finally, *finally* pulled the shirt all the way up, whipping it over his head after doing something quick and tricky to that collar, flinging it aside with a toss of his mass of black hair. It settled around his shoulders like a silk curtain.

I stared up at him, gaping like an idiot—and for the sake of my dignity, hopefully not actually drooling.

Raven smiled, eyes alight, and ran his hands down from his throat to the waistband of his pants.

"Well?" he asked. "What do you think of my skills?"

"Ungh," I groaned, my tongue practically hanging out. "Fuck."

With a saucy wink, he rolled off of me, flipping his legs around so quickly I couldn't follow his motion. He landed next to the bed as lightly as a cat, fingers already busy with his button and zipper.

When he started to lean down to work on his boots, I rasped, "Turn around for that. Pro tip."

Raven peeked up at me through his hair. "You won't keep your hands off if I turn around. I told you, I don't trust you." His flashing grin took the sting out of the words. And a moment later he'd peeled off the pants and boots at least as quickly and gracefully as one of the Lucky or Knot guys with our specially designed easy-off outfits, and was climbing back onto the bed completely bare.

His cock stood fully erect, glistening at the tip, exactly as pretty and perfectly proportioned as I remembered.

Which did I want more, that in my mouth, or his mouth on my own cock? Both at once wouldn't work well with our height difference. One at a time. Except that clearly wasn't what he had in mind, because he settled himself over me again, knees wedged against my hips, his ass resting on my thighs. If I reached out and lifted up his balls, I could see that lovely tight hole. Or I could pinch his nipples, make him squirm…

"Fuck, can I—"

"No," he said, cutting me off firmly and categorically. "No."

When he reached for my cock, he had a bottle of lube in the other hand. As if he'd conjured it out of nowhere. Fairies, Christ. He probably had.

"Will you—"

"No."

My buried claws flexed involuntarily, one of them catching on a mattress spring, bits of shredded bedding floating up into the air. I tasted blood as one of my fangs dug into my lip. Sweat dampened my shirt and trickled down my temples, and my limbs had gone rigid with the strain of *not doing anything.*

"For the love of—"

"I want you like this," he said. The faintest tremor ran through his voice. "Exactly like this, and I'll do what I want with you."

Bravado, not confidence. Even though I couldn't hear much over the staccato thudding of my own racing heart, I could hear that.

And so I forced my head back until my neck ached, scraped my claws through the bed's torn-up innards, dug my heels in, and stayed in place through sheer force of will as he unfastened my jeans, peeled them open in front, and tugged the waist of my boxers down. When his hand wrapped around my straining length I groaned and bucked but didn't otherwise move, vision blurring as he rewarded me by stroking all the way up, running his thumb over my swollen cockhead, and then stroking all the way down again, gripping me hard around the base of my cock.

I throbbed in his grip, the part of my shaft that would swell into my knot already thickening and tingling.

He'd reached around behind himself, arching his back, somehow managing to prep his ass while he kept up his stroke-and-twist…as if he did this a lot. Practiced, it looked fucking *practiced*, and the edges of my vision went blood-red and sparkly as I realized why.

But he'd chosen this. Chosen me. I had to remember that.

Raven let out a soft moan and brought his hand back around, giving his own cock a teasing tug. The glitter of his eyes and the deep, rosy pink of his parted lips and flushed cheeks didn't look like they belonged to a man who wished himself elsewhere.

He paused, biting his lip, one hand barely wrapping all the way around my thick cock and the other with a much better grip on his own. He squeezed us both at once. My head pressed into the pillow as my back arched, and I groaned, the thrill of it rolling up my spine and lodging in what I had left of my brain.

For an instant I pictured what someone watching us would see. Raven's slim, naked figure poised over me, hair flowing down around him, long legs splayed open around my big body, with only my cock out of my clothes and standing up like a flagpole, and my shoulders and arms rigid with straining muscle, my eyes glowing.

If we had it on video, we'd make a killing on a porn site. And it had very little to do with me. Alphas were pretty standard in porn, but Raven…

…And then the vision dissipated as he moved, shifting forward and positioning himself over my cock, his balls brushing over the head tantalizingly as he did.

As he settled, my cockhead pressed against the slick softness behind them and the slight give of his wet hole. Did I dare to thrust up and into him? Probably not. He might stop like he'd threatened. So I held perfectly still except for my chest heaving as he lowered himself, muttering curses as my cock slipped and he had to re-center, and then finally shoved down with his hips.

The head of my cock popped inside him, the sudden heat and tightness exploding stars behind my eyelids as my whole body went stiff.

Fuck. *Fuck*, no one should feel so good on the inside, my cock sliding into hot honey, the silky grip of his inner flesh, the texture of him. Without needing to think about moving my body, thrusting, holding him in place, my focus narrowed down to the way he clenched and released as he got used to the stretch and fullness, the slow rotation of his hips.

His gaze sharpened, eyes boring holes in my face. What was he looking for? I didn't know, and I wouldn't have lied and given him what he wanted even if I knew how. Raven had finally been honest with me, and he deserved the same.

And even if he hadn't, lying to him in this moment, as he gave himself to me, would've made me pond scum.

Nothing to say came to me, anyway. Nothing seemed like enough. There were times when I liked to talk during sex. Encouragement, praise, demands, or narration, depending on the occasion and the other person. But like last time with Raven, I couldn't even find words to describe how it felt to be with him, to be inside him, to be connected to him so intimately.

Raven leaned forward and laid his hands on my chest, hair swinging forward and swishing over my sides. Gods, I wished I'd had my shirt off so I could've felt it tickling my skin.

But Raven didn't want my shirt off. He wanted me exactly how he'd arranged me, and he probably didn't get to fuck the way he wanted all that often, did he?

Fuck.

"If you were mine," I choked out, as he pushed down, seating his hips, my cock buried as deep in him as he could get it, "fuck, if you were—gods, that feels—you'd always have me however you wanted me."

For a moment his mouth dropped open in shock—nearly as much as my own at having said it in the first place. And then he bared his teeth at me, eyes flashing.

"I'd never be yours." The words pierced my chest and lodged there, but I didn't have a lot of time to think about it before he lifted up on his knees, the thick length of my cock sliding almost all the way out of him, the air cold on my wet skin, and then slammed down again, hard. "I couldn't."

Another lift, agonizingly slow, and then he forced himself down, whimpering as I stretched him open again, the squeeze around my shaft on the edge of pain. And also on the edge of making me come, my gods.

"This doesn't mean—oh," he gasped, because I couldn't take it anymore, and I braced my feet and thrust up with my hips, my embedded claws giving me even more leverage.

More stars behind my half-closed eyelids, black and red, as he retaliated with a sudden constriction of his inner muscles that throttled my cock and imprinted the texture of his insides onto my shaft.

The world spun around one fixed point: Raven, his head hanging down, fucking himself on me harder and harder, his fingers digging clawlike into my chest. I met him on every thrust, grinding my cock into him, opening him up for the knot that had started to form at the base of my cock as I came closer and closer to losing control.

The bed creaked and thumped underneath us as we bounced up and down, and Raven's hair flew around his head as if it had a life of its own, his slim shoulders peeking out through the strands. He held me tighter and tighter between his knees and rode me as if he didn't care if it hurt.

Raven must have been close to coming too, he had to be, because I needed him to come first this time. No hands, no mouth for kisses, so what could I do to...but I did have my mouth, didn't I?

"You have me at your mercy," I gritted out, wishing it was only meant to get him off and not a hundred percent true. "You going to come all over me? Hmm? Paint me with that pretty cock?"

He looked up sharply, wild-eyed, hair flying around his face. "Yes," he panted. "Yes?"

His expression twisted into something desperate, and he thrust his hips back, impaling himself harder and deeper.

Through the pounding roar of my own blood in my ears, I managed to say, "Come on, Raven. Hold me down and make me knot you."

Self-serving too, maybe, but good enough for him, because he stopped, shaking, coming in pearly ribbons all over my shirt, and clenching so hard that it ripped the orgasm out of me, my back arching and my clawed fists tearing up what was left of the bed underneath us.

Raven cried out, high and wild, trailing off to a little whimpering moan as I filled him with pulse after pulse, thrusting up to stuff my growing knot inside. He writhed, pushed back on me, and took it—and then toppled forward and landed on my chest with a long, low sigh. My whole body shuddered with aftershocks, every one of them jolting through him and rubbing my knot against his sweet spot. More small moans, and his fingers flexed against my shoulders.

But he didn't move, even though he'd lain down in his own sticky mess. Gods, I wanted to lick it off of him. Instead it'd just ruin my shirt. What a waste.

I closed my eyes and drifted.

Chapter 10

My vision unblurred as my heart slowed a bit, and I blinked up at the ceiling, staring at a crack in the paint until it came into focus again. Raven still hadn't moved, his hands resting on my shoulders. His fanned-out hair concealed his face completely. If I tucked my chin slightly, I could feel it, silky-soft and cool. The scent of it mingled with sex and sweat and magic, all lemony sweet and musky.

His relaxed weight on my chest gave me an ache deep inside it that had nothing whatsoever to do with compression of my lungs—he wasn't big enough for that.

Raven probably hadn't gone to sleep, but he had gone totally limp.

As if he trusted me. Not to hurt him, not to take advantage of having him tied to me with my knot...and possibly even to protect him.

He'd said he didn't trust me, but maybe he really had meant it only as a commentary on my clumsiness and not in a more general sense.

Although if I were him, I might not trust any alpha, anywhere, ever, and in that post-nut clarity that swept over me as I lay there in the quiet, scenting Raven's bone-melting deliciousness and savoring his slight body draped over mine, I wished to all the gods I hadn't said that stupid bullshit about "if you were mine." That must've sounded like more of the same to him. Another day, another alpha wanting to own him.

No doubt he'd be really impressed if I explained that it wasn't the same at all, because I was nothing like Cunningham.

Right.

On the other hand, my hands ached like a bitch, so I'd need to at least convince him to let me free them from the mattress.

"Raven," I said softly.

"Tony," he murmured without moving, and something that felt like one of my ribs, but wasn't, cracked and twanged.

"I'm going to get my claws unstuck. Half my arms are buried in the bed." Nothing. "Am I allowed to touch you now?"

His slight motion in response could've been a shrug. Anyway, he hadn't said no, so I started dragging my hands out of the fluff and springs and threads that had wound around them, my claws scraping unpleasantly as I tried to retract them.

Raven shuddered. "That's a horrible noise," he complained muzzily, lips moving against my chest.

My sudden desire to protect him from all horrible noises in the future had to be a sign that I'd finally lost my grip on reality.

At last my hands tugged free, bits of mattress stuffing floating up into the air and settling around us like dusty, sneeze-inducing snow. I flexed my fingers, getting my claws retracted all the way, and then—he really hadn't said no. With infinite care, holding my breath, I let my hands drift down onto his bare back, one in the center and the other on his ass, honestly, not his back. But I couldn't resist that soft curve. So smooth, so round, so lightly jiggly. And when I squeezed his cheek, I felt the tug of it inside him, around my knot, in his tightly plugged hole full of my come—

"Is that a purr or a growl?" Raven asked, sounding slightly more alert, if breathless. "I can feel it more than I can hear it."

"No, tigers can't purr," I said without thinking.

His head popped up, eyes glittering, hair hanging all around his face in a tangled, silky web.

"Ha!" And then, "Ha!" again. Raven grinned at me, a dimple appearing in one flushed cheek. "You really aren't all that much smarter than you look, are you?"

I really, really wasn't.

"You," I said, getting a firmer grip on his perfect handful of an ass, "really ought to be more careful," and I braced my feet, "about what you say to the weretiger who has you—"

"Oh!" he cried out, his eyes growing round. I shoved off and flipped us in a move fully worthy of someone who'd spent as much time working a strip club stage as I had.

"—knotted and pinned," I finished in a low growl, as his head bounced on the pillow and I landed on top of him, his legs around my thighs.

I'd held him flush against me so that my knot couldn't pull painfully on his stretched hole, but he whimpered, eyes sliding shut, as I thrust down into him, circling my hips, stretching him even more.

"I may not be much smarter than I look," I said, "but that doesn't mean you can get away with anything you want."

Raven opened his eyes and blinked, fluttering his lashes. "I'll be more circumspect in future." His voice quivered, and the corners of his mouth twitched. Oh, for fuck's sake, what now... "In fact, it'll be—oh, ha, it'll be—grrreat!"

And his face scrunched up and went rosy pink as he dissolved into helpless chuckles, his eyes shiny-bright.

For a long moment, I simply couldn't believe my ears.

Grrreat!

Fucking son of a bitch.

My parents had been blissfully unaware of the connotations of being a weretiger named Tony, American cereal ads not having been a part of their Turkish cultural consciousness. A few thousand miles had been enough to keep them ignorant.

But a fairy, an actual magical being from across the divide of our mortal realm, somehow apparently knew about Tony the Tiger.

I stared down at him open-mouthed as he howled with laughter, vibrating with it, muscles clenching rhythmically around my knot, massaging me. He had my half-hard cock, fuck, my *hardening* cock, buried inside him, and he had the nerve—oh, he was going to get it.

Bracing my knees, I shoved deep into his wet heat. Raven choked, his laughter cutting off in a long, shaky moan. Another thrust, working my knot against his sweet spot, my cock splitting him open as I stirred his insides, and he moaned again, head thrown back against the pillow, staring up at me transfixed.

"That's right," I said, and thrust again. "You want to play that game? I can play that game."

"What—oh, gods above—what game? I'm not playing any—oh!"

"Yes, you are, and I'm winning."

Jesus Christ, yeah, I was winning, because I was balls-deep in the most beautiful man I'd ever met, ever even imagined, fucking him in earnest, now, pounding him into the shredded remnants of the bed, making him mine. At least for now. For tonight. For this stolen moment out of the twin chaos of our fucked-up lives.

I lifted him up with the arm I still had wrapped underneath him, holding him close, feeling his legs tangled around mine and his arms winding around my neck and my cock inside him and the sweaty heat between my muscled chest and his soft skin, our combined scents twining around us and making me lightheaded.

Or maybe that was just the oncoming rush of another orgasm, as irresistible as a tidal wave.

Raven's hair brushed my lips and cheek as I turned my head to find his mouth—and he twisted away from me with a pained-sounding murmur.

That stung, gods, sending a lance of pain all the way down into my stomach, but I latched onto the side of his neck instead, sucking hard, the flavor of him bursting on my tongue, bright and sharp and sweet.

If he really did belong to me, I'd mouth down to the juncture of his shoulder and bite, mark him, claim him.

Sparks burst behind my eyelids as I thrust harder, impossibly deeper, into the grip of his body, and filled him again, with a sudden cresting thrill that verged on agony.

He cried out, a counterpoint to my muffled roar, and more wetness spread against my stomach.

Nothing existed but him. My whole body shuddered, the twisting aftermath of my climax tugging me inward, and I let my head drop down to rest a bit above his, forehead on the mattress.

Somehow, even after being flipped like a pancake and vigorously fucked with a knotted alpha cock, he'd managed to keep himself perfectly centered on the pillow.

Maybe I was lucky he'd snuck out the other night. Three times his size, and I just knew I'd have ended up clinging to the edge of the bed with no blankets or pillows.

Or on the floor.

He wouldn't be sneaking out tonight, magic or no. My arm tightened around him without any conscious input from me, and he *mmph*ed at me as his ribs creaked.

"Sorry," I mumbled into his hair, and forced my arm to relax.

Tucked all the way under me like this, he had to be either suffocating or crushed even without my too-possessive grip, and I started to push up.

Raven's surprisingly strong hands dug into my shoulders, tugging me back down again. Well, all right. No arguments from me. Missionary position was the worst for knotting in some ways, because then you had to hold a plank for half an hour if you didn't want to squish your lover. Maybe Declan was onto something, taking another alpha as a mate. He'd be durable.

Of course, Raven seemed like a good middle ground. Not an alpha, which was great, because I wasn't attracted to guys who looked like me, and most alphas ran to the big and muscled and rough. But...shockingly durable for someone so delicate-looking. And fresh-smelling, despite two rounds of sweaty, knotted sex. Mmm. I nuzzled into his apple-blossom-scented hair.

"I wanted you to kiss me," Raven said, so abruptly that it startled me out of my impending slide into total relaxation.

That statement demanded my full attention, and I pushed up to look down into his face. Christ, why did he have to be so...so...he hadn't been crying this time, because I'd have noticed, but the shiny corners of his eyes and the tightness around his mouth caught at my heart in a way no one else's emotional displays had ever done. Usually I figured people would sort out their own crap unless they directly asked for my help, and I much preferred it that way.

Not with Raven, damn it all.

Gods. He'd wanted me to kiss him. The bubbly sensation in my chest made me a little bit embarrassed to exist.

"Then why didn't you let me?"

He turned his head a bit and met my eyes. The gods only knew what mine were showing him, probably too much. But his had clouded over, the shimmering polish of his jet-black irises dimmed.

"You've heard about eating fairy food? What can happen to someone from this plane of existence?" His mouth turned down at the corners, and I'd never wanted to kiss him more, even as the pit of my gut started to sink like he'd dropped a brick into it. "It's all true. It's a very bad idea. You can't consume something that's not of the mortal world without it having an effect, usually unpredictable and even more usually undesirable."

"And your bodily fluids are the same. If I consume them. Is that what you're telling me?" Fuck me. The headaches and the longing and the protectiveness...not that he hadn't warned me. Although. "You know, you could've tried a little harder to explain why I should keep my mouth to myself."

Raven's eyelashes swept down and up again in a slow blink that was almost more catlike than an actual cat, and I should know.

"My general attitude toward alphas can be summed up as 'go knot yourselves and die.' I made quite an effort, considering." I raised my eyebrows at him, and he sighed, one corner of his mouth quirking up. "Unfortunately for my total lack of concern for your well-being, you haven't been completely dreadful. In fact, in some ways, you're grr—oh!" He pressed himself back down into the pillow. "That's what your actual growl sounds like. Ah."

Good to know he could take me at least a little bit seriously, for fuck's sake, although the way he lay still and lax under me, my cock slowly starting to soften inside him, suggested I hadn't actually scared him.

Even better.

And anyway, I had more questions.

"Is it cumulative? I mean, you said it might wear off. You thought. And by the way, if you think that counts as quite an effort, you know, try harder." A slight nod was all I got in acknowledgment. Little fucker. "But if I kiss you now, will it actually make it worse? Whatever the hell you've already done to me? And don't pretend it was only the effect of kissing you. You whammied me to knock me out the other night."

"It's also the effect of licking me. My sweat isn't any better than my saliva."

"Not an answer," I gritted out. "And way to make it sound gross instead of hot, dude."

He tensed up slightly, sending one last ripple of sensation through my now truly exhausted cock, his fingers digging into my upper arms.

"If you call me 'dude' again," he said primly, "I'll use my magic to change your name from The Hammer to Tony the Tiger on every piece of promotional material your club puts out from now until the end of mortal time."

That cartoon tiger in a glittery G-string...wearing my face?

I dropped back down against the edge of his pillow to hide my expression, but my shaking shoulders gave me away, and he poked me in the ribs until I pinched his side and made him squeak and cut it out.

"Fuck," I wheezed. "Fuck. But you really overestimate the good taste of Lucky or Knot's clientele, Raven. I'd sell out the house as Tony the Tiger. All I have to lose is my dignity."

"Will you pinch me again if I point out that you don't have a lot of that to lose?" The warm, relaxed amusement in his voice took all the sting out of the words.

After all, when I fell down on stage the other night—still his fault, I hadn't forgotten, simply chosen to forgive—it'd been all right when they were laughing with me instead of at me.

"It's the glitter," I finally managed. "It doesn't leave you with a lot of dignified high ground."

And then I remembered what I'd said to Dominic about girls and corvids, and I lost it again, whooping with laughter, my soft-at-last cock slipping out of Raven as I shook with it.

I rolled over and off of him, our bodies unsticking in a way that made me wince, and flopped onto my back, the bed giving a horrid screech under me.

With my arm still trapped under him, it only took one quick

motion to tug him with me and nestle him against my side. A little to my surprise, he didn't resist, his arm coming to rest over my chest. The weight of his head on my shoulder, the silkiness of his hair…I stared up at the ceiling, not laughing anymore.

It'd been on the tip of my tongue to say something about how next time we needed to find a sturdier bed. *Much* sturdier. Did any super expensive hotels offer beds made out of titanium?

But it hardly mattered. There wouldn't be a next time. Why the hell hadn't I insisted he meet me earlier than midnight, of all the stupid times, so that we had more of the night together? It had to be two in the morning already, and now that I'd focused on it, the seconds seemed to be racing past, galloping their way to the inevitable end of this. The gods only knew how Raven had gotten away from Cunningham for a few hours, especially since he'd been with me two nights ago, too. I knew alphas, and I knew toxic, asshole alphas, and suspicion and jealousy and controlling scrutiny came with the territory. Someone like that would keep tabs on Raven. Obsessively, even.

And Raven had sounded close to panic when I demanded to see him. At the time, I hadn't cared much. What a difference a couple of hours could make.

"How are you getting away with this?" I asked, when the silence had stretched to the boiling point.

Raven tensed up against me, but he didn't waste his time, or mine, pretending not to understand what I meant.

"The bargain we struck gives him a great deal of power over me," he said, his voice surprisingly steady. The wild heartbeat hammering against my side told a different story, and his body had gone almost rigid. So much for post-coital relaxation. "But I'm powerful too. Even if I can't use my magic to hurt him, and I'm obligated to belong to him for now, he's not stupid or naïve, and when I tell him I require time alone to commune with the air, he knows better than to push too hard. And I'm very good at covering my tracks, luckily for you and your lease on life. Besides, he has his own obligations that keep him busy much of the time. I'll pay for it, though," he added, in a weary little undertone that made my teeth clench.

Given my previous total focus on making Raven pay for the way he'd cheated me, which I finally had to admit to myself had been a cover for my desperate need to get him under me again—which had, in its turn, probably been a function of having kissed and licked him too much for my magical health—I hadn't spent a lot of time thinking about the bargain's terms and the coin's bizarre behavior.

But now...

"So why didn't it work? Paying me for a mirror image of what he paid you for. You said it needed symmetry, right? Why?"

"If I knew, then I'd obviously have done something else," he snapped, sounding much more like himself. "And it needs symmetry because it does. Because that's the way these things work. It's not something I can explain to someone who doesn't simply feel it in his bones."

Christ. "You can try to explain it, at least. I'm not actually a complete fucking moron—"

"Then stop acting like one!" He wrenched himself out of my hold and landed on his feet beside the bed, moving with the lightness and grace of someone who really could command the air—or commune with it, whatever the fuck that meant. Raven stood with his back to me, shaking out his hair, clearly putting himself together mentally and physically.

Getting ready to leave this room, and me.

I shoved up to sitting a lot less gracefully and swung my legs over.

"Don't," he said tightly, without bothering to turn or look at me. "Don't touch me again."

"I won't if you don't want me to, but—"

"No. You won't." Raven's voice rang with total finality.

Something like panic wrapped a big hand around my chest and squeezed. "Look, come on," I said, hating my own pleading tone. "No. We need to talk about this. You used me for this crazy plan of yours. Now I'm involved, whether I like it or not. I can feel the effects of your magic on me, okay? You owe me."

Raven spun on me, hair flying and floating in the air, and glared down at me with that innate magic of his sparking in his eyes and shimmering around his pale, perfect body. Most people looked silly or vulnerable when they were naked, one reason why stripping took more skill than we usually got credit for.

Not him. I gazed at him, transfixed, a shiver working its way down from the tingling crown of my head to the soles of my feet.

Magic. He was pure magic. And for a moment, I almost pitied Cunningham: he might think he had the upper hand, but he was playing with fire, trying to own and tame an elemental creature like this.

Almost. Because Cunningham deserved to burn. And in the meantime, Raven was trapped and suffering.

"As I already told you, I fulfilled my side of our bargain," he snarled, vicious, teeth bared, a feral wild thing struggling against its fetters. "I said I could offer you the coin. And I gave it to you. I never guaranteed that you'd keep it."

"You know damn well that's wrong! No, not incorrect," I gritted out, as he opened his mouth to argue, "morally wrong. And I know you're not actually angry with me, because I haven't wronged *you* in any way, and we both know that. So get off your damn high horse."

A shadow of something like guilt flashed across his pointy little face and was gone again. He lifted his chin.

"I'll do no such thing. But you're right. I'm not angry with you, I'm frustrated by your stupidity and stubbornness. I'm going to shower, and I expect it to take me quite some time. I'd be very grateful if you were long gone by the time I emerge."

And with that, he spun on his heel and strode for the bathroom.

As if I didn't even exist for him anymore.

But I was faster than he was, and I launched myself off the bed and into his path, forcing him to fetch up short, inches from touching me. He stumbled back a step.

"I'm not just going to leave," I said. "Not without—"

"Without what?" he demanded. "There's nothing to say. Nothing to do here. Fuck, fine. If you truly feel that I owe you, as soon as I'm reasonably able to do so, I will send you the equivalent monetary value of the coin. You have my word. Are you happy now? Will you please stand aside? And then go. Please."

If it hadn't been for that second *please*, which never would've left his mouth if he hadn't been desperate, I probably would've done any one of the dozen things I burned to do. Grab him, kiss him breathless, bear him back down onto that wreck of a bed and wreck it, and him, a whole lot more.

But he'd said it. He'd asked me not to touch him, to leave him alone. He'd *asked* me.

It took every bit of willpower I had. Raven standing there nude and gleaming and rumpled, with my come dripping down his beautiful thighs, could've tempted a saint. And I wasn't any saint.

I clenched my fists, claws pricking my palms, and I stepped aside.

"Oh," Raven gasped, and he hesitated, eyes darting away from my face and then back again.

Had it shocked him that much that I hadn't simply taken what I wanted? Gods. I held my breath. Maybe he'd change his mind…

And then he walked past me, eyes fixed ahead of him, and shut the bathroom door behind him with a terribly final click.

The shower came on with a rattle and whoosh, but I couldn't hear anything else, and with my alpha hearing in play, that meant he had to be standing perfectly still and practically not breathing. He hadn't locked the door, either. I'd have heard the extra snick from the doorknob if he had.

Was he waiting for me to ignore him and follow him into the bathroom? Take him in my arms and get in the shower with him, and then, what, whisper to him that I'd make everything all right? Protect him from Cunningham, help him think of another way out?

My laugh echoed bitterly in the quiet of the room.

Yeah. Right.

That was my fantasy, not his. He just wanted me gone, a complication that he'd enjoyed more than he expected to, maybe, but that he really didn't fucking need.

So I dressed as quickly as I could, ignoring that I needed to piss and wash up myself. The alley behind the parking lot would take care of the first, and I'd be home soon enough to get in my own shower for the second.

To make it clear to him that I'd done what he wanted, I tossed the room keys on the nightstand, and then I slipped out and shut the door firmly behind me before I could rethink it yet again.

For a long moment, I stood there in the hall, letting the miserable gray and brown of the carpet and wallpaper blur in my vision, my mind's eye full of Raven: in the shower, tipping his head back so he could slick his long hair down his neck; leaning against the wall, forehead resting on his arm, the water beating down on his round, rosy ass and washing away every trace of me.

And then stepping out of the bathroom, towel around his waist and hair dripping everywhere, all shiny and scrubbed and pink.

Looking around for me, maybe. Even though he'd commanded me to go, somehow I knew he'd be taken aback by the gloomy, sordid emptiness of the dingy room and the ruined bed. He'd see the keys there. He'd know I'd really gone.

Would he be relieved or secretly, horribly disappointed?

I'd probably never know.

I shook my head and walked away, every step feeling like I had weights on my ankles.

But I went. And I didn't look back.

Chapter 11

Morning dawned at last after a sleepless remainder of the night, and the day crawled by in work and laundry and mundane bullshit.

And then another night. And another day.

Thoughts of Raven crowded into my mind more or less all the time: in the shower, making a sandwich, rubbing glitter on my abs, dancing and smiling and pretending I gave a shit.

Cold desert winds whipped through Vegas, bringing the scent of mountain snow. And even though shifters ran hot and alphas even hotter, a chill settled in my bones and wouldn't leave me.

I had Raven's phone number, and anyway, we were probably within a mile of each other on a daily basis. Practically shouting distance; definitely a tiger's roaring distance.

And yet he might as well have vanished back into whatever godsforsaken fairy place he'd left when he'd chosen to come to the human world and get in trouble.

Desire beat in my blood and burned in my nerves, but I gritted my teeth and forced it down. I shifted and ran through the desert for a full night, terrifying the ever-loving shit out of every poor fox and lizard and mouse that usually lived a naturally and blissfully tiger-free existence.

Early morning, the fourth after I'd left him at the Silver Lode, found me high up on a rock overlooking the desert and the rising sun to the east, with Vegas a weird glittering lump off to the west.

I shifted back to my human form, shaking out my fur as it vanished into me, and flopped down to stare up at the sky stretching above me, pink-washed blue, endless nothingness except for a single wheeling raptor, probably looking for one of those scared mice.

Simple. A predator, prey, life and death, night fading into day.

No magical coins or debts owed, no manipulations or tricks or lies.

The rough stone under my skin would've been much more comfortable in a tiger's furry body, but while shifters kept our ability to reason while in our animal forms, it took effort. The scents of desert flowers and prey, the brush of the wind in my whiskers, the faint far-off rustles and squawks and yips of the desert's life came to the foreground with a tiger's senses.

But now that I'd shifted back, I could think clearly again.

Genuinely clearly.

Because either the shift or just the passage of a bit of time had finally driven out the last of Raven's magic, that I'd absorbed with my poorly judged licking and kissing. It was far more obvious now in its absence than while I'd been under his spell.

Unlike the hawk and its intended victim, nothing about Raven or his situation was simple, at least not on the face of it. Alpha magic might have a lot of advantages—strength, healing, keen senses, an innate ability to dominate and command—but it didn't lend itself to anything requiring subtlety. His magic, on the other hand…it wound itself around you like smoke, seeped in along the edges, manipulated and tricked and lied. If anyone had the perfect skill-set to deal with a bad bargain and a fairy-wrought coin with a mind of its own, he did. I didn't. So the logical thing would be to leave him to it.

And the logical, human part of me, the part that could understand how incredibly not-simple Raven and his predicament really was, knew I ought to continue my trajectory of the other night. I'd walked away. I should keep walking.

But even human-shaped, even free of magical influence, I had to recognize that my instincts and the deepest part of my nature insisted that no, it really was incredibly fucking simple. He was mine. He belonged to me, and he was in trouble, and I had to protect him. End of story. Cunningham and the bargain and the coin were nothing but obstacles in the way of what had to be. Difficult obstacles, maybe, but not complicated.

It felt like that moment in the club all over again, when Raven had made his proposition and I'd had to admit to myself that I'd been negotiating terms, not disagreeing with the underlying premise. The instant I'd seen him, possibly even the instant I'd scented him, it'd been all over.

Now I had to face the same uncomfortable realization: there'd never been the faintest chance in hell that I'd shrug and let it go, the way Declan had—correctly but unrealistically—told me I ought to.

It had nothing to do with Raven's literal enchantment of me. He'd enchanted me much more lastingly with his very being, with his laughter and his tears and his stubbornness.

I had to get him the hell away from Cunningham. Ideally, I'd rip Cunningham's face off and feed it to him sideways in the process. And then…well, then Raven would probably rip me a new one in turn for interfering in his business.

…Except that he'd cried. He'd taken my knot, and he'd cried because I hadn't hurt him, and he'd told me that he'd wanted me to kiss him.

Whether he'd ever admit it or not, he needed my help.

And he'd get it. Whether he liked it or not.

Tigers had a particular talent for basking, and even in my human skin I could bask like a motherfucker.

So I lay there on my rocky perch until the sun had fully breached the horizon, basking in my new understanding, blinking lazily up at the brightening sky and tracking a second raptor that'd joined the first in its morning hunt.

A predator seeking prey, life and death, a new day beginning.

Raven was mine. And he needed me.

Simple.

***

Since I'd already taken the day off work, knowing the club would be too loud and claustrophobic after a night spent in my wild tiger's body and mind, I went home to shower and then headed straight back out again to do some recon. Raven's DMV records might not be the most accurate—I mean, Ty Tania—but Cunningham's Audacity Hotel, where Raven had claimed to live, seemed like the place to start.

A few calls to other service-industry friends I'd met during my year of hanging out in off-Strip bars late at night got me the phone number of a parking valet at Audacity, with a warning that he wouldn't talk to me unless I brought him weed. A text to the same friend at the Silver Lode yielded a potential introduction to his cousin's girlfriend, who worked as a concierge assistant at Audacity four days a week. (Luckily for his job and our friendship, he'd laughed himself sick when he saw the bed, filmed the damage to post anonymously online, and then colluded with housekeeping to cover it up.)

The girlfriend apparently had gone on vacation, though, so I tried the valet first, texting him with the name of our mutual friend and an offer to meet up and smoke on his break.

His reply was encouragingly enthusiastic, although I'd had no idea phones even had that many emojis relating to smoking pot.

Half an hour of driving around buying weed later found me leaning against the wall of a parking garage near Audacity, as casually as a weretiger stripper waiting to bribe someone with drugs could lean. The alley boasted an inspiring view of concrete dust, traffic cones, and a chain link fence with a couple of used condoms caught in its gaps and fluttering limply in the cold breeze.

Christ. The things we did for—lust, possessiveness, and a sense of responsibility. I'd go with that. Even alphas didn't fall in...other things that weren't lust...that quickly. Not even when every sense and instinct recognized the object of the not-other-things as the epitome of everything I didn't even know I'd been looking for.

The way he'd looked at me when he'd practically begged me to leave him...

The faint scuff of footsteps had me turning toward the front of the alley a couple of seconds before a tall, lanky dude in a tacky purple-and-gold valet uniform slouched around the corner of the building.

For fuck's sake, Cunningham really was a blight on the world. What kind of asshole made his employees dress like that?

"Hey, Tony?" he said as he approached—not too close, and sounding a little wary, and I didn't really blame him. Jeans and a long-sleeved blue T-shirt were innocuous on most people, but when you came right down to it, my bulging-biceped, unshaven-red-stubbled picture was in the dictionary next to "guy you don't want to approach in a seedy alley."

"What's up? Sean? Thanks for meeting me, man. Jake said I could trust you, so I appreciate it." I put all the friendly harmlessness I could muster into my tone.

Sean relaxed a bit and came within arm's reach at last, so apparently I hadn't growled too much.

"Happy to help," he said, and actually smiled at me, a surprisingly charming expression on his thin, plain face. Dirty blond hair flopped down into his eye, and he shoved it back. "You said something about taking a break...?"

Right. I pulled out my purchases from the dispensary, and his eyes lit up. "I don't really smoke much pot," I said, the understatement of the century, and he nodded, swooped the baggie of pre-rolled joints out of my hand, and produced a lighter from seemingly nowhere.

His happy little sounds as he took his first drag had me suppressing a laugh. Yeah, if I had to cosplay a gilded eggplant and park people's cars all day, I might be eagerly ready to get baked out of my gourd on my break, too.

Sean quirked an eyebrow and held out the joint after a polite three hits, and I shook my head and propped up the wall again, biding my time as patiently as I could until he'd finished his smoke.

At last he dropped the smoldering end on the ground with a satisfied *aaah*, and leaned back next to me, gazing out at the condom-decorated vista.

"So what's up?" he said. "I checked in with Jake. He said you were looking for someone who works at Audacity? You need a job there or something? He told me you work at Lucky or Knot. I've never had the balls to like, go in there and check it out."

Sean was into guys? Shit. Maybe his hesitation when he saw me had been based on more than just my intimidating size. Did he think I'd hit on him?

"Text me if you want to come by some night." That sounded neutral, right? "I'll make sure you get a drink on the house. No one's going to come on too strong. We're all cool, I promise."

He laughed. "If they're all like you, then I believe you. Thanks for the smoke. You want the rest of…"

"No, keep it for your next break. I have a favor to ask."

He hummed thoughtfully, and when I glanced over at him, I found him eyeing me a lot more alertly than I'd have expected from someone who'd put down a joint in three minutes. Well, double shit. I'd seriously considered what to say to him, but no matter what story I gave, anyone with half a brain would know I was leaving a lot out. I'd hoped the weed would get him down to more like a quarter of a brain, but it seemed not.

"The guy who owns Audacity, Arnold Cunningham. You ever meet him personally?"

I'd thought that would be a nicely oblique way to start the awkward conversation, but his face changed the instant Cunningham's name came out of my mouth. Sean had pale skin to start with, but he went pasty.

"No, thank God," he said. "No. He's—you should stay away from him. I mean, don't quote me. He's fired and blacklisted people for talking shit about him on social media or whatever. But he's not cool. He has this vibe, you know? Like you want to stay out of his line of sight. His own security deals with his vehicles, so I never have to get near him. But I've seen him coming in and out. That's enough for me."

Raven crying, Raven terrified that I might damage his clothes and bring Cunningham's violent wrath down on him…

"Yeah, that's what I've heard." Sean jumped and edged away from me. "Fuck, sorry. I'm not angry with you. I'm—sorry. Don't mind me. Seriously."

"I haven't spent much time around alphas, or shifters at all," he said after a second, giving me a quick, shy, up-and-down glance. "I guess you guys are kind of, you know. More intense than some people? It's okay."

"Is that why you want to check out Lucky or Knot?" I asked him, trying to lighten the mood. "See what we're like?"

He quirked a smile and gave me the once-over again through half-lowered lashes. "That and the, you know. Obvious reason to go. Um. I thought Jake maybe gave you my number because he knew I uh, you know."

Okay. I'd never claimed to be the sharpest knife in the drawer, but the penny finally dropped. If I'd been alone, I'd have face-palmed. He hadn't been afraid I'd hit on him, he'd been expecting it, probably assuming I'd wanted to get him high in an alley as the prelude to some kind of hook-up.

The thought came unbidden and unwelcome: Raven would've laughed his ass off if he'd been here—or maybe he wouldn't have, and I'd have liked that even more. If Raven ever cared enough to be jealous…my chest hurt.

"Yeah," I answered, forcing my mouth to form coherent words even though I wanted to roar and batter my fists and claws into the wall until I bled and the parking structure came down around my ears. "I know. Um, you're really cute," and that was only sort of a flattering lie, because I might've even gone for that hook-up if my interest in all non-Raven beings hadn't vanished into the ether, "but I'm here because I'm having a problem with, okay, fuck."

He watched me patiently, with a slightly disappointed down-turn to his mouth, but mostly with sympathetic curiosity in his clear blue eyes. I wanted to trust him. If I had any chance of getting what I needed, I probably had to trust him. The risk to Raven…fuck. But I needed someone to help me, and I knew for sure Declan, my only other source of information, wouldn't go any further for what he perceived as my own good.

And Jake had vouched for Sean.

I had to take the risk, or there was no point in my being here at all. It wouldn't have made any sense to someone without a shifter's senses and instincts, but underneath the pervasive odor of strong cannabis, Sean smelled honest.

And I was desperate.

"There's a guy," I blurted out.

The words *There's a guy* came nowhere near encompassing Raven, or the strange, aching space he'd carved out for himself in my tight chest so quickly and definitively, but Sean nodded as if he understood completely.

"Cunningham," I began, and then chuckled despite everything as Sean's eyes widened in total horror. "No! Not Cunningham, I mean, he isn't the guy. Have you ever seen Cunningham's boyfriend?" Referring to Raven that way made my gut clench, but I couldn't think of a better way to say it that wouldn't get into the details. "Short, long black hair, dresses like the king of the goths circa 1996?"

Sean's eyes went, if possible, even wider. "Oh, fuck," he choked. "You—that's—*there's a guy*? Are you suicidal? Are you insane? You're insane. Jake set me up with a maniac. I'm going to kill him. If you don't kill me first. Are you a serial killer?"

"No one's killing anyone, I promise." Except Cunningham, and anyone who got between me and him, but details. "So you've seen him. You know who he is."

"Everyone who works at Audacity knows who he is. He lives in one of the suites of the penthouse Cunningham uses when he stays here. He's, like, you know those rich ladies who always have those little purebred dogs they carry around in designer purses, that have diamonds on their collars and shit? I don't know if boyfriend's the right word for what he is." He swallowed audibly, looked around nervously, and lowered his voice to a paranoid whisper. "How did you even get close enough to him to like, have him be a guy to you without dying?"

Sean and Declan should probably get together and have a drink so they could agree on how incredibly stupid I was.

"I shouldn't tell you and you don't want to know. But I need to know more about his routine. And Cunningham's. How they spend their time, where they go and when. And that's—the favor," I finished lamely. "That's why I asked Jake for the intro."

Sean stared at me. "So you can get me fired and killed too?"

"Bright side, if you get killed you won't care about getting fired?" The look that earned me could've blistered paint off a wall. "Sorry, that wasn't a great joke."

"Yeah, don't try to incorporate stand-up comedy into your stage act anytime soon," he said. "Tony, I can't help you. I'm sorry. You smoked me out and that was really cool of you, and I'll even pay you back whatever you spent, no worries. But I can't."

He pushed off the wall, and I knew I had about a two-second window to change his mind. "Free drinks at Lucky for life, and I'll talk to Declan MacKenna about giving you a job at the Morrigan once this is over," I promised wildly. "You won't have to wear that shit. Or work for that motherfucker Cunningham." His mouth tightened. He was about to say no again. "Please," I said, Raven's voice echoing in my head as I did. "Help me, and I swear to all the gods I'll make sure nothing happens to you. This isn't about me. This is about, shit. Does he look happy, when you see him? Cunningham's, you know, the guy."

Sean hesitated, sighed, and said, "He doesn't look like anything. I mean, blank. Like someone who's—there's rumors. More than rumors. About the way Cunningham treats people." He slumped back against the wall and rubbed his hands over his face. "Damn it," he groaned from behind them. "I get what you're not saying. Now I'll feel guilty as hell."

My heart gave a pathetic, hopeful thump, and I pressed my advantage shamelessly. "You won't have to feel guilty if you help me. Help me help him."

He dropped his hands and shot me a sour look. "We both know you probably can't do anything to actually help him get away from Cunningham, since I figure that's what you're trying to do. That's assuming he even wants to, and you could just be a crazed stalker, even if you're not a serial killer. Plus there's no way you can actually protect me from someone like that, and I have my doubts about the job. I'm sorry, like I'm not trying to be rude, but looking at you, I feel like even the free drinks might be kind of a stretch."

Christ, forget my optimistic estimate of half a brain. I'd managed to find the one person on Earth who actually got smarter when he smoked pot instead of stupider. Totally unfair.

How was I supposed to argue with someone who had made a series of valid, inarguable points?

I came up with, "Me being a crazed stalker and him wanting to get away from Cunningham aren't mutually exclusive."

Sean blinked at me, shook his head, and stuck a hand in his pocket. "I need to be a lot more high for this. Like, exponentially more high."

Chapter 12

While Sean smoked another one of the joints, he'd given me a quick rundown on what he knew about Raven and Cunningham's typical activities. On the weekends, Cunningham had the usual round of filthy-rich pretentious-douchebag-appropriate social occasions, to which Raven accompanied him. Sometimes he hosted lavish parties at the hotel, or more rarely at his estate.

On weekdays, Cunningham worked, and Raven tended to either stay completely out of sight or go out doing the things that one might expect of a wealthy man's kept boytoy: shopping, spa days, the salon.

Cunningham fancied himself an art collector, and frequently traveled to various private auctions around the world. He'd been on one such trip earlier in the week, and Sean was pretty sure he'd gotten back Thursday evening—which explained Raven's panic when I'd demanded he meet me that night at the Silver Lode. The gods only knew what explanation he'd given. Something about "communing with the air" or some other hocus-pocus fairy bullshit, I figured. Had Cunningham bought it? I could only pray that he had.

After Sean went back to work half-panicked himself at the idea of being my informant and also high enough to float, I had nothing to do but loiter around and hope he got back to me with something more concrete, as he'd reluctantly promised me he'd do.

Fuck, Raven was probably *right there*. From my current lurking spot on the roof of the parking garage where I'd met Sean, he was maybe…I eyed the top of the towering blue-glass expanse of Audacity, to which I had a clear line of sight over a cluster of shorter buildings. Shit, I'd need the Pythagorean Theorem if I wanted to know how far away he was.

Not like I had anything better to do but worry and brood. I pulled out my phone and looked up the height of the building, did a couple of calculations.

About 1300 feet, as one of his fellow corvids would fly.

Now I could worry and brood with more mathematical confidence. Fucking great.

It felt like it took forever, standing there in the sunshine listening to the honks and shouts and random bursts of shitty music that drifted up from the street below, breathing in car exhaust and dust, before my phone pinged with a message.

I scrabbled to unlock the screen so violently I nearly dropped it over the edge of the roof.

If I get killed for this, I'm going to make sure I take you with me, he said. Thanks, Sean. Not that I blamed him. *Someone told me your guy went to the Endless Sky Spa out in Summerlin for the afternoon. And there's going to be an over the top party here on Friday night, but it's private. That's all I have.*

I texted back a thank you and a thumbs up, and after a short wait got a series of emojis that I couldn't interpret clearly but that seemed to indicate mental distress of some kind. A second later, a marijuana leaf emoji followed in its own message.

That was clear enough. *Will do, I owe you,* I sent back. He didn't reply.

Two minutes later, I was in the car and on my way to the Endless Sky Spa. Weird name, and equally weird that he'd chosen to go outside Audacity, which had one of the best spas in the world, I'd heard, let alone Las Vegas.

Then again, maybe he took literally any excuse to be out from under Cunningham's watchful eye for a couple of hours. In fact, maybe he hadn't even gone there, and it really *was* an excuse.

Maybe he'd found another alpha and tried again, since it hadn't worked with me.

My heart tried to pound sideways out of my ribs and my vision blurred for a second, and I nearly ran off the road.

I straightened out, cursing, with someone honking in the other lane.

Fuck. Fuck me, maybe he had. Of course he'd keep trying to get out of his magical bondage. He wouldn't shrug and give up because his first attempt had been a failure. I'd already been forcing myself not to spend every minute freaking out over what Cunningham might be doing to him, and now that I'd thought of this...someone else might hurt him.

Cunningham was already hurting him, or at least using and terrorizing him, except that everything added up to Cunningham keeping him around in part as a status symbol, a beautiful thing he owned. He probably wouldn't damage something he valued that much too badly, right? I'd been clinging to that thought, trying to keep myself on this side of storming Audacity and challenging Cunningham to a fight to the death. Raven had been enduring him for a while already. He could hopefully wait a little longer until I could find a better way.

But some fucking random alpha might not have even those scruples, or that level of selfish investment in Raven being in one piece on the other side of whatever encounter they might have.

My claws sprouted uncontrollably, one hand's worth of them digging into the steering wheel, and a gold haze fell over my vision. I had to be breaking the speed limit by a whole hell of a lot, but fuck it.

I screeched around the final corner and slowed down enough to come to a reasonable stop in the parking lot of the strip mall where my map app had told me I'd find Endless Sky.

And there, pulled up right in front, was Raven's shiny black coupe.

I parked on the other side of the narrow lot, backing in so that I could watch his car and the front of the spa, and slumped my forehead down onto the steering wheel, slowly working my claws back out of it and breathing like I'd been running all the way here instead of just driving like a maniac.

Once I'd calmed down a bit, I opened my window, shut off

the engine, and settled in for the duration. The urge to barge inside and find him immediately rose up strong, but screw bulls in china shops—a glowing-eyed, six-foot-four-inch alpha weretiger in a day spa took that concept to a whole new level. If I had any chance of getting Raven to talk to me, I had to wait.

So I waited.

And waited, as the sun crept down toward the horizon and shadows lengthened across the parking lot.

Fucking Christ, how much rubbing and lotioning and pedicuring did one small fairy need? He was already so beautiful, and it had nothing at all to do with the efforts of a team of salon employees.

My sister liked going to the spa. Maybe she'd know how long it took. She'd called me the other day, and I'd dodged, texting her that I was too busy to talk.

What would she say if I called her back right now and told her where I was and why? She'd shit a brick. Always on me to find a mate and settle down, but if she knew what I—

My thoughts came to a halt more screeching than my entrance into the strip mall's parking lot.

A mate.

The scar of my alpha bite on Raven's slender, perfect neck, right at the base of it. Off to the side slightly so that it wouldn't be visible unless one of his high collars slipped down, the only mark on all of his silky white skin. His smile when I kissed it, his soft sigh as he tilted his head and leaned into me...

The parking lot reformed around me as the fantasy shattered into a million pieces. My claws had embedded themselves in the steering wheel again. My erection threatened to bust through the front of my jeans and do the same.

And I knew, at last, exactly how fucked I was. Raven wouldn't want that. Any of it. Fantasy-Raven didn't exist, and real-Raven would be horrified to know what he got up to in my fevered imagination.

Worse than that...

A mate.

My mate.

Something I'd never really planned to have, because no one had roused the part of me that would crave so deeply, desire so powerfully, that no one else would ever be good enough again.

No one before Raven. And I knew, down to my bones, there wouldn't be anyone after, either.

Oh, Raven had gotten it right when he said I wasn't any smarter than I looked.

Sort of right, but also sort of wrong. Because I was even fucking stupider than that. The "Dominic could run intellectual rings around me" kind of stupid.

It took me another ten minutes to get my claws out of the ruined steering wheel for the second time, and to will my cock down to half mast, and by then the last of the dusk had faded and all the lights around me had come on. The front of the spa glowed a subtle sort of greenish-purple with little twinkly lights on strings making patterns across the curtained windows.

Fairy lights.

The Endless Sky.

I turned my head toward my open window, closed my eyes, and concentrated, taking deep breaths and consciously focusing on the sensory data my body usually processed instinctually.

Yeah, that was the scent of magic. Faint and almost muted somehow, sort of like that weird underwater light coming from the spa windows. But definitely there, and it didn't smell like Raven. Any scent of him in the parking lot had dissipated before I arrived.

Was this what he'd meant by communing with the air? Did the Las Vegas fae community have some kind of secret hideout inside a strip-mall day spa?

I didn't have long to wonder, because another fifteen minutes later, the door opened, the first time it had done so while I'd been parked here, I now realized.

Raven stepped out and let the door swing shut behind him, frowning down at the phone in his hand and with his car keys in the other. He was in all black again, but of course, and had his hair up in a messy bun.

My breath caught, the sensation starting to become familiar with repetition: a little hitch of wonder that he even existed.

He looked up.

And he stopped dead as our eyes met and held, even through my windshield and across the dim parking lot.

His lips pressed together in a flat line.

I tensed, my hand on the door release. He'd never make it into his car before I intercepted him.

But it wasn't necessary, because he slipped his keys and phone into the pockets of his jacket and strode toward me, shaking his head at me as he did.

An instant later he'd opened the passenger door and climbed in, shutting it behind him.

Chapter 13

Raven filled my senses: his sweetness mingled with the scent of some herbal and slightly spicy spa product or other, the warmth of his body, the tingling presence of him all along my right side. When he half turned in his seat to face me, we were only a foot apart, and the jet black of his eyes glittered, reflecting the strip mall's overhead lights. A flush spread over his cheeks, and one waving tendril of his hair that had escaped the bun curled along his jaw.

"I would ask how you found me, but I'm not sure I want to know," he said. "And I'd ask what you're doing here, but I'm afraid that I do know."

I had to lick my lips and swallow before I could force my throat to push any words out. Every cell in my body strained to touch him.

"I doubt you do, actually," I rasped. "You probably think I'm here to try to fuck you."

A shadow passed across his face, so briefly I almost missed it, and then he'd composed himself again, impenetrable.

Blank, Sean had said. The face Raven showed the world at large.

And now me, apparently. I felt like a starving man plastered against the bulletproof glass window of—nothing as mundane as a grocery store, obviously. Maybe the kind of bakery that listed its pastries' fillings in a language you didn't know and which they refused to translate for you, but that you knew would be able to sell you the most delicious thing you'd ever tasted.

"That possibility had occurred to me," he said levelly. Too levelly? Or with genuine indifference? "But that would be better than the alternative, that you want to...*talk* to me." His tone suggested that "dead, bloated, stinking fish" would've been the right synonym for "talk."

Since I'd come here to talk to him, that took most of the wind out of my sails.

What I had left, anyway, after sitting here across from a fairy probably-not-really-massage joint for hours, facing up to the fact that I'd landed myself on the wrong side of doomed, unrequited feelings.

"Maybe I am here to fuck you," I said, since he'd left me without a next scripted line. *I want more than your body, Raven. I don't want to own you. I want to help you. We need to talk.* Not so much, damn it. "Or maybe you could tell me what really goes on in there, since no one else has been in and out all afternoon and it smells like fairy magic."

He lifted a hand, fingers spread, and waggled it a few inches from my face. "Endless Sky doesn't take many appointments, because the clientele is exclusive. And as you see, my nails are now purple. Completely different from the last time you saw me. They take time to dry perfectly, and my toes must match, so of course I was there for a while."

Raven tried to drop his hand back to his lap, but Christ, I had to touch him or I'd explode, so I caught his wrist before he could get away. His pulse jackrabbited under my fingers, and when I rubbed my thumb over the back of his hand, a faint shiver ran through his arm.

"Purple" apparently meant super pale purply iridescent, in this case. Last time it'd been more of a creamy silver, I was pretty sure, although I never would've noticed if he hadn't pointed out how "completely different" they were.

"I've never noticed your nails," I lied through my teeth. "But it looks nice."

He tried, without success, to pull his wrist away. I leaned in and kissed his knuckles, flicking my tongue, a wave of helpless want rolling through me all the way down to my balls as I tasted the faintly salted-honey warmth of his skin.

The hitch in his breath mimicked my own when I'd caught sight of him.

Encouraged, and dizzy with all the blood rushing to my suddenly rock-hard cock, I kissed up his hand and sucked his index finger into my mouth. He didn't taste or smell like nail polish chemicals, surprisingly—score one for fairy salons. Only, and intoxicatingly, like him.

Raven's gasp turned into a low moan, quickly cut off. A glance up showed me his teeth digging ferociously into his lower lip, and he'd half-closed his eyelids. Sultry. I'd never used that word before, didn't even realize I'd known it, but nothing else captured the way he eyed me as if he wanted me to eat him—but not until he'd driven me insane first.

Redundant effort, you already got there without even trying, I could've said, if I hadn't had two fingers in my mouth now, rough-textured tongue prodding and teasing at the juncture between them.

His scent intensified, now tinged with arousal, musky and tart and absolutely unmistakable.

Maybe I should fuck him after all. My shitty old sedan had plenty of room in the back seat compared to a similar model. He could probably ride me if I slid down as far as I could go, and maybe cut off my feet.

The base of my cock throbbed, right where my knot would swell inside the wet, hot grasp of his pretty little hole.

And my own groan echoed in the car, half muffled by his fingers and all the more obscene for it. His cock down my throat, my tongue driving him crazy...I'd love that too. Although given the space constraints of the front seat, it might make more sense to have his soft lips wrapped around my cock, head bobbing up and down in my lap as I wrapped my hands in his hair...

"Stop imagining all the things you want to do to me with that ridiculous tongue of yours," he complained. "And stop, oh, Tony, you...oh." I captured a third finger and sucked like I meant it. "*Oh.*" He'd started squirming in his seat, the car jouncing lightly. Shit, maybe my shocks couldn't take fucking in the back after all.

Plus we were in public. But yeah, professional stripper. My fucks given were zero on that particular issue.

Deep-throating his fingers would make me come in my jeans, so I pulled off and kissed the tips of them. Raven had blushed velvety, rosy red, eyes glittering and lips parted. More hair tumbled down from his messy updo.

"If you'd answer any of my questions, maybe I'd be paying attention to that instead of thinking about fucking your mouth. Or doing more with my tongue, you aren't wrong," I admitted, in the spirit of fairness.

Not that he ever bothered with fairness. Maybe I could set a good example.

"I'm not wrong about anything, oh, don't—" I bit his fingers, and Raven broke off in a whimper, swaying toward me as if the gravity well between us had suddenly doubled in magnitude.

I dropped his hand in favor of wrapping my arms around him and hauling him halfway over the center console, my mouth finding his unerringly. Soft lips, a wet, flicking tongue, the smoothness of his teeth and the hot roof of his mouth, and I explored it all, devouring him, swallowing his little moans and clutching him close as he writhed in my grasp. Too possessive, and too desperate, but his efforts weren't directed at escaping from me. He seemed to be trying to climb me, to press himself against me until not even our clothes would fit in the space between us.

Fuck it, I didn't need the back seat. With a good yank, I got him out of the passenger seat and almost into my lap.

With a wrench and a shove, he broke the kiss and pushed away with both hands flat on my chest.

"Why do you keep doing this to yourself?" he demanded, and his breath against my face had me shuddering with the need to do it some more. He evaded my lunge for his shiny, kiss-swollen lips by tilting his head all the way back.

That exposed the line of his throat.

My low, rumbling growl vibrated the air between us.

Strong, slim fingers caught a fistful of my hair and yanked my head up and back. The console under him eliminated our height difference, and I found myself eye to eye with a furiously glaring fairy.

"Yes, eyes up here, please," he snapped. "I can't even imagine the complications of that on top of everything else. I hate alphas!"

By *that*, he surely meant me losing control and adding my own magic to the mix. And Cunningham, what would he do to him if Raven came back with another alpha's bite on his neck? It didn't bear thinking about.

"I wouldn't do that unless you wanted it," I said, because I wouldn't, no matter how my fangs dropped and my mouth watered. Blood didn't taste particularly appealing to most predator shifters in our human forms, but his…I didn't want enough to hurt him. Just enough to know him down to his bones. "And you don't hate me."

"There are exceptions to every rule, not that I'm saying you are one." The tiny smile he couldn't seem to suppress belied that.

"Not biting," I whispered as I leaned in, and he stopped pushing, letting me press the softest possible kiss to the hollow of his throat between his collar bones. He quivered in my arms. "I'm an exception. The only exception. Say it."

I nuzzled the side of his throat and flicked my tongue.

"Ah," he gasped. "In, mmm, Endless Sky. We have a portal to our own lands. It's not really a spa for humans, but they do, oh, they do paint nails."

"Interesting, but that won't work. Say it." I licked a stripe up to his chin, nipped at the little point of it, breathed out, "Tell me I'm the only alpha you'd ever want."

"He can't keep me from my own people, they'd take that very poorly," Raven babbled, "so that's why I can come here, to—" And then I kissed him again, and again, until he sagged in my arms and gave in, head tipped back and mouth yielding.

One of my hands slid down his spine, and his pants were stretchy today, enough that I could get my fingers down the back of them and tease into the crease of his ass. Raven jolted like I'd electrocuted him, hips thrusting against nothing. I found the tight clench of his hole with one finger. A knuckle's worth of penetration had him clinging to me and shaking, practically sobbing into my mouth, and gods, I'd have given anything to be inside him—

anything except the triumph and the perfection of holding him as he came apart, knowing that he didn't need to say a gods-damned thing about exceptions. Words weren't needed.

Raven would never moan and whine and come in his expensive pants for another alpha.

This was mine. He was mine. The hot, sweet come he'd spilled into his clothes was mine, along with that honeyed alkaline scent that wafted up to me. Someone else might technically own him, and that motherfucker's days were numbered, but the panting, gasping mess of previously elegant and composed fairy in my arms belonged to *me*.

I pulled back enough to appreciate the sight of him, damp with perspiration, hair a rat's nest, lashes fanned out over glowing cheeks. He'd slumped sideways with his head leaning on my upper arm, twisted up on top of the center console in a way that would've had anyone without his natural flexibility headed straight to the chiropractor.

He'd do anything I wanted right now. Let me spread his legs. Or suck me off, if I told him to. I knew it the way I knew my own name. Some combination of fairy obligation, desire, and the submissiveness that came out at odd moments when I'd pleased him would make him agree to whatever I asked for.

My erection hadn't subsided in the slightest. In fact, watching Raven come had almost tipped me over the edge.

But my arousal felt...not quite distant, but secondary. Pleasing him had been enough for me. Proving he wanted me, whether he'd say it or not, had been a nice little side bonus. And more than any of that, in the context of his relationship with Cunningham—if you could call it that—the thought of asking for sex acts he didn't volunteer for made me sick.

So I eased him back down into the passenger seat, keeping my arm around his shoulders for support, and pulling my other hand out of his pants. That left me leaning uncomfortably over the center of the front seat, but the brush of his hair against my neck and cheek more than made up for it. I could've sat like that for a long, long time.

But of course Raven stirred and opened his eyes, tension

returning to his relaxed body.

"My mouth is available if you need some relief," he said. But his tone didn't suggest eagerness.

The last of my overwhelming need drained away. Yeah, still hard. And yeah, later on I'd jerk myself raw thinking about his mouth, probably twice. But no.

"No," I said, and it came out harsher than I'd meant it to. Now the arm I had around him felt weird. Half of me ached to grab him again and pull him close, but I slid it out from behind him and dropped back into my own seat, staring out at the sickly violet glow still radiating from the "spa's" windows. What he'd said to me when he'd been trying to distract me replayed in my head—the big one, which finally had a bit of blood going to it. "Wait a second. You have family, or whoever, who'd be pissed if Cunningham kept you away from them? So how come they haven't helped you? I assumed you were on your own. You can't use your magic against him, you said. But presumably they can. What gives?"

His long, deep sigh could've indicated a lot of things from annoyance to regret, but the law of averages suggested disgust at my stupidity.

"Of course they can't interfere with a bargain I entered into freely." Yep. Shocked disgust. I'd called it. "However, their power gives me more leeway than he might allow me otherwise. They can't release me, but they could make his life…uncomfortable. Which he'd then take out on me, of course. So no one wants that."

Fairies. Fucking fairies, man. If my family had a choice between a cultural technicality and leaving me in what amounted to sex slavery, no rules existed that they wouldn't be willing to violate.

"Your family sucks," I said, because I simply couldn't find any better words. "Christ. That's—uncomfortable?" I rolled my head on the headrest to look at him. He'd kept his gaze straight ahead, also fixed on the eerie lighting, as far as I could tell. The clean, pointy lines of his profile gave nothing away. "They'd make him fucking uncomfortable, and that's it? That doesn't compute. You need their help!"

Raven shrugged one shoulder, and his lips pressed into a flat line, but he didn't reply. Probably that was as close as he could get, within the constraints of his species and upbringing, to agreeing with me. I'd have to accept that.

Still. If I ever met his family…realistically, they'd turn me into a diseased frog.

Cunningham. I had to focus on the enemy I could defeat. A bunch of nail-painting fairies who wouldn't get off their asses to rescue their own family and friends even though they were overpowered to do so were obviously out of my league.

"Look, we should—"

"No," he said, echoing my earlier harshness, but with a weary undertone to it. He turned his head to meet my gaze steadily. "You're about to start talking about it all again, aren't you? I really wish you'd stop this. It only makes it worse. There's nothing you can do. I'm starting to think there's nothing I can do, either," he added, wearier than ever.

"Not with that attitude." Jesus, I sounded like my dad. Raven raised his eyebrows disdainfully. "Sorry, that was a joke?" His lip curled. "Fine. Not funny. But obviously there's a way out, right? You said fae magic likes symmetry. There has to be some other way to flip the bargain you made with Cunningham that we haven't thought of yet. Also, and stop me if I'm missing something important, but killing him seems like a pretty valid solution."

His eyes widened.

"Killing him," he rasped, and cleared his throat. "Killing him? Tony, have you ever killed anyone?"

"Tigers are natural predators, and Cunningham's a fucking piece of shit."

Raven glared at me. "I'll take that as a no, then? Well?"

"No," I admitted.

"Well, hopefully this doesn't surprise you, but neither have I. And aside from the moral implications, and yes, thank you, I do have something like morality, it would be complicated and messy and dangerous, and I obviously can't do it myself or to be frank I probably would have by now despite all of that, and if you try to do it, you'll get yourself killed or put in prison for the rest of your life!" He broke off to suck in a couple of deep lungfuls, since he'd ranted all that at me in one breath. "There are prisons strong enough to hold you here in the human world, aren't there? Or would they just kill you? The authorities, I mean, not Cunningham's security team. They'd definitely kill you."

"Aren't you a ray of fucking sunshine, and yes, there are prisons that would hold me. If they could get me there. But you could use your magic to hide me if it came to that, right? Take me to the spa or something." I tried for another joke. "Paint my claws purple."

He didn't even dignify that with a response, simply countering with, "And then you'd never see your family again, and reading between the lines, you seem to like them rather a lot. Killing him isn't an option. At least not for you."

Not for me. Right. The only person who seemed to be showing the desire, will, and possibly even ability to get it done. "Let me guess, your fae buddies won't do it because it'd be cheating your bargain."

He shrugged again. "That, and we don't really kill. That's not our way."

"More of the 'ensnare for a thousand years of confused torment that you didn't really deserve' kind of people, huh?"

"Yes," he said primly. "It's more fun that way."

"Endless torment and nail painting," I remarked absently. "Thematic."

To my shock, that won me a soft laugh. "I won't take you to the spa with me, then," he said. "But I enjoy it. Aside from seeing my people. Facials are lovely."

No, I wouldn't say it, even though I could feel the words forming on my tongue and a leer on my face.

Coming all over his face had a certain amount of appeal, but the way he was looking at me, open and soft (for him, anyway), head leaned back and the parking lot's lights gleaming on his white neck, stirred up stronger impulses. Less crude ones.

Slightly less crude, anyway. I'd never claimed to be a poetic romantic.

"What now?" I asked. "Since you don't want me to kill him. Although full disclosure, I might not be able to resist if the opportunity comes up. But a thousand years of torment sounds okay, if that can be arranged. I'm open-minded. As long as you end up free of him." *And all mine.* But I knew better than to say that. And it wasn't true, anyway. I wanted him free of Cunningham whether he ended up mine or not.

"Now?" He couldn't meet my eyes, eyelashes sweeping down as he fixed his gaze on his hands where they rested on his thighs, running a thumb over his brand-new completely different (identical) shiny nails. "Now I go back to Audacity. And you go to work. Nothing. There's nothing you can do, Tony. You shouldn't have tracked me down today."

Every time he protested that he wanted me to go, or that he wished he hadn't been with me, it sounded less and less convincing, and it gave me a thrilling swoop in my stomach that I didn't know what to do with.

I reached out and laid my hand over both of his where they twisted together in his lap. My much bigger hand covered both of his, enclosed them. Gods, I wished I could wrap myself around him like that, physically and in a more metaphorical way.

What the hell could I say to him that'd convince him to stop arguing?

"Your magic wore off. The kissing thing? This morning. I felt it dissipate." That snapped his gaze back up to me. "I mean, now I've kissed you again, so who knows."

"You," he said, and stopped. "You, ah, you. Came to see me, with no magical compulsion at all?"

That would've been the perfect time for a cheesy line. *Your sweet ass is magic, baby*, possibly followed by a wink.

Jesus, I'd been a strip club stage performer for way too long.

"You really thought I'd left you for good when I walked out of that room, Raven?"

"Yes," he whispered, and his eyes had gotten suspiciously shiny. So had his lashes, gleaming wetly. He blinked and a drop fell. "I did, and I didn't, I didn't—"

With a gun to my head—actually, strike that, a gunshot or two wouldn't even kill me. With an aircraft carrier to my head, I couldn't have resisted.

Raven collapsed against my chest as I caught him in my arms

and gathered him close again, and he shuddered and shook, the front of my shirt instantly soaked through, his freshly painted nails digging furrows in my sides.

I buried my face in his hair and held him, temporarily safe from the world, knowing as I did that I'd inevitably need to let him go.

Chapter 14

It shouldn't have surprised me that Raven turned out to be one of those people who looked beautiful even when he'd cried his heart out into a rough T-shirt. Actually, he'd gotten as puffy-faced and creased around the edges and disheveled as anyone else, objectively. Maybe it said more about me than it did about him that I could've worshipped his swollen lips and reddened eyes and the damp, pink tip of his nose until the end of time.

Yeah, it definitely said more than a few things about me.

But after he'd peeled himself off my chest, and I'd kissed him for a while and mumbled the kind of nonsense people say at times like that, I reluctantly had to let him go. As I'd known I would at the beginning of that stolen hour of petting him and kissing his hair and taking comfort in the fact that no one could hurt him while I was there.

Knowing didn't make my chest ache any less, or quiet the growing storm of panic that'd started to echo around in my skull.

"Stay with me," I said, because I couldn't help it, as he started to fuss with his hair, pulling down the sun visor to peer into the little mirror there. "We'll deal with him together. You can't go back to him."

I might lose my mind if you go back to him.

He glanced at me, and it took him a moment to tear his eyes away. I knew I had to be looking grim: glowing eyes, pale around the mouth, clawed fists clenched, barely restraining myself from a roar that would've shaken the strip mall's foundations.

"I already have gone back to him from you, twice." He twisted his hair together and fastened it, and then passed his hands over his face, muttering something I didn't catch but that made my ears feel like someone had poked them with a feather. When he took them away, the traces of his tears had vanished. "And I need to do it again. If I don't fulfill my obligations, my magic will wither, and there won't be anything left of me for you to keep."

"I don't give a fuck about your magic. You think that's why I want you?"

Raven flicked the visor back into place and turned on me, eyes flashing. "My magic *is* me. You of all people should understand."

That hurt, unexpectedly deeply. "You wouldn't have any use for me without my alpha magic, is that what you mean? If I were a human guy?"

"It's a moot point, because I never would have sought you out if you were a human guy. No, don't look like that. You also, ah." A dark flush had crept up from his neck and stained his cheeks, and he avoided my eyes as he said, "There's more to you than that. If you lost your alpha-ness, you'd be as—what you are. Even though you'd probably miss it terribly, and that's what I meant when I said you'd understand. But if I lost my magic, that's the entire fabric of my being. There's nothing else. I'm not partly human, the way you are. I mean it, Tony. I'd die."

Sincerity rang in his voice. For once, Raven wasn't feeding me fae half-truths. I nodded. "Then I won't ask you to stay, but…be careful." Don't ask, don't ask…I couldn't stop myself from fishing for that hinted-at compliment, pathetic as it was. "And what am I? With or without my alpha magic?"

Raven reached out, brushing his fingers down my cheek, the saddest smile I'd ever seen teasing at one corner of his mouth. Whatever he'd done to his face, it hadn't fixed him completely, and his upper lip still had that soft, trembly look to it. His mouth had tasted like salt and misery when I kissed him a few minutes ago. It felt like years ago already.

"You're an exception," he said, and whisked his hand away, opening the passenger door and slipping out before I could even process the words, let alone respond to them.

He shut the door behind him and strode across the parking lot toward his own car, hand in his pocket and already beeping it open.

My muscles and joints locked into painful rigidity with the effort of staying put.

But he was right. He had to go back for now, and killing Cunningham would be...I watched Raven get into his car, back out of the spot, and pull away. He didn't turn his head to look at me, but his hands were white-knuckled on the steering wheel.

A last resort, I decided. Killing Cunningham, with the associated risks of being killed for it by his guards or his friends, or of going to a supernatural supermax prison for the rest of my life, would be my last resort. Raven would be free. He could use his magic to scoot back to his own world, either via Endless Sky or some other portal, and any guilt he felt over my fate wouldn't last forever.

Not that I wanted any of that to happen. But I'd committed, now. Made a choice. And I'd see it through no matter what that entailed. My glimpse of Raven's face as he drove away fighting back a new wave of tears made that a certainty.

I waited a few minutes, until there was no chance at all of my catching up to him on the drive back from Summerlin, before I started the car and headed home.

***

Sometimes, when I had a seemingly insoluble problem, I had to exhaust myself until I couldn't think anymore. With my conscious mind out of commission—and let's not kid ourselves, it wasn't all that useful most days anyway—my unconscious could range far and wide, ideally coming back with a solution I'd never have come up with if I'd wracked my brain about it.

Two days of working doubles at Lucky or Knot certainly exhausted me, keeping me dancing and gyrating and glittering from noon to four AM on Tuesday and Wednesday. But when I woke up around lunchtime on Thursday, stomach growling and glitter still visibly clinging to my eyebrows when I staggered into the bathroom and peered in the mirror, no bright ideas had appeared.

In the shower, I leaned down with my arm braced against the wall, staring at the water swirling past my toes, and took a few deep breaths.

We had time to come up with something. Raven hadn't told me exactly how long he'd been with Cunningham, but if he'd only started seriously hunting for a way out recently, it couldn't be more than a few months, I didn't think. A long time when you were in a situation like his, but in the grand scheme of things—particularly for a magical being with an indeterminate lifespan—not something to panic over. A few more weeks while we worked something out would be fine, even a couple of months, although every second of Raven in Cunningham's hands and bed and control would be a hell of Raven's misery and my fury and terror.

But he'd be fine. I had to believe it. I'd hire a shaman to help, maybe. Find a rogue fairy who didn't mind breaking his people's stupid rules. Figure out a way to kill Cunningham without getting caught, now there was an idea.

So I got out of the shower slightly more hopeful, and much less glittery, than I'd been in days.

That mood lasted until I'd tossed my towel and padded into my bedroom. The phone I'd left at the foot of the bed had lit up like a Christmas tree.

I grabbed it immediately, heart lurching—it could be Raven.

It wasn't. I had two messages from Sean and one from Louie. I opened Sean's first.

Hey. So I just got to work and heard about it. Boss had a fit last night, threw a chair through a penthouse window and barely missed a tourist down on the ground. He's moving out of the hotel and into his house in the hills

The second read: *I'm out of anything for my break so hit me up*

That muffled roar had to be my own blood pounding in my ears, and the faint creak…shit, I'd nearly broken my phone. I loosened my grip with an effort, forced my claws to retract, blinked against the gold haze of the alpha glow. The few droplets of water left on my skin felt chilled, congealed, like chunks of ice.

Cunningham knew. That had to be it.

Raven had been gone too long, or he hadn't managed to magic away all the traces of my scent or his tears or his orgasm. Cunningham had gotten a clue. And somehow, last night, he'd become certain.

What had he done to him? In that plush, luxurious penthouse, full of chairs heavy enough to go through windows that were probably unbreakable without an alpha's strength.

An alpha's strength, up against a small fairy who couldn't use his magic to defend himself.

I'd done that to him, as surely as if it'd been my alpha strength he couldn't fight. Tracked him down, forced him to talk to me, touched him, kissed him, fucked him with my fingers, made him cry, put him in danger.

My fault. My responsibility.

The blood boiled in my veins, the pressure unbearable, and I roared with it, raged, black and crimson and gold flashes like lightning, and came back to myself at last, shaking and running with sweat, one clawed and orange-furred arm embedded in the wall by the bathroom door. Bits of drywall peppered the floor like snow. The silence rang around me. My rasping breaths punctuated it.

Fuck. Fuck me. I dropped my forehead against what was left of my bedroom wall and forced it down, all of it, the fur retreating, the claws pulling in, tugging my arm from the wreckage, my vision starting to go back to normal.

The sound of my own hollow laugh made me jump.

Yeah. An exception, Raven had called me, and I'd lived on those two words ever since, treasuring them up. Some fucking exception. If I'd been in a penthouse, I'd have thrown a chair through a window just now myself. Violent, and uncontrolled, and selfish. Too focused on what I wanted and what I arrogantly thought I could do for Raven to understand how much of a risk he'd taken every time he saw me.

No, he was right to hate alphas. Including me. Especially me.

He might be hurt right now, bruised and broken, crying again—although I suspected he'd die before he cried in front of Cunningham, and it broke my heart all over again, leaving me breathless and twisted up inside, to know that he'd trusted me so much and then I'd let him down.

My fault.

And any time that I'd imagined I had to come up with a plan had run out. If Cunningham meant to move to his house, which I'd be willing to bet more resembled a fortified compound, it was because he wanted to lock Raven up somewhere he couldn't come and go freely, the way he could at Audacity. What would he do to him there? What was he doing to him *right now*?

I swallowed down bile and swayed against a wave of dizziness.

Cunningham wouldn't be alone, he wouldn't be vulnerable, and yes, maybe I could fight my way through his security with their magic and claws and guns and get to him and tear him to bloody shreds…but maybe not.

And if I got myself killed in the attempt, Raven would truly be alone.

Even a stupid, selfish, arrogant alpha had to be better than no one at all.

The urge to call Raven, to run out the door naked, to do any number of ill-considered things, rose up strong.

I resisted. From this moment on, I had to think everything through carefully, plan it like a game of chess.

Fuck, talk about playing to my own weaknesses. My favorite board game had always been Monopoly, and I usually lost.

So I got dressed, and I texted Sean, and I told the club scheduler that I wouldn't be in later, and I glanced at Louie's message, which told me to call him or he'd call my parents. Christ, hadn't had one like that since high school. What the hell kind of regressed mess had I made of my life? Raven had been right not to take me seriously.

Of course, Raven had also been right that I couldn't help him, that I'd put him in danger.

Keeping my cool while I drove the ten minutes to the dispensary, and then the ten further minutes to the parking lot, felt like a monumental effort, every cell in my body screaming at me to go faster and claw out and fucking *do something* as I braked and gripped the steering wheel and gritted my teeth and nearly crawled out of my own skin with impatience.

Right across the Strip from the parking garage, I hit traffic and stopped dead. Everyone honked and yelled, and in my rearview, a cop car edged its way through the jam and toward whatever bullshit had gone down.

The steering wheel let out an ominous creaking crack.

In desperation for something to do, I called Louie back, since I had to get that over with anyway.

"Tony, I'm glad you—"

I didn't have the patience for whatever smarmy, sneering crap he had in mind. Louie liked to lean into the loan shark persona, indeterminate accent and gold pinky ring and all. Motherfucker.

"Get to the point," I snapped. "I've got some of your money, not all of it, I'll get you a payment…" Shit, when would I have the time? Later today, I'd take him the whole pile of cash I'd made in two busy, successful days at work, because I wouldn't need it for rent, right? I'd be killing Cunningham and going to doublesupe, what the guys I knew who'd done time always called the supernatural maximum security facilities. "…tonight, I have cash for you. My parents are broke so don't bother, I already told you that. Also, my mom might eat you. Anything else to add?"

A short pause followed, kind of like the moment of quiet before the tea kettle whistled.

"The fuck did you just say to me?" Louie demanded. "You threatening me? With your *mom*?"

"You threatened to call my mom, so I'm not sure—yeah, fuck you too! No, that wasn't for you. I'm in traffic. Fuck you too, though, Louie, now you fucking mention it."

A low chuckle and some static crackled out of my phone, where I had it precariously leaned against the dash with the speaker on. My car was too old for Bluetooth, or I'd have sold it to pay Louie a long time ago.

"You'll regret that," he said, totally failing to make me give a shit. Raven would be able, and probably willing, to take care of Louie and get him off my parents' back while I was in prison, I figured. Not that they'd care about their house once I went away. "I fucking own you, Tony."

"Yeah, yeah," I growled absently, because the cop had made

his way through at last and it looked like we were all merging right, and if I didn't manage to get some forward motion of some kind—Raven crying, Raven bruised, Raven cursing my name, fuck—I was going to vibrate out of the car and into another dimension. "Fucking move! Not you. Louie, dude, if you call my mom before I get to you with the cash, I won't bring it. So up to you. Later."

And I poked the end button hard enough that the phone went flying down into the passenger footwell.

A minute later I finally screeched across Las Vegas Boulevard cursing and gesticulating, the way the gods intended, made it to the garage, and parked with a jolt.

Fuck Louie, Jesus. What a son of a bitch. It wasn't like I hadn't been paying him off in increments. *I fucking own you.* Right, as if that'd stand up in court outside of some Shakespeare silliness. Maybe a fae court.

Maybe a...fuck me sideways.

For a second I simply sat there, staring at the filthy marks on the concrete wall in front of my car, frozen into stillness.

Louie thought he owned me. Which meant he'd probably be willing to sell me.

By shitty fairy law, Cunningham did own Raven, in exchange for that coin.

The coin that wanted symmetry, that would only leave Raven and free him from Cunningham if he could somehow flip the deal he'd made on its head.

Paying me for the same thing he'd been paid *for* hadn't worked. But what about using the coin an alpha had used to buy him...to buy his very own alpha in turn? Louie had one for sale. Not the highest quality, maybe, and preowned always came with risks. But definitely available, and beggars couldn't be choosers.

Anyway, I'd do the begging for both of us.

Please, fuck, let him be all right.

I got out of the car, slammed the door behind me, and set out to put my plan into motion.

Chapter 15

Sean was waiting for me this time, fiddling with his phone and frowning.

"Shit, fuck, I'm sorry I'm late," I said, and handed him the dispensary bag as he looked up. "Light up if you want, but I need information. And a favor." He really wouldn't like that, but then...shit. "And another one after that, probably. If that party's still happening, I need to get in. First info, though. Did Cunningham leave the hotel? Did he take, uh, my guy with him?"

I had a hundred other questions running through my mind, and the energy of momentum fizzing in my blood, but I forced myself to shut up and give Sean a chance to answer.

Gods, maybe I could get around killing Cunningham and ruining the rest of my life. Not that Cunningham didn't deserve to be killed, but with a tiny bit of hope for another solution now glimmering in front of me at the end of the tunnel, I could admit that Raven had a point. There were better ways.

Sean produced a lighter, eyed me with his brows furrowed, and said, "Okay, we'll come back to the favors, but I really don't know much. I think they went to the house last night after the chair thing. His limo left. And your guy's not around this morning. I guess he went too."

Just hearing *your guy*, Raven referred to by someone else, made my heart skip a beat. Gods. I needed to get a grip.

Raven had been moved, okay, that sucked, but I'd suspected

as much. Of course, that was the best case scenario, that he'd been sitting tight-lipped and frightened in that limo. Worst case…

I couldn't. Not if I wanted to function. I pushed it back, pushed it down, forced myself to focus on the here and now.

The lighter clicked, Sean inhaled deeply, and a plume of smoke trailed past me, borne on a fitful little breeze that whistled mournfully around the corner of the garage.

"He hasn't canceled the party, as far as I know," Sean said after another deep inhale, in that weird, suffused, holding-a-lungful stoner voice. "Still happening tomorrow night. And—"

He broke off in a raw-sounding coughing fit, smoke exploding everywhere, and I winced, ground my teeth together, and felt my eyes begin to glow. *I will not shake it out of him. I will not rip his fucking face off.*

"I can't get you in," he said at last, right as I thought I might burst into flame myself. "There's no way. Everyone's ID gets checked. You talk to MacKenna about that job yet?"

Fuck.

"I will in a minute," I said. What the hell. Now I'd need to ask Declan if he could get me into the party, anyway, since I knew from the tone of Sean's voice that if I pushed him any further on this, I'd lose what little help he'd still be willing to give me. So I might as well annoy Declan once instead of twice. "Right now I need the first favor. A smaller one," I added, as he shot me a look. "I need you to make a call from your phone."

I took out my phone and pulled up Raven's number, messaging it to Sean. "Call the number I just sent you and say you're a scheduler needing to change a massage appointment," I said. "Put it on speaker. And then ask if he has a minute to talk to a manager."

Hopefully the tone of Raven's voice and his response to that would let me know if it'd be safe to take the phone and talk to him myself. Not the greatest plan, but it was all I had. Calling him from my own phone was too damn risky.

Sean shook his head, but he got his phone out and poked at the screen.

"I'm calling your guy, aren't I," he said. "Fuckin-A. You owe me a job. And those drinks."

He dialed, hit the speaker button, and took a hit off his joint.

One ring. Two. My heart thrummed, and I held my breath.

Click. "This mobile customer is not available," said a bland, tinny recording. "Thank you."

And the line went dead.

I nearly keeled over dead myself, the sun-baked asphalt of the alley and Sean's concerned face and the condoms on the fence flapping in the breeze all going spinny for a second.

Cunningham had taken Raven's phone. Somehow, I hadn't expected that, even though I should have.

"You think he switched providers?" Sean said, and I choked on something between a laugh and a groan. "Or, you know, not?"

"Not," I ground out. "Thanks for trying. Give me a minute, okay?"

"Okay," he said dubiously.

Okay. Another sign that Raven was now an actual prisoner changed nothing. It simply meant I'd have a harder time getting to him, and I'd never expected it to be easy.

I switched over to a new message to Declan. He'd say no. But I still had to ask. Anyway, if I ended up storming Cunningham's mansion after all, I wouldn't have another chance to keep my promise to Sean, so no time like the present.

Hey, sorry to bother you. Cunningham's having a big party at Audacity tomorrow night. Are you invited? Any chance you can get me a plus one? I need to get in there. It's urgent. Also, a dude I know needs a valet job. Is the Morrigan hiring? I owe him. He's all right, just kind of a stoner.

The message went through, Sean lit up a second joint, and I breathed shallowly and waited.

Within a minute, much sooner than I'd expected given Declan's busy schedule, the phone buzzed in my hand.

Let me guess, that valet works at Audacity and already tried to get you in, and that's why you owe him, Declan sent, proving once and for all that he was a lot smarter than me—if the fact that he owned a major casino hotel and a successful strip club and I worked on the stage of said strip club hadn't already made it clear. *Every valet in Vegas is a stoner. I was when I was one. Tell him to send his resume to my attention, it'll go on the top of the interview pile.*

After a second, another message came in.

I'm not invited, I'm glad to say. Heard what happened last night. Don't get involved.

If he'd already heard, he could've passed that on to me immediately instead of sitting on it, that sneaky fucker.

Thank you, Sean will email, I sent back. And then after thinking for a second: *I'm already involved. If something happens, my parents will need someone to tell them. Sorry.*

His reply: *I'll take care of it, but don't let it come to that.*

And that was that from Declan, I knew. He'd made up his mind.

"Email your resume, and put his name on it, and you'll get an interview," I said, in lieu of a lot of obscenities. "I may not see you around, Sean. Thanks for everything."

He called after me as I walked away, his tone somewhere between worried and pissed, but I let it wash over me. At least I'd taken care of my obligation to him. That was something.

Next, the cash for Louie, and then I'd have to make the call. Kill Cunningham, or try to add another option to my dwindling list?

But as it turned out, another option came to me.

My phone rang as I walked in my apartment door. Not a number in my contacts, and it had an area code I didn't recognize, either.

If Raven had managed to steal a phone…I fumbled to answer it so fast I almost snapped a claw. "Yeah?"

"Tony?" said a pleasant, medium-pitched male voice that distinctly wasn't Raven's. "I'm Blake. We haven't met. Not through any fault of mine."

Blake. Declan's mate, who wanted to hang out at Lucky or Knot, much to Declan's horror.

With or without Declan's brains, I knew he couldn't possibly know Blake had called me.

Fuck, exactly what I needed: Declan MacKenna hunting me down in a jealous rage. Great. I had to get Blake the hell off the phone before he somehow talked me into letting him in the back of the club when Declan wasn't looking, or something equally suicidal. Like I didn't already have enough problems with other alphas wanting to kill me for being involved with people they thought of as theirs.

"Blake," I said warily. "Nice to meet you. Um, I'm not working for a few days, so I can't really—"

He burst out laughing. "I'm not trying to get you to take me to Lucky or Knot behind Declan's back," he said, and then laughed some more. "That would be hilarious, just not for you. I'm not that much of an asshole. I used to be, and that would be…ha! Okay, no. But you still can't tell him I called. He told me about you and your problem, and I have an idea." His voice had been quivering with barely suppressed mischief, and now he lowered it—clearly for dramatic effect, because he had to be a mile away from Declan and his alpha hearing if he expected this phone call to be a secret. "So…Tony. How do you feel about posing as a trained circus tiger?"

***

In the face of Raven's precarious, dangerous captivity, how I felt about posing as a trained circus tiger obviously didn't matter much, if at all.

And yet.

It was Friday afternoon, the sun pouring down out of a cloudless sky into the narrow parking lot attached to a local shaman's office and workshop. I tilted the small paper bag I held toward the light, illuminating a brown, grainy, waxy lump of spell components—that I was supposed to swallow before I shifted that afternoon, for fuck's sake—and wrinkled my nose against an odor that gave notes of oregano, maple syrup, unwashed socks, and most disturbingly, tiger piss. Not even mine, either. I hadn't given the shaman a sample.

"This is probably the worst idea of my entire life," I said, as soon as the door to the shop closed behind us and the weird, cranky old shaman who'd made the lump presumably couldn't hear us anymore and get offended. "Actually, strike that. I'm not taking responsibility for this. Blake, this is the worst idea of anyone's entire life."

I glanced at him sidelong and found him grinning, blue eyes sparkling with delight. He "used to be" that much of an asshole, huh? Yeah, I wasn't going to be the one to break it to him, but I doubted he'd changed as much as he thought. Dick. A helpful dick, and possibly an evil genius, but a dick nonetheless.

"I just wish I could be there to see it," he said with a sigh. "I haven't been to a party that sounds this fun in years. But Declan would lose his mind. He obviously couldn't come with me to keep an eye on me, because Cunningham wouldn't let him on the property, and Declan's a little overprotective."

Coming from an alpha, and about an alpha, that statement carried more weight than it would have otherwise.

Translation: Murderously, obsessively possessive.

Well, I couldn't blame Declan. Raven had inspired some similar feelings in me, and anyway, Blake would be most people's idea of a strong nine, maybe even a ten if you went for charming blonds.

"No worries," I said, choosing not to comment on their relationship. After all, I'd only met Blake an hour ago, when we rendezvoused at the shaman's shop. He hadn't wanted to miss out on any of the prep for his crazy plan to get me into the party, and he needed to be there for the next part of it anyway. "With my luck, someone's going to film it and put it online."

"Gods, I fucking hope so," he said, with a level of relish I found off-putting. Ugh. Strong nine or not, Declan could have him. Did he know what he'd gotten into when he'd mated this guy? "Anyway, I'm great at blackjack, but my poker face isn't the best. It's probably just as well."

I got in the passenger seat of Blake's car, since Blake had sweet-talked the shaman into letting me leave mine there for now while I used his magical concoction. After all, I'd be arriving at Audacity in a form that didn't lend itself to operating a motor vehicle.

Besides, I'd spent last night, after I'd gotten off the phone with Blake, making some alternate arrangements for transportation.

My buddy's cousin's girlfriend the part-time concierge still hadn't gotten back from her trip to Mexico, but she'd responded to my desperate, begging text messages from a poolside bar, according to the photo she'd also sent me of sparkling blue water viewed through a sparkling blue cocktail. She hadn't spent a ton of time in the fanciest parts of the hotel, but she'd given me a few pointers on how the staff got in and out, and a couple of shortcuts through the labyrinth of service corridors that crisscrossed Audacity's multiple buildings.

And with that information jotted down, I'd had to text Sean again, hat in hand. After a tense negotiation, he'd agreed to leave one of the valeted cars, unlocked with the keys in the glove box, in a discreet corner of the parking garage near a set of emergency stairs. Only my oaths, on my life, that I'd get him a job at either the Morrigan or Lucky or Knot when he inevitably got fired for negligence convinced him to agree.

Also, it sounded like he had his eye on a specific casino regular's car. It really didn't pay to piss off the valets, it turned out.

"So I met this big cat trainer guy because I broke up a fight he was having with his brother at a roulette table at the Morrigan," Blake began as he started the car.

And then he was off to the races, chatting to me about all the craziness he'd seen at Declan's casino, about how he missed rainy weather and generally spending time outside living in Vegas, and which fancy restaurants in town—exactly zero of which I could afford to eat at—had the best cheesecake, ranked as a top five with two honorable mentions. Good thing Declan had a lot of money, because Blake sounded eager to spend it. To be fair, he also couldn't say Declan's name without smiling and turning pink, and he smelled the way Declan did: like contentment, satisfaction...love.

Envy gnawed at my guts. I'd give a lot to make Raven look and smell that way when he talked about me. Declan and Blake hadn't had the easiest path to a deliriously happy mating, though, so maybe there was hope for me yet.

Blake didn't seem to need any replies to his nonsense, so I tuned him out, staring out the window at the passing suburbs. All I saw was Raven. I'd dreamed about him the night before during what little fitful sleep I'd managed to get. He'd walked away from me, and I'd called his name and chased him until I fell into a pit and woke up.

Finally it dawned on me that Blake had fallen silent.

"I'm sorry," I managed. "The, um. I'll have to try it some-time."

"I wasn't talking about cheesecake anymore," Blake said after a second. "But if you really want to try Declan giving you a foot massage while you drink martinis, I guess you could ask him."

My head whipped around and I stared at him, unable to tell if he was fucking with me or not.

"You weren't really talking about that." I was glad I'd missed it, if so. Some things, you just didn't want to know about another dude.

Blake grimaced. "Yeah, actually I was. You weren't listening, so I wanted to see how far I could go before you noticed. Sorry. Not sorry? Anyway, I get why you're so distracted. I genuinely am sorry about that, and I wish I could do more besides wish you luck tonight. Declan actually wanted to help you, not sure if you picked up on that. But he has a lot of enemies, and he can't afford to stir them up, not while he's still getting the new Morrigan off the ground. Also, he didn't think he could morally justify helping you get yourself killed."

"You're doing enough. I can't believe you figured out who Cunningham hired for entertainment tonight, and managed to get him to agree to this."

Blake shrugged. "He owes me. Also, you know. People tend to talk to me. I hear all kinds of things about what's going on in town."

"I owe you too, now," I said, and meant it.

Crazy or not, Blake's plan promised to get me into the party, anonymous and unsuspected. The edible spellbag on which I'd spent the money I should've given Louie would make me smell like a normal, non-shifter tiger, fooling all of the supernatural beings who'd be present at Cunningham's party. Blake's acquaintance the trainer had agreed to leave his regular tiger at home and take me along in its place to—I didn't know what, exactly. Perform on a stage? Surely I could do that as well in my tiger body as I could in my human body. Hopefully they wouldn't want me to wear glitter or shake my ass, because that'd be a really fucked-up party.

In a few hours, I'd be in the same room as Raven. At least, I hoped and prayed I would be, and that he hadn't been locked up somewhere, or hurt too badly to appear in public—and no, I had to shut that train of thought down before I lost my shit.

Blake shifted a little in his seat, probably smelling my anger, or simply feeling it in the air. "I'm sorry again," I said. "I keep thinking about him. About what could be going on. I'll keep it together."

"Declan had to bail me out of some trouble one time." Blake's tone suggested a massive understatement, there. "He thought it was his fault. It kind of was his fault, actually. But he was so fucking worked up—I get where you're coming from, Tony. And I promise we both have your back if you need it. Declan might not have wanted to encourage you to get yourself in trouble over a fae who probably wouldn't reciprocate, but I'll talk to him later on tonight once it's too late for him to do anything about it except wait to see what happens. If he gets mad, I'll work my magic."

Oh, and there was an image I both did and didn't want. There didn't seem to be much to say to that except thanks, and Blake managed to keep his mouth shut until we pulled up in the dusty driveway of a small ranch and circus training facility on the edge of where the suburbs became the desert.

A short, crazy-haired young guy in a white suit who seemed way too nervous and jumpy to work with big cats came out to meet us, shook our hands, introduced himself as Axel, and ushered us into a large barn. There weren't any actual cats present, unless you counted me, but there was one of those livestock trailers like you'd see on the freeway carrying horses around, only much sturdier.

"So we'll take this to Audacity," Axel said. "Like I talked about with Blake on the phone, we need to head over pretty soon, and we won't have a lot of time to prepare once we get there. My team's already on their way, they'll do all the setup, so it'll just be us in the trailer, in case you, um. I don't know, need to change back for some reason? The tigers I work with respond to voice commands, so I guess that won't be a problem, right? I mean, you understand English as a tiger?"

My instinctive revulsion for the cage-trailer must've shown on my face, because Blake smoothly stepped in between me and Axel, hiding my reaction, and said, maybe a little bit pointedly, "Tony's a professional stage performer in his human form, so you'll be able to work smoothly together. I know," and he cleared his throat and glared at me, a lot pointedly, "that you have a reputation as a tiger trainer and that you're doing us both a favor, so just tell Tony what the schedule is and what's next. And hey, he won't bite you if he's in a bad mood, so win win."

Axel nodded, looking less like he'd run away any second now. Blake really did have a gift with people when he wanted to, seemed like.

"I wouldn't count on it," I muttered, low enough for only other alpha shifter ears to pick it up.

Blake's lips twitched. "Behave," he whispered back, and followed Axel, volubly running through all the polite small talk that I simply couldn't manage.

Christ. A fucking cage on wheels. Voice commands? I mean, this was demeaning for a non-sentient tiger, let alone a weretiger. Maybe a rabbit or something, they didn't have any dignity to lose. But a tiger? An apex predator? Ugh.

Raven's smile as he pointed out that I didn't have a lot of dignity left to lose flashed through my mind, and that little aching knot under my sternum that hadn't gone away since I saw him last gave a twist and a throb.

Dignity be damned. This was how I could get to Raven.

The shaman had promised me that his magical glob would give me a full twenty-four hours of not smelling like any kind of shifter, so I took it out of the bag and bit the bullet, literally and figuratively. Blake produced a bottle of water from somewhere or other, and I took it and guzzled every drop, forcing the spell down my throat.

Definitely tiger piss, and no amount of maple syrup, or bottled water, could cover that up.

Fuck my life.

As I undressed, I folded my clothes and handed them to Axel to put somewhere in his truck. I probably wouldn't get a chance to retrieve them if all went to plan. But I had to pretend to Axel that I'd be leaving with him and not causing any trouble at the party, or he wouldn't cooperate. I'd taken inspiration from Raven's story the night we met, suggesting to Blake that he tell Axel I'd lost a bet with another weretiger. Axel had agreed, since he'd thought it was harmless enough, but I knew one wrong move and he'd bail on me.

Blake took my phone, wallet, and keys. We'd discussed it while we waited for the shaman to fill our order, and he'd promised to drop them off at my apartment. The apartment door locked automatically when you closed it behind you, and if and when I ever got home, I could always ask the property manager to let me in, or break the door and worry about it later.

At last I stood at the foot of the ramp leading up into the barred trailer, and I turned to Axel, who'd turned bright red and was staring fixedly at my face.

I smirked at him—and then remembered that Declan MacKenna's mate was there looking at my naked alpha body too, and stopped being amused. Hopefully Blake would leave this part out when he told Declan about it later.

"I'll tap a paw or blink once for yes and twice for no," I said. "I'll have the same comprehension, but a tiger's vocal apparatus won't form human words. And if you make the mistake of actually treating me like an animal you've trained when we're not performing, I will bite you. And then I'll transform back to human and kick your ass. Got it?" Axel nodded convulsively, eyes wide. I sighed, but it had to be said. "Also, if you say anything about my name, my species, or anything relating to cereal, you're dead meat. And thank you," I added belatedly. "Blake, wish me luck."

"Good luck," he said, and I started my shift, flowing into my tiger form, bones and joints twisting around, muscles lengthening and strengthening, all the sounds around me suddenly gaining depth as my vision narrowed down to a desaturated palette full of tiny details that even a human shifter's eyes wouldn't catch.

I prowled into the trailer, sniffing the traces of two other tigers, one male, one female. The scents indicated relative contentment, at least, not anger or fear. And come to think of it, Axel had all of his limbs, protruding parts, and presumably his internal organs, some of which I'd expect to be missing if he made a habit of mistreating his cats. Twitchy or not, maybe the guy wasn't so bad after all.

Mmm. That smelled like someone had been feeding these tigers some incredibly fresh wild boar, at some point recently. All right. Axel might not be the worst.

Resigned to my fate, I flopped down onto the more or less clean trailer floor, and Axel shut the door behind me.

We were on our way to Cunningham's party, and Raven.

Nothing else mattered.

Chapter 16

Parking garages smelled even worse as a full tiger, and the sour tang of Axel's nerves didn't help matters. Plus, the random echoing noise hurt my ears. I swiveled them around a bit in an attempt to shake it off.

Axel was having a conversation with some of Cunningham's security team about the night's details. The back gate of the trailer hadn't been opened yet, so I had nothing to do but sit there.

"You seem kind of nervous," said one of the security guys, in a tone that had my hackles up. Paranoia seemed to be the name of the game around here. "Everything okay? I'm going to need to take a quick look at your tiger."

Fuck. I rearranged myself into more of a springing position. Did they suspect something? Even without seeing them, I knew the security were shifters by their scents. Mostly coyotes. Not much of a threat, really, but if the shaman's magic failed, they'd smell me as quickly as any other kind of were. If I had to take them all out, I could, but then my plan would go to hell, and it'd be a race to find Raven and not get killed in the process.

"Sorry, yeah, this is a big night for me," Axel said, hardly missing a beat. Apparently I'd underestimated him. "Mr. Cunningham's really influential. You know that. It's a huge deal to be here. My tigers are rescues, so it's super important to me to be able to fund my nonprofit—"

"Great, that's cool," said another security guy dismissively. I flicked an ear, flexed a dinner-plate-sized paw, and mentally marked him for some biting if I had the chance. Axel's tigers were rescues? I really should've been nicer to the guy, starting with not getting him involved in this at all. "Let's see the tiger, huh? And get going, you're on in half an hour. Your people are already up there."

The gate rattled, Axel offered a few boilerplate warnings like "don't get your face bitten off," and I froze. What the hell did normal tigers do? Like most shifters, especially the predatory ones, I never went to zoos, and I'd never fucking interacted with actual tigers. Our scents freaked out the normal animals. Shit. Fuck. Be a tiger. Act casual.

I ended up flopping down on my side and half-lidding my eyes, leaving my claws partially out so as to project a hint of menace.

Three faces appeared in the gap at the top of the trailer door: Axel's, and two guys in suits with earpieces. They both sniffed the air, glanced around, and withdrew, apparently satisfied.

Well, give a point to the shaman and his piss-wax lump of awfulness.

Axel flashed me a nervous grin and opened the door the rest of the way.

"All right," he said, in a voice that might have been intended to sound soothing to tigers, or to sound to the security team like it was meant to sound soothing to tigers. My head hurt. "Let's get ready, hmm?"

He took a huge leather collar, a chain leash, and a whip from where they hung on the wall of the trailer.

"I'm so fucking sorry," he mouthed, barely audibly even to me. "The whip's for showmanship. The uh, collar. Please don't eat me?"

Shrugging felt odd in my tiger body, and it looked odd, too, by the puzzlement on Axel's face. I stood up, shook myself out, and blinked once, trying to indicate acceptance.

"Is that yes, you're okay with it, or yes, you're going to eat me?" Axel hissed.

Christ. I stared at him, trying to telepathically communicate that he needed to ask a fucking yes or no question.

"Crap," he said, comprehension dawning. "Um. Are you going to eat me?"

I blinked twice, and he slumped a bit, nodded, and got the collar on me with a minimum of fuss.

Raven, I repeated to myself. *This is for Raven.*

Stalking past the security guys without taking a limb or two required all my self-control. Two of them took point, and two more fell in behind at a respectful distance. Axel stayed close to me, looping up enough of the leash to be only a couple of feet from my head. Did he show that much trust with his actual tigers? Would anyone notice a difference? But no one challenged us as I padded into a service elevator, sat quietly at a word from Axel while the display on the panel ticked from G all the way to PH, and then padded out again into a utilitarian hallway.

We went a couple dozen yards along, the sound of a party starting to grow in volume from a faint, distant murmur to distinct chatter, clinking dishes, and music—some super pretentious-sounding jazz. Of course, all jazz ranged from pretentious to unbearable, until it got smoky vocals, and then it turned into dancing and/or sex music, but this shit was bad enough to make me flatten my ears.

"I'll go check on how it's going out there," one security guy said, and pushed his way through a swinging door. "I think they're almost ready for you."

The other who'd been in front of us went a few more feet down the hall and ushered us through another door. That led to a green room of sorts, with a couch and some bottled water. "We installed a ring for the tiger's leash, right there. And the sound guy's coming to mic you," he said, and left.

The sound guy came in and they fiddled with Axel's lapels. So as not to freak out the tech, I lay down meekly in the corner next to the metal ring they'd bolted to the wall, and I indulged in some silent panic.

They're almost ready.

Maybe they were, but not me. My heartbeat juddered down to the tips of the pads of my toes. A tiger's resting heart rate was about the same as a human's, and this felt at least twice as fast as that.

More than a year of stripping in front of an audience dozens of times a week, and my paws seemed to have riveted themselves to the floor with the worst case of stage fright I'd ever imagined, let alone experienced. Stage fright, shyness, and anxiety in general had never been a problem for me.

Until now.

Fuck. I had no idea what I was doing. And if I screwed up, Raven could pay the price for my stupidity. Again. What I was supposed to do, or look like, or…

"Come on, it's showtime," said a pleasant voice, pitched remarkably well to be soothing to tigers when necessary, it turned out. "You'll be awesome."

Axel, being a bro. And then he put his hand on my shoulder for a second, and it probably looked like a pet to anyone watching, but it felt more like the type of bracing pat a buddy might give you before you went to rip your pants off for a bachelorette party.

Deep breath. I could do this.

We left our little green room and then into the same door the first guy had gone through.

As the door swung open, I could've sworn I caught a faint, curling tendril of Raven's scent. It floated, delicate and haunting, over the heavier reek of alcohol and shrimp and steak and the perfumes and colognes of a whole mass of rich people sweating in their evening clothes.

It didn't exactly calm me down, but it focused me.

Honed me. Sharpened my senses and my resolve.

First I had to see him. I had to know he was all right, present and accounted for. Then…then I'd wait for the right opportunity to grab him and get the hell out of there.

Axel adjusted his grip on the whip, holding it at a more theatrical angle, and led the way through another service area, with gawking tuxedoed waiters pressing themselves against walls as far from me as they could manage. Then we were walking through a much nicer set of doors and into a full-size freaking ballroom, of all the things to have in the penthouse of a hotel.

The near end of the huge room held round dining tables half full of guests sitting and lingering over coffee, eyes and jewelry glittering in the subtle shaded lighting in the centers of the tables and the chandeliers above. We went right through, close enough to people's chairs that there were some *oohs* and *aahs* and discreet, ladylike shrieks of terror as I padded by. Axel bowed and smiled, working the crowd.

Up ahead, a double rank of seats ringed a large dance floor, and those were packed with Cunningham's friends or business associates or maybe people he fucking hated, all in evening clothes holding glasses of champagne. Behind them were cocktail tables with more guests at them.

So many fucking people. Christ. So many potential witnesses, so much potential for collateral damage.

The dance floor had—oh, fuck me, a couple of those godsdamned round platform things like at circuses, and a trio of giant rings, all supervised by three guys in spandex and capes, clearly Axel's team. Colored spotlights whirled. Someone with a microphone announced Axel and me, giving a spiel about Cunningham's support of good causes like tiger rescues.

But none of that was important. None of it mattered.

Because at the other end of the dance floor, seated next to Cunningham on a fancy settee thing at the edge of the low band platform, was Raven.

Even though colors weren't really the most important part of a tiger's vision, and even though Raven's white skin and black hair and black clothes should have had him fading into the background, he dazzled me, like stepping into the technicolor Land of Oz after spending my whole life in a gloomy, muted nightmare world. His tux had cropped trousers, showing off strappy stiletto sandals on those elegant feet, and instead of a bow tie he had some kind of silky white scarf that dipped down to show the soft hollow between his collar bones. A severe bun with a pair of chopsticks stuck through it at precise angles confined his mass of hair.

Every detail of him imprinted itself on my retinas. And as he glanced to the side, as one of his fingers twitched, as he shifted his foot, I caught it all, my tiger eyes attuned to the faintest movement of the prey I hunted.

Raven. Alive, and mostly well. Enough to sit up and be on

display for Cunningham's world to stare at, anyway.

Until this moment, I hadn't quite been able to let go of my fear that it'd be otherwise.

Relief rushed through me dizzyingly, leaving me aching with determination. I'd keep my cool and keep my cover. I'd wait for my moment. And I'd seize it when it came along.

I stared at Raven and Cunningham while the announcer wound himself up to a crescendo. They sat close together, and as I watched, Cunningham put his hand on Raven's thigh.

Raven's leg tensed up. Tigers really could see the most minute movements even at a distance, and I saw Cunningham's fingers dig in slightly in response, even though his bland smile didn't waver.

In person, he projected an aura of violence that his photos hadn't captured, closely-cropped graying hair and narrow-set eyes giving him a look that blended middle-aged executive with contract killer. His tux had to have cost more than my car, maybe by a factor of three. The alpha-magic smell of him twined with Raven's honeysuckle and lemon, wrapping around and choking it like invasive vines, the combination nauseatingly vile.

Raven's pale, blank mask was clearly meant to give nothing away.

But to me…

…Cunningham's mouth open in a shriek of terror, claws sprouting too late to defend himself from my rending fangs…

Axel's hand landed on my shoulder again, this time with a lot more force.

I started, stilled, and forced myself to stop growling.

"Easy," he said, low-voiced but high-pitched with worry. Shit. "Easy. Please?"

And then we were walking into the center of the ring.

Raven hovered in my peripheral vision, always and forever the focus of my attention, but I forced myself to tune in to Axel's commands.

The performance space had been set up kind of like an obstacle course, I realized, with platforms and rings alternating around in a circle. The last ring had…oh, for fuck's sake. Little jets that would spout flame, no doubt at a dramatic moment before I jumped through it. There didn't seem to be a good way to communicate "if my whiskers get singed, I'll sue you and then gnaw the arms off your lawyer" with blinks and paw taps, so I settled for a speaking glance up at Axel, who paled slightly under his bronzer.

He recovered instantly, launching into his patter, voice rolling out of the sound system with surprising force given how tentatively he'd spoken to me so far.

"And now, this ferocious ruler of the jungle will show you how elegantly he can entertain you, ladies and gentlemen..."

He waved his whip at the first round platform, a drum roll sounding out of the speakers. And it was surprisingly less humiliating than I'd expected. It simply felt unbearably stupid. When I glittered up and pasted on a lecherous grin and shook my package at the crowd in my human shape, that was also stupid, and it didn't humiliate me because it wasn't really *me*.

All of a sudden, everything fell into place.

I tossed my head, my fur rippling, and pulled my lips back in enough of a snarl to display my fangs to the awed crowd without making them think I was about to go for someone's jugular. Meanwhile, I paced forward, paws in a precise line, the very picture of prowling, feline grace. This wasn't any different than the choreography I used on stage at Lucky or Knot. I could do this.

Wild applause greeted my leap onto the platform, the size of which required me to put all four of my paws fairly close together. Rearing up onto my hind legs and doing a bit of a dance tempted my shitty sense of humor, but I remembered just in time that a lot of people would probably die tonight if I outed myself as a shifter.

But then I made the mistake of giving in to Raven's irresistible pull, glancing up at the band platform as I landed on my own.

Our eyes met, his jet black and mine golden-orange streaked with brown—the same color as in my human body, although they were a different shape and size in this one, and the shaman's spell had suppressed my alpha glow.

Raven's eyes. Gods, and his scent, a thread of it teasing at my nose even through the huge ballroom's currents of air conditioning and people's movements, unmistakable even tainted with Cunningham's reek and filtered through all the other smells generated by a crowd.

For a crucial instant, my knees went weak. One paw slipped off the edge of the platform, and my reflexes compensated in the nick of time, my stumble lasting only a fraction of a second.

It was enough. As I perched neatly, wrapping my tail primly around my paws, I saw the minute change pass over Raven's face, there and gone again. A widening of the eyes, a slight part to those plush lips, before he pulled himself back together and went neutral.

But his eyes blazed.

And he *knew*.

If I'd been equipped for it in my current body, I'd have laughed. Normal animals didn't get as large as my shifted form, and I had—I'd have really, really liked to think, anyway—more intelligence in my eyes than the average tiger. Besides, Raven had spent two nights with me, in my arms, with me in him. Cried on me. Told me some of his secrets, trusted me, learned more about me than most people did, to be honest, because I tended to keep it pretty surface-level. It would've been nice to believe that he'd recognize me in any shape, as I'd have known him anywhere and in any guise.

But it had to be my clumsiness that clued him in, not any of that. Of course it did.

Humiliating as that might be, to be recognized by the most graceful and seductive person I'd ever met primarily for my lack of those qualities…thank the gods. Because making myself known to Raven without tipping anyone else off had been one of the night's biggest hurdles, and that had now been accomplished.

The rest of the performance went smoothly, because Axel announced each upcoming trick to the audience right before his gestures and commands that would've been an actual tiger's cues. Even jumping through the flaming hoop went well, and I landed on the final tiny platform without toppling over onto my back with my dick waving in the air. Small victories.

Some cymbals clashed, everyone applauded, and the announcer informed everyone that the show would go on after a fifteen-minute intermission.

Axel led me out the way we'd come in, and fuck, fuck, Raven was right there. I couldn't catch his eye again, and if I tried too hard it'd be obvious. Fifteen minutes. I had fifteen minutes to figure out what to do next.

Worst case, I'd take on my half-shifted form, charge the band platform, and carry Raven away by main force. He'd have the coin with him; I didn't even have to wonder. That was part of his fae nature.

We could fight our way out. Surprise would give me an advantage. I had to believe that. Get down the emergency stairs that the concierge girl had told me how to find, which would take a while given we were sixty floors up, but I could move faster than nearly anyone. Jump in the car Sean would have left for me, and get to Louie to hopefully complete the mirror-image deal.

That had sounded simple last night when I'd cooked it up. Now, as I followed Axel back through the catering area, it seemed impossible.

Gods. How stupid could one tiger be? I seemed determined to push the limits.

As soon as the green room door shut behind us, Axel collapsed into a chair, sucking in heaving breaths and wiping sweat from his temples—carefully, so as not to disturb his makeup.

"Oh, God," he whispered. "God. You were great, by the—oh no," he said, going greenish white. "Don't eat me! I didn't mean to use that word!"

For fuck's sake. I rolled my eyes, the only reaction available to me in this body. I could shift to human and try to verbally reassure him, but I had no idea who might walk in any second. And shit, there were probably…I glanced around, pretending to yawn, because a circus tiger looking for security cameras wouldn't be fucking suspicious or anything. Yep, there it was up in the corner of the ceiling. Hopefully no one thought too much of Axel talking to me like he had been a second ago. On second thought, no. A guy like Axel, with his rhinestone-encrusted white suit and his semi-tame tiger, could probably get away with nearly any eccentricity without raising any eyebrows.

In lieu of any better response to Axel's worry, I lay down on the floor, as nonthreatening as seven hundred pounds of muscle and claws and desperation could be.

Axel's Adam's apple bobbed as he swallowed convulsively. Not very nonthreatening, then. He sucked down most of a bottle of water and leaned back to rest.

And then jumped halfway out of his chair as a firm knock sounded on the door. I tensed up too, hopefully ready for anything.

"Come in," Axel called shakily.

The door opened to admit one of the more senior security guys, at least going by his particularly sour expression and his fortyish face and hair. I let my eyes drift halfway shut.

"Mr. Cunningham's companion wants to meet the tiger," he said. "You'll need to restrain it."

Mr. Cunningham's companion. A jolt like an electric shock ran through me, and it took everything I had to stay still, to pretend like I hadn't understood, like I wasn't trembling with eagerness. Raven, gods, clever Raven, who'd probably sweet-talked Cunningham with any number of promises that I'd rather die than let him fulfill in order to be allowed this indulgence.

But he wouldn't have to. I'd get him out before that.

Axel stood up, and his glance at me spoke volumes. I waited. He waited. *Come on, come on...* it twigged at last, that while I'd understood what the guy wanted, I couldn't admit it. He picked up my leash, snapped his fingers, and tugged gently, and I did my best to act like a tiger responding to a trainer, ambling the few steps over to the ring in the wall and sitting politely while Axel secured my collar by a short length of chain.

The guy nodded and withdrew.

"I'm sorry," Axel whispered. Had he really not noticed the camera? Fuck it, a guy like him would totally apologize to a tiger. I'd bet he watched TV on an extra-large couch with his actual tigers and apologized when they didn't like his choice of movie.

Axel stood next to me, his hand on my shoulder, probably trying to make us look totally safe to be around.

The security guy stepped in again, nodded his satisfaction, and held the door all the way open.

A waft of mouthwatering scent preceded Raven's entrance into the green room, and then he was there, close enough to reach out and touch. Cunningham's nasty odor clung to him, but I could erase that within seconds, holding him, kissing him, stripping him bare, sitting him on my cock and stuffing him with my come and then plugging him with my knot.

Flexing my claws did absolutely nothing to relieve the strain of staying still. And thank the gods I'd sat down with my front legs positioned just so. No bodyguard, no matter how well trained to ignore the weirdnesses and vagaries of rich people and their entertainers, would be able to overlook the trained tiger's massive erection.

Raven's gaze flickered over me and Axel. His lip curled slightly, and a dangerous gleam sparked in his eyes.

"Leave," he said imperiously, without specifying who he meant.

"Mr. Cunningham's not going to like it if I let you get hurt," the bodyguard said, but he looked like he'd only take a little convincing. Maybe he'd seen Raven use his magic and felt stuck between a rock and a hard place, his employer's cruelty to Raven and Raven's powers and anger, which were as precariously leashed as my enormous tiger's body.

But then Axel chimed in with, "I can't leave my tigers alone with anyone. It's not safe for you, or for them. I'm really sorry, sir."

Fuck, fuck…if Axel stuck to this principle of his, I was so screwed. Although there was still that camera, too. My mind flailed around in a circle, basically chasing its tail. And I had no one to blame but myself. My plan had been sketchy as hell to start with. And Axel had no idea that getting myself alone with Raven had been the entire goal of the exercise. He was fucking me over completely in his attempt to help me stay under the radar.

"Both of you," Raven said, and this time the faint, stern impatience in his tone had even my spine straightening. "I'm not human, those rules don't apply to me. The tiger won't hurt me, and I certainly wouldn't harm a dumb beast."

Dumb beast? Christ. When I'd gotten him out of here, and gotten him free, we'd be having a conversation about his sense of humor.

Very lightly, praying that it didn't look weird to the security guy, I shifted my shoulder under Axel's hand. And then I deliberately lifted one paw, let it hover, and set it down again.

Yes. Please take a fucking hint. Yes.

"Oh," Axel said, and cleared his throat. "*Oh.* Yeah, you're fae, maybe? You're good with animals, right? Maybe I can make an exception?"

I lifted my paw again, held it, and set it down.

Raven raised an eyebrow, clearly catching on. The bodyguard just looked bored.

"Thank you," Raven said, and sauntered farther into the room. "That's all."

The bodyguard held the door for Axel, who hesitated, mumbled a few more words of warning, shot me a look somewhere between confusion and apology, and scuttled out. The guard followed and shut the door.

And Raven and I were alone.

Chapter 17

Raven closed his eyes and took a deep breath. His exhale—gods, it sparkled, like dust motes lit up by a beam of sunlight, only green and pastel orange and some color human language didn't have a name for.

When his eyes opened, he found me gaping at him in wonder. That probably looked pretty stupid on a tiger's face.

Raven offered me a small, pale smile, and even in that dull, windowless little room, the sun came out.

"The camera's taken care of for now," he said. "And no one will hear us through the door. But that only lasts as long as they leave us alone, and I don't dare to lock it. Tony, you shouldn't be here. You can't be here. He'll kill you."

No amount of blinking or paw-tapping would do at this point. The camera wouldn't catch it, so fuck it, and if someone came in, I'd have to start the carnage sooner than I wanted.

Flowing from tiger to human took an instant's more thought than usual, because I'd been so laser-focused on looking and acting like a normal tiger no matter what, but when I shook my head to clear it, I had hair and not fur, and my ears had migrated down to the sides of my head. The collar hung loose around my neck, and I'd paid attention to how Axel fastened it. A moment's fumbling and it fell to the floor with a clink of chain, and I stood up, fully human, naked, my cock rampantly erect.

Raven's eyes dropped down, lingered, and then skimmed back

up to my face. A trace of pink tinged his white cheeks at last. The only color in his face before had come from the purple shadows under his eyes.

And around one of them. Around…as if someone's fist had…

Rage nearly blinded me, and I lunged for him, needing to wrap him in my arms and crush him to my chest and never let him go…

"Don't," he hissed, stumbling back. "Don't! My clothes, and your scent on me!"

I jerked to a stop inches away from him, clenching my hand into a fist around nothing to keep myself from touching him.

That was how I'd gotten him in trouble in the first place. And I'd almost done it again, fuck.

Except that…

"It doesn't matter," I said. "I'm here to take you away with me. You're not going to be with him for one more fucking night."

He bit his lip, glaring up at me. "Don't even say that. You know I can't, that I'm stuck here, and—Tony, this only makes it worse. Seeing you. Having you make me feel like you could protect—you can't keep doing this to me!"

Gods, if I could only kiss him, let him feel what he meant to me. But I wouldn't, not until he agreed to my plan. He had to say yes. If he didn't, I'd be as bad as Cunningham.

And there'd be time for kissing and comforting and everything else. All the time in the world, if I could only get Raven out of here, safely away where no one could ever hurt him again.

"I'm not, I promise," I said. Begged. The air between us quivered, pulsed, with the force of my need to breach it. "I thought of a way out. A way to break your bargain with him."

He went rigid. "You?"

Christ, I probably deserved that. But it hurt.

"Yes, me! And I have a plan to get us out of here. Okay, it's not the very best, but it's all I could come up with on short notice. It'll work."

"You," he said again, even more unflatteringly. "You have a plan to get me out of this. Tony—"

That repetition of my name, in that soft tone he couldn't seem to help even when he was annoyed with me for being an idiot, nearly broke my resolve. I needed one taste of that pretty mouth, one nibble of those lips…my head spun, in a way it usually took a couple of bottles of strong liquor to achieve.

His eyelashes fluttered, as if he felt the same way. The plan had to work. It had to.

"Me." This time the word had more confidence behind it. "You have the coin with you?"

"Yes, but—"

"No buts, just yes. Raven, do you trust me? Even a little bit? I get that this seems really half-assed, what with pretending to be a performing tiger—"

"Pretending to be?" he muttered, and I filed that away next to "dumb beast" in the "get my revenge later on when there's time" folder.

"—and not being able to save you from—Raven, sweetness, I'm sorry, I'm so sorry, I can see the bruise on your face, and I know there's more I can't see, and I swear to you, if I'd been able to—"

He was the one to lunge at me, winding his arms around my neck, and he tugged me violently down into the kiss that'd been on the tip of my very being, his tongue darting into my mouth, his lips clinging to mine with feverish strength. When he let go and tore his mouth away, leaving me reeling, he tried to slide down my body, as if he meant to go to his knees in front of me.

I caught him under the arms and hauled him back up. "What are you doing? Raven, gods, you said not to do that. Is that a yes? Please tell me that was a yes, because you can't go back to him like this. Look we're here together, you have the coin, I have a car waiting." Hopefully. "I'll explain on the way, but the short version is, you can buy me from a loan shark to break the spell on you."

Raven's mouth fell open, and then he snapped it shut again, chin jutting, eyes wild. "Buy you from a—see, I knew your plan would be something absurd like that. That won't work. So I'm going to get on my knees and suck your magnificent cock, because we only have a few minutes left and I'll never have another chance, and that'll make you happy, and you can finish capering through hoops and then go home. And I'll deal with the consequences of seeing you one last time."

Seeing you one last time. Suck your magnificent cock.

Dirty pool, fuck. Under literally any other circumstances, in any other place, I'd have been willing and eager to forget my own name, not to mention sign away my own soul, if he offered to "suck my magnificent cock."

I leaned in, nose to nose, glaring at him so ferociously I didn't need the alpha glow. "It's not absurd, for one thing. And for another, I was capering through those hoops *for you*, because I'd do literally anything for you as it fucking happens, and if you think you on your knees is what would make me happy? We've been over this. You not being a fucking prisoner of a sadist makes me fucking happy! Or will, once you get with the program!"

I gave him a shake, not enough to hurt him, but enough that his mouth formed a startled O and a chopstick came loose, a tumble of glossy hair falling over one ear.

"We're going. Now. Are we fucking clear?"

He swallowed, throat working, eyes so big and wide and shiny I nearly fell into them and drowned.

"If it doesn't work, I'll die," he whispered after a moment. "Should I trust you enough to die if you're wrong?"

Well, when he put it that way. Fuck.

"No," I said, reluctantly but honestly. "But you should trust me enough to come with me and try. If it doesn't work, I'll...damn it. I'll carry you down the hall and out. If it doesn't work, you can come back," I lied through my teeth. "It'll look like an insane, naked alpha kidnapped you, and then you escaped."

"Escaped," he said, on a bitter, high little laugh. "From you. Right. Why not? Half shift," he added. "It'll make you less recognizable and give you a chance to get away later, as long as you leave Vegas and lie low for a while."

Yes, gods, yes, he'd said yes! Adrenaline jolted through me, setting every nerve alight with triumph and relief.

And ignoring that nonsense about leaving Vegas and lying low seemed safest, because he might change his mind if he realized my plan B wasn't running away with my cowardly tail between my legs and leaving him with Cunningham, but stashing Raven somewhere safe whether he liked it or not, and then coming back and killing Cunningham until the motherfucker was *dead*. No matter what happened to me after that.

Half shifting wouldn't do much good, either, because one shifter running away plus one missing tiger equaled one weretiger. We weren't exactly common, and species went on official government records. If Declan could bribe or hack the DMV, so could Cunningham.

"Okay," I said, instead of any of that. "I'll put you over my shoulder and bust out of the room and run. Feel free to struggle as much as you want to make it look realistic. I'll be able to keep you where I want you regardless. You won't slow me down."

"Oh," he breathed. "I wish we had the chance to explore that concept further, under other circumstances."

It took a second for that to compute. Yes. A hundred fucking times yes, and if Raven wanted that too, then nothing was going to stop me from getting us the hell out of here and through all this bullshit to somewhere with a bed.

"We will. You ready?"

He swallowed hard, bit his lip, and nodded.

My half shift wasn't something I showed people all that often, if for no other reason than it had, in retrospect, probably been the original inspiration for my sister calling me Smilodon. When I allowed the magic to well up and transform me, fangs lengthening past my lower lip and claws extending to their full, razor-sharp length, my jaw heavier, fur sprouting on my shoulders and chest, Raven stared at me with glittering eyes, flushed and speechless. Hopefully not with horror, but I wasn't about to waste time asking.

"Showtime," I said, and scooped him up to sling him over my shoulder. With my left arm wrapped around his ass, I wrenched the door open with my other hand.

As the door cracked off its hinges and went flying behind me, Raven and I were, for a split second, the eye of the storm: everyone around us—which included Axel, two of Cunningham's security team, and a passing hotel staff member carrying a towering stack of linens—froze, their mouths open in shock and disbelief.

And then Raven shrieked, loud and shrill enough to leave my

ears ringing, and all hell broke loose.

Axel dived for the door behind me, eyes practically popping out of his head, and I didn't know if he wanted to hide or get his stuff or he'd just panicked or what, but I practically tripped over him as I turned to run down the hall.

One of the bodyguards did trip over him, cursing and lunging for me, and the other shoved the staffer out of the way to get to me. That guy screamed as napkins flew up in the air and everywhere, and I bowled Bodyguard Two over, kicking his legs out from under him and racing away at alpha weretiger speed, leaving them all to wrestle and yell and untangle themselves.

As we passed the service elevator, I hesitated for a precious half-second—but no. I could already hear the security guys shouting into their radios, and we'd have the fucking National Guard waiting for us the second the doors opened at the bottom.

I bolted past, Raven still screaming and waving his arms around, and in the distance there was an uproar: the party dissolving into chaos, I suspected. Good, maybe that'd buy us some time. Maybe Axel and his team would slip out unnoticed in the confusion. I hoped so, but I didn't have time to worry about them. My feet slapped the polished concrete floor, the hallway narrowed down into a yellow-lit gray-walled nightmare tunnel, the stairwell had to be—there, the red emergency exit sign glowing above it. I skidded to half a stop, yanking the door open and using the momentum of it to fling myself through, remembering just in time to strafe to the right so Raven's head didn't whack into anything.

Behind us, the service elevator dinged, and then a new hubbub of shouts and frantic commands arose. Good thing I hadn't waited for it, because it seemed to have disgorged a whole security team.

I'd already made it down five flights, flinging myself around the corners, praying that Raven's fae magic could protect him from whiplash, when the team burst into the stairwell.

By the cacophony of new scents assaulting me as they clattered after us, they were mostly shifters themselves, a mix of coyotes and wolves, but they wouldn't be able to catch up.

But a bullet could, and the overlapping, overwhelming chorus of echoing shouts and running footsteps suddenly shattered in a horrendous, earsplitting bang. The shot ricocheted from the wall two feet in front of me, concrete chips flying and ripping gouges into my thighs and stomach.

Raven cried out, for real this time, and I managed to catch a glimpse of a tear in his trouser leg, blood welling through from crimson-painted white skin.

He'd heal, fuck, it was only a scratch, but I ran faster and faster, swooping around and around the square stairs and their central well. Another gunshot rang and boomed.

"Stop, you'll hit the boss's boy!" someone shouted, and thank the gods for that authoritative someone's common sense, but sweat poured down my back and my feet were slippery with it, and with the blood running from my wounds and Raven's, and I ran just as fast but slammed into walls as I took the corners now, without enough traction to prevent it. My shoulder would be ground beef, and the pain nagged at me, but my grip on Raven with my other arm hadn't slackened in the slightest.

The stairwell whirled past me, sickening and dizzying, and Raven moaned. The number 42 flashed by, big white blocky numerals next to a door. About eighteen floors down, nearly a third of the way.

If Sean had the car waiting, if I could even find it, if I didn't pause for anything, if they didn't start shooting again...my heart hammered to the beat of my frantic thoughts, and my frantic feet, and then I caught a glimpse of 33, we were leaving pursuit behind, we might actually fucking make it, 24, then 19, and then...

Down below, a door slammed, and another wall of sound echoed up to meet the noise from above.

Two heads appeared, craning up, and there were more moving shapes, more voices.

I skidded to a stop, bracing myself against the wall, squeezing my eyes shut to try to blink away the stinging sweat. My chest heaved. Even my powerful alpha body needed a second to catch its breath.

We were fucked. Enemies coming up from below, more above, closing in now that I'd stopped. Cornered. Nowhere to run. Out of the stairwell, and I'd be lost in the hotel's maze and end up cornered somewhere else. Raven would probably get killed if I tried to fight our way through, too high of a probability to risk.

A triumphant call and response went up as they realized the same things I had.

"Put him down and back away from him," the same voice yelled from above, the one who'd told his subordinate to stop shooting. "Now! Put him down!"

My arm tightened, and Raven squirmed, twisting around and obviously trying to get a look at the situation.

"Put me down, do what he says," Raven said, loudly enough that everyone could hear. "Stop moving, he could kill me," he added, even louder, and the footsteps slowed down, but I could still see the guys down below creeping up one stair at a time. A glint of halogen lighting on bare metal suggested they were trying to get in position for a clear shot. "He'll put me down. Right? You don't want to die here, do you?"

Hopefully only I caught the quaver in his voice, the faint crack, the signs of weakness. Everyone else would probably think it was fear *of* me, rather than *for* me, but I knew better, and a horrible suspicion started to slither up my throat from my churning gut and choke me.

Raven raised his voice again, calling out, "If you crowd him, which one of you morons wants to explain to Arnold that I fell down a stairwell and went splat? Give him your word he can go. And then he'll put me down and hand me over, and you won't have to."

I could have roared—or wept.

I'd been right. Raven was trying to trade the very last of his currency as something valuable to Cunningham for a chance at my survival.

No. Not a fucking chance in hell, in any sense of the word.

Fell down a stairwell and went splat.

Less than twenty stories to the bottom. Splat, indeed, for a normal human. Maybe for a more durable fairy, too, although I knew even regular people sometimes survived falls like that under freak circumstances.

But I *was* a freak circumstance, wasn't I? Mostly mortal

flesh—but with the supernatural strength and healing magic that ran through my every nerve and vein and bone and cell, a lot less mortal than most people.

Death might be more pleasant than the agony of healing a couple of hundred broken bones and a dozen-odd ruptured internal organs.

On the other hand, I'd promised Raven he wouldn't spend one more night with that piece of shit Cunningham. I'd promised I'd protect him.

Fuck it. Splat it had to be.

I bunched up my muscles, crouched, and leapt, my spring through the air high enough and graceful enough to do any tiger proud, whirling up into the center of the stairwell, flailing like Wile E. Coyote—and then plummeting straight down, as all of the security team shouted and panicked, their shocked faces and the railings and the lights on the walls nothing but blurs as we fell.

In the couple of seconds of freefall, I yanked Raven around, getting one glimpse of his horrified face as I pulled him over my shoulder and clutched him to my chest.

Air whistled by my ears, I banged a foot into a railing, and then…

Splat. Or more of a deafening thud and a crunch, really.

The impact knocked the wind out of me first, and my head hit and everything went black, and the last things I heard before unconsciousness took me were Raven's scream and the snapping of my spine.

Searing, pounding agony.

And then nothing.

Chapter 18

The bliss of unconsciousness didn't last nearly as long as I would've liked.

So much pain, everything, everywhere, the instant my brain woke up again, and I wanted to curl in and die and tuck it into my center and smother it, but I couldn't move a single splatted muscle.

My eyelids lifted for a second. Raven, his hair hanging down over me, his black eyes so wide the whites were showing, tears falling like crystal jewels.

He was yelling into my face, sobbing, braced on my chest.

Not hurt.

Not dead. I'd kept him on top of me, and I'd broken his fall. A human might still have been badly hurt, but the fae were pretty resilient by comparison.

Thank the gods. The pain didn't stop, but I remembered why I'd welcomed it.

Raven. The pain crested as my bones started to knit, my organs repairing themselves, my lungs finally sucking in a bubbling, labored, choking breath of air.

I was gargling my own blood, fucking gross, and I managed to turn my head and cough it out, wracking agony in my chest as I did.

No sensation from my legs, because of that broken spine, but the stabbing torment in my vertebrae suggested that it'd started to heal.

Not quickly enough, because they'd be following. Chasing us down the stairs. Precious seconds lost to this bullshit.

"Tony, Tony, please," Raven's voice finally coalesced into words through the screeching pain in my skull. "You fucking idiot. Tony!"

Gods, he sounded so terrified. For me, and that was both the best and the worst thing ever.

My throat had cleared enough for speech, maybe. I worked the muscles, coughed again, forced my eyes open. Raven caught me by the chin and turned my head, peering down at me. So beautiful. Worth all of it. And in a second, I'd get up off my broken ass and get him out of here.

But when I did manage to speak, all that came out was, "Ow."

"Ow," Raven repeated, in a tone of disbelief. And then his chin lifted and he drew himself up. "Fuck you. Up! Now! Move!"

He scrambled to his feet, and the lack of his usual fluid grace worried me, but then I couldn't think about that anymore, because he'd shoved an arm under my shoulders and heaved, and every nerve in my body fired at once, and I twisted into knots again, letting out a very not-stoic groan.

Raven whispered a few odd, sibilant words, and his magic twined around me, tugging on all my limbs.

Oh, that was strange, because I was moving—up, as he pulled on me, as if I'd suddenly lost about a hundred pounds of weight.

Raven dragged me to my feet, wrapped his arms around me, and began lurching and stumbling us through a propped-open door, out of the stairwell and into a parking garage. The garage, the car...

"There's a car," I mumbled. "A c-car. I had a..." Fuck, I couldn't get my throbbing brain to function. Concussion. That'd be healing too, but not fast enough, and I could hear the sounds of pursuit, the shouts and rapid footsteps from the stairwell.

"Move faster," Raven gasped. "You're alive, you can walk. Fuck. A car, yes, thank you for that brilliant idea," and there was a car in front of us, a sleek black luxury vehicle in a line of other sleek black luxury vehicles. Cunningham's. Shit. Not Sean's car, not that I'd have been able to find it in this state.

Raven propped me against the side, panting for breath, got the back door open, and toppled me through it with no ceremony at all.

I faceplanted into a leather seat, nearly lost consciousness again, and couldn't help at all as he stuffed my legs in and then slammed the door.

A moment later, he flung himself into the driver's seat, said something else in his own language, and the engine revved to life. Fairy magic. Now there was a way to hotwire a car that had never occurred to me.

As he screeched into reverse, I flopped down into the footwell, my face mashed into the edge of the seat, blood smearing fucking everywhere. And then he gunned it, tires squealing, shouts of alarm and three gunshots ringing out as we peeled out of the garage. Or at least I assumed we had, by the rending crash of what had to be one of those barrier gates breaking over the hood, and the violent scrape of the suspension as we swung crazily to the right.

A chorus of honks broke out around us, and Raven punched it.

"Tony! Are you still alive?"

Trying to pull myself up onto the seat again was taking all my attention and effort, but I mumbled something that could've been a yes, and Christ, this was impossible, digging my claws into the seat for leverage, managing to get sort of onto my knees as the car swerved and weaved, more honks breaking out, and a few screams. I was kind of glad I couldn't see anything from my angle.

"Good, because I need you to tell me where to go—oh no, hold on—" A wild, spinning turn to the left flung me back down into the footwell, and I lay there, gasping, everything feeling like it'd broken all over again, and gave up on moving for now. "Where are we going? Now, please?"

"You should've left me," I managed.

"Not helpful," he gritted out. "And not possible. There's no going back now."

No, there really wasn't. Louie. We needed to get to…he had an office, but at this time of night, he was always in a shitty strip club way out past the end of the glamorous part of Vegas. I managed to mumble the name of the place and the intersection, and then I breathed deep, focusing every bit of energy I had on healing.

Raven slowed down slightly, but he still drove like a maniac, changing lanes and gears with reckless abandon. Beautiful. Magical. Brave and resilient. Quick-witted and loyal. And he handled the car like a professional getaway driver, to boot.

Fuck me. That spreading warmth in my chest, the smile I couldn't suppress even though smiling hurt…it couldn't be anything else. I'd already known, but I'd been trying not to give it a name. Now I simply couldn't deny it.

"Gods, I love you," I said into the torn-up leather of the back seat.

The car gave a lurch, quickly corrected. "What the fuck did you just say to me?" he demanded. "You can't possibly have said what I heard!"

Something in my abdomen felt like it flipped over and strangled something else, a crescendo of agony that had me clenching my teeth and arching my back in a rictus. Everything faded for a second, blurred, came back after a moment, with more blood pooling in my mouth. I'd bitten my tongue, fucking damn it. On the other hand, I probably had one more organ functioning again. Healing like this was a bitch, zero out of ten, would not recommend.

What had he…I blinked into the semi-darkness of the footwell. Right. He needed clarification.

"Then I'll say it again," I said. "I love you. I love the way you drive. I love everything about you."

Raven didn't reply. Well, that was kind of discouraging.

He cursed a lot, though, and I couldn't tell if it was directed at me or at all the other drivers trying to survive being on the road with him.

By the time he jerked to a stop a few uncommunicative minutes later, I'd healed enough to hoist myself up onto the seat, breathing easier and able to think clearly, at least, if still battered enough to look and feel like I'd gone a few rounds with an angry meat grinder.

We were in the parking lot of Louie's club, flashing neon pink lighting giving the interior of the car a surreal glow. My eyes met Raven's in the rearview mirror. His were black pools, reflecting pink. On. Off. Pink again.

"I lost them for now," he said, continuing to completely ignore the whole *I love everything about you* thing. "But these cars all have GPS tracking. They'll be here soon. So what now?"

"Now we go find Louie. He's inside. I hope. And you make a deal."

Raven grimaced and got out of the car without another word.

I followed him more slowly, but my strength had finally started to return now that most of the major damage to my body had healed. We limped the few yards to the door of the club, where a pair of bouncers stood staring, their cigarettes dangling forgotten from their fingers.

"Oh, hell to the no," one of them said, and the other stepped forward and added, with more bravado than common sense, "Get the fuck out of here before I call the cops. You can't come in here like that."

Right. I was naked, covered with nothing but healing abrasions and blood.

I was also out of patience and time in a way that I couldn't even begin to put into words. Instead, I extended my claws and flexed my hands. Both the bouncers took a step back.

"Go ahead," I snarled, pretty confident in that offer. I'd been in this place a couple of times, and my professional eye had caught more than a few things the LVPD would've enjoyed levying heavy fines for, if not arresting everyone on the spot. "We're here to see Louie. You going to stop me?"

"I don't get paid enough for this shit," the first bouncer muttered.

The other remained silent.

"That's what I thought," I said, and Raven and I walked past them and pushed open the door.

The pounding music and flashing lights hit like an assault, but I pushed ahead, past a cocktail waitress who leapt out of the way with a cry of surprise, through another bouncer whom I simply pushed into a booth, and around several tables of drunk guys and topless girls, who all whooped with laughter.

Louie always held court at the best booth near the far wall, a big circular table with a commanding view of the whole place.

He had a couple of goons with him, and they both crowded forward, starting to protest, while Louie himself, bald pate and gold chains gleaming in the lights from the stage, went still, drink halfway to his mouth.

"I'm here to pay you," I called over the music, looking only at him and ignoring his men. "All of it, and then some."

Louie stared for a moment longer, shook his head, and started to laugh. "Let him through," he said, and his guys glanced at each other, clearly unhappy, but stood aside.

Raven slid in first, opposite Louie, and I started to sit down next to him.

"Fuck no!" Louie said. "Your naked ass doesn't go anywhere near my velvet seats."

My distaste for Dominic's jock strap and the locker room couch at Lucky or Knot flashed through my mind, and for the first and probably last time ever, I sympathized with Louie.

"Fine," I said, and leaned down and braced my fists on the table instead. Let the goons ogle my naked ass instead. Not like I wasn't used to it. "You're talking to him, anyway." I gestured at Raven, who looked up at me, lips tight and jaw set.

Come on, get it together, that look seemed to say. *I need my straight line, and we're in a hurry.* I turned back to Louie, heart pounding. I'd staked everything on this throw of the dice. Everything for me, and everything for Raven. Cunningham's furious security were about to bust through the door any minute. Our lives depended on my getting this right.

No fucking pressure or anything.

"When we talked yesterday, you said you owned me," I told Louie. Only yesterday? Years, it felt like. Jesus. "He's going to buy me."

Louie's eyebrows rose, and he took a long drink of his cocktail. "Buy him?" he said at last, laughing again, turning his attention to Raven. "Why? And with what, pretty boy? You got a suitcase full of cash hidden in those tight pants?"

My fists itched with the urge to knock that leer right off his smug face, but Raven drew himself up, back straight, chin lifted, eyes glittering dangerously, every inch a powerfully magical fae confident in his superiority. Even with his hair a tangled, matted mess, his clothing torn and disheveled, and the healing cuts and bruises, he managed to leave no doubt of what he was.

I could've kissed him. And a lot more than kissed him. Would he kill me if I took a moment to tell him again that I loved him? Yeah, probably.

"My kind deal in less vulgar payments than suitcases," he said, voice crisp and hard and cold, somehow making the word *suitcase* sound like the kind of thing only a peasant would use. Louie wilted visibly, his cheeks going red. "I will give you this."

He took his hand from under the table and laid it on the table palm-up.

And there was the coin. Louie and I both stared at it, our attention riveted, mine in wonder and Louie's in avarice more naked than my ass. It practically glowed, more golden than any gold had ever been, the other side of it that I hadn't seen before exposed: a raven with its wings outspread.

Of course. I'd wondered why the coin had called to him so potently that he'd been willing to give himself to Cunningham to possess it, but how could he have resisted magical fairy gold that bore the image of his namesake?

The coin looked much bigger than it had before, nearly covering Raven's palm, and thicker, too, heavier. A light buzzing started in my ears, in my brain, a tickle inside my skull, a hum below the spectrum of normal human or even shifter hearing. Warmth, satisfaction, eagerness.

As if the coin wanted this. As if it approved. As if we'd finally figured out the right answer that it'd been trying to lead us to all this time.

Apparently, even this piece of magical metal thought I was a little slow on the uptake.

"This was crafted in my own world by a fae workman," Raven said. "An artifact of great value beyond its weight in gold. Even melted down for its price by the ounce, it would be worth more than the debt he owes you. But I strongly recommend you don't try to do that, because it would work out very badly for you," he added, with typical fairy understatement and a strong overtone of fairy threat. "I will give it to you free and clear and resign all ownership of it. In trade, you will give me Tony, and renounce any claim over him in the future."

Louie shook himself like a dog clearing water from his ears and tore his gaze away from the coin with a visible effort, looking up at me.

"You got anything to say about this?" he asked, unexpectedly—because I wouldn't have imagined that Louie would have any moral qualms about making a deal to sell me into fae slavery. "You okay with this guy buying you?"

Would I be okay with Raven owning me, body and soul, until the end of time? What a stupid fucking thing to ask.

I glanced down at Raven and met his gaze. Also questioning, even though I had no idea why he'd have any doubt. Hadn't I already given my answer in the car?

"Yep," I said, not bothering to even look at Louie. Raven's eyes. He already owned me, and this was nothing more than a fairy technicality. Maybe the coin had known that all along. "Fine with me."

The faintest flicker passed over Raven's sharp features. Relief, maybe. Maybe more than that.

"Do you accept the bargain?" Raven said, turning back to Louie. "Do we have a deal?"

"You people can't lie about stuff like this," Louie said. "Right?" Raven nodded. Debatable, and I could've given him some pretty pungent opinions on that subject, but in this case, what Louie didn't know probably wouldn't come back to bite him in the ass before Raven and I were long gone. Couldn't happen to a nicer guy, and all that. "Then we have a deal."

Louie reached out, fingers practically twitching with eagerness. Raven delicately laid the coin in his hand, fastidiously making sure not to touch him.

The moment he lost contact with the coin, something in the

air shifted.

Like a pressure change, an oncoming storm. Or maybe a storm passing, the clouds drifting apart, the sun shining out, a fresh breeze whisking all the darkness away.

And I could've sworn I heard a weird, high, mocking laugh.

It had worked. I knew it down to my bones. My crazy, idiotic idea had actually gods-damned *worked*.

Louie's hand closed around the coin, and everything went back to normal. Mostly. Because there was something inside me, centered on a part of me that didn't have a name or a physical location, a tug...it felt like the leash Axel had used, only lighter and sweeter, not a burden at all. It wasn't pulling me, exactly. More orienting me toward Raven. Like when you turned a compass, and the little hand swung around toward north no matter how you moved its container.

Actually, it felt kind of like a gentler version of how I'd always heard other shifters describe a mating bond.

Well, fuck me sideways. Raven surely hadn't anticipated that. But being tied to me had to be better than being tied to Cunningham, right? Especially when this magic clearly flowed the other direction, signifying Raven's ownership rather than the reverse.

I turned to Raven, drinking in the slight smile teasing the corners of his mouth, the wonder on his face, the way he suddenly looked like he'd shed a two-ton weight, opening my mouth to...I didn't get a chance to find out. At that moment, screams broke out at the front of the club, and I whirled around, claws already sprouting, to see a dozen men with guns pouring into the room with Arnold Cunningham in their midst.

Chapter 19

"Nobody move!" Cunningham's head minion shouted, and then there was a chaos of curses and more screaming and tables getting knocked over as patrons and staff alike did the exact opposite, the drum-and-bass from the speakers playing over it all for a few more seconds before the DJ cut the music.

He also turned on the house lights, and we were all suddenly bathed in an unforgiving glare.

It didn't do the shabby club any favors, or Cunningham, either, because if I'd ever seen a person intended to be viewed under flatteringly dim lighting, it was him. The lines starting to show in his late-middle-aged face hadn't been carved there by laughter and smiles, that was for sure—more by the type of expression he wore now, a scowl like a thundercloud, with an aura of vicious menace wrapping around him like static electricity.

Hatred hadn't ever been one of my primary emotions. I usually couldn't be bothered, barely even knew how it felt.

It turned out to feel like acid searing each and every one of my veins individually from the inside, rushing up to fill my face and my scalp with a roasting, roaring, teeth-gritting cold rage.

My eyes glowed, I could feel it, the shaman's spell burned out by the force of my alpha fury.

"Fuck, what the fuck is he doing here," Louie stuttered, sounding two seconds from a heart attack. He clearly recognized his uninvited guest.

"Shoot him," Cunningham growled, and Louie let out a shockingly high-pitched shriek for someone with his chest measurements and then dived under the table.

"He didn't mean you," I said, even though Louie had the right idea. Cunningham meant me, and Louie was close enough to be in the line of fire.

I took one step to the side, making sure Raven was completely behind me. A couple of bullets would barely slow me down. I'd take the first barrage so I could shield Raven, and then I'd charge. Maybe Raven could throw some magic into the mix.

But as Cunningham's men raised their guns, a new commotion broke out in the front of the club, Cunningham's men and someone else they were confronting. There were shouts of alarm, an argument, and cutting through that, a cool, sardonic voice I recognized.

"You won't like how that works out for you, believe me," Declan MacKenna said in reply to someone's threats as he stepped into the club, brushing aside one of Cunningham's bodyguards with total nonchalance and possibly more force than necessary. Right behind him clustered several of his own security team—and Blake, who had a look on his face like a kid who'd been caught with both hands stuck in the cookie jar.

I winced, both on his behalf and my own. If I lived long enough for Declan to chew me out for dragging his mate into this kind of fuckery, it'd be a humiliating half hour.

Everyone turned to look at the newcomers, even Cunningham.

"What the hell is going on?" Raven complained, shoving at my back. "Move aside!"

"Not until they put their guns away," I said, and shoved him back, a lot more gently.

Which they hadn't, although they'd been lowered in response to this new influx of high-profile witnesses.

Declan's eyes were sharp and assessing, darting around and taking it all in, and I recognized the flex of his hand: claws at the ready. His men were shifters too, and they also had guns. Killing our kind wasn't easy, but there might have even been enough combined firepower and natural weaponry in the room to pull it off.

Silence fell for a long, pregnant moment.

It was kind of like the famous standoff scene from that Clint Eastwood movie, with the music everyone hummed at times like this. Only instead of the good, bad, and ugly, we had the contemptuous, the frothing, and the naked—and the terrified, if you counted Louie.

"This has nothing to do with you," Cunningham said, his voice thick with rage. "This is a private matter. Get out before I deal with you, too."

Declan opened his mouth, but Blake stepped up to his shoulder, stared Cunningham down, and said, with the utter confidence and arrogance of someone who'd actually used that line in the past and gotten the reaction he felt he deserved, "You've got to be kidding me. Do you know who I am?"

"What?" Cunningham said, after a beat. "*What?*"

"Yes," Declan said, and his deadpan delivery didn't do much to hide the grin breaking out on his face, "you're never going to get away with this, not in front of one of the eminent Castelli pack." Blake made a face and elbowed Declan in the ribs. "Former, anyway. Now my mate, and I know you know who the fuck I am. Cunningham, this is over. You're not going to commit murder. Not in public, and definitely not with us standing here watching you. Enough."

"He stole from me," Cunningham said, and his voice had gone guttural, his shift starting to take over. "He stole my property. He's going to pay." He turned to shoot us a look over his shoulder that would've killed if it could. "They both are."

It was my turn to grin. Because Cunningham couldn't possibly have handed me a better cue if he'd tried. And while he'd have been able to refuse and have his guys shoot me with only his own people and some humans as witnesses, he couldn't possibly wriggle out of it in front of Declan and Blake, two other wealthy and prominent alphas who'd be only too happy to publicize his cowardice.

In some ways, shifter culture hadn't evolved much since the eighteenth century. We didn't use swords, but then again, we didn't need to.

"Happy to," I said, and stepped forward. "Clearly you want to settle this the old-fashioned way. I accept your challenge. Alpha to alpha."

Declan raised an eyebrow, Blake started to laugh, Cunningham stared at me in horror, and his men all turned to each other and muttered amongst themselves.

Behind me there was total, ominous silence. I turned to glance at Raven, whose expression had gone fixed, his posture rigid. "This isn't necessary," he said, strain in every syllable. "There are—I had plans for those thousand years of torment. We already discussed the reasons why you shouldn't do this!"

The thousand years of torment. Right. And if I believed that was really his problem with me doing this, maybe he had a bridge to sell me. He'd already watched me almost die once this evening, but he couldn't imagine this was a fight I'd lose. Not if Cunningham didn't get help from his men, and Declan wouldn't let that happen. So it couldn't be that, either.

I flashed back to that moment of clarity after I'd ripped up my bedroom wall, how I'd realized Raven might've been as afraid of me, in my blind rage, as he was of Cunningham's violence.

Retribution from Cunningham's minions aside, the possibility of prison time aside…Raven didn't want to see me become a killer. And I couldn't blame him for that, not at all.

"This is necessary for me," I said, because Raven deserved honesty. "But I won't kill him," I conceded, with a lot less regret than I'd expected. Raven's happiness and comfort and trust in my ability to control myself mattered more than my own visceral satisfaction. "I promise."

Raven tilted his head, examining me, and finally seemed to find what he'd been looking for, his shoulders losing some of their tension.

"Fine," he said, and then added, in a meditative tone, "You know, I'd be lying if I said I didn't want to watch you beat him to a living but miserable pulp. As an appetizer for the thousand years of torment, of course."

"Your wish is my command." I winked at him, and he flashed

me half a smile. Good enough, given how cheesy that wink had been. I turned and sauntered into the middle of the room. "Are we doing this or what?"

"No, of course we're not—me, waste my time with some low-life?" Cunningham hadn't moved, and the stink of fear had started to waft to me across the broken-furniture-strewn space between us. "I wouldn't dirty my claws with the likes of you," he said desperately.

"Not much danger of that," some smartass muttered—Blake, of course.

Declan laughed out loud, and Cunningham went a ruddy purplish color from his collar to his hairline. "Go on, then," Declan said, still chuckling. "Or not, and every shifter in Vegas is going to be laughing with me by morning. And outside of Vegas. And in all the investment banking boardrooms—"

"Go fuck yourself," Cunningham snarled, and stepped forward out of the protective circle of his bodyguards at last. "Come on, you animal. I'll kill you while that little bitch watches."

Unlikely, but since Blake had already made that joke, I kept my mouth shut. Although "little bitch" was going to get him a few extra claws through the spine. He'd heal, but I had recent knowledge of how much that fucking hurt, and I wanted him to get the same.

We circled each other for a few seconds, while he drew his magic around him, the air crackling with it, and half shifted for the advantages of size and strength it would give him. The fangs and claws and glowing eyes gave him a strange look in his designer tux, and the way the seams were ripping along the sides from his increase in mass only made it weirder.

I hadn't been planning to bother, myself, because I didn't need any more advantages. But what the hell. Somewhere along the line, I realized I'd already made up my mind, and I wouldn't be going back to Lucky or Knot. Stripping had been fun, profitable, and a great way to kill some time while I figured out my life, but I wanted Raven more than I wanted anything else, and I suspected that he wouldn't want to stay in Vegas after everything that had happened here. Since this was going to be my last nude performance in a strip club, then, I might as well give it my all.

So I flexed—subtly, I had it down to an art form by now—and drew myself up to my full height of rippling muscle, letting my fangs protrude to their Smilodon maximum, holding my hands up to display the gleaming edges of my claws, widening my stance to show it all off.

Cunningham had gone from red to pale. Good. I wanted him afraid. Knowing how helpless he was, how he was about to get hurt. He needed a dose of that. I doubted it'd make him a better man, but if it made him a crying, broken, screaming man who'd gotten every bruise and moment of fear he'd ever inflicted on Raven back on him a few times over, that'd be enough for me.

Someone wolf-whistled. Blake again, I was pretty sure, dammit, confirmed when Declan said quietly, "And that's why we don't go to Lucky or Knot, darlin'," and then laughed.

"You're no fun," Blake muttered. "I'm just encouraging him."

"Don't think he needs it," Declan replied dryly.

And I really didn't. Despite everything I'd done and endured over the last few hours, I'd never had more energy coursing through me, more focused power, in my life.

Cunningham lunged first, in a move that was probably meant to appear bold and dominant, but that had more of an air of losing his nerve. I swiped at him, raking my claws down his back as I sidestepped, shreds of Italian wool drifting through the air and blood welling up in their place. He howled, spun, and went for me again, and this time I punched the claws of my other hand straight through his side, the sensation of scraping along his ribs setting my teeth on edge.

I ripped out my hand, his blood pouring off my claws in rivulets and splattering the floor. Cunningham staggered, shook his head, and came at me again, eyes glowing and wild, rationality gone, past the point of anything but rage.

Toying with him some more had its appeal—but I glanced up, over Cunningham's oncoming rush, and saw Raven standing there by the booth, his posture unnaturally stiff again and one hand gripping its back hard enough that his tendons stood out.

Shit. Fae appetite for vengeance or no, stated desire to see me beat up his abuser or no, he looked like he'd had enough violence and blood and alpha anger for one night. Possibly even forever.

Time to end it.

I indulged myself with one powerful uppercut that took advantage of my own strength and Cunningham's momentum, snapping his head back in a way that would've instantly killed a human, the impact shuddering all the way up my arm and into my shoulder in an immensely satisfying way. Cunningham went flying, landing on his back on the ground.

He tried to sit up, failed, groaned, and went still.

Gods fucking damn it. I'd missed my chance to sever his spine a few times. Still, I'd splatted him pretty well.

The room erupted in noise and chatter and argument, Declan's voice above it all, taking charge, ordering around his own men and Cunningham's with equal authority. Two men rushed forward and started dragging Cunningham away. Louie had at last crawled out from under the table, and he'd started yelling at everyone indiscriminately.

But none of it really mattered. None of it mattered at all. Cunningham's still-warm blood on the dirty, gritty linoleum felt truly disgusting under my bare feet as I crossed the room back to Raven, but I didn't care.

Raven. His eyes wide, his cropped tux nearly in tatters, the scarf he'd had around his neck long gone, gazing up at me silently. He didn't have a trace of color in his cheeks or lips. Yeah, he'd had enough. What I'd done had been necessary, because to break a shifter's power and authority you had to do it our way. But I made a promise to myself, unspoken but as binding as any fae bargain, that he'd never have that kind of violence in his life again, not if I had anything to say about it. I stopped a foot away, so close, but not touching. I'd need a shower, maybe three, before I was fit to touch anyone, let alone him.

Well, maybe a little bit of touching.

I remembered to retract my claws before I reached across the gap, gently taking his hand in mine, squeezing his fingers. He squeezed back, and his attempt at an exhausted smile lit up his face and the room and my whole fucking life.

"Can we leave now?" he asked, voice unsteady. "We've run for our lives, fallen to our certain deaths down a stairwell, negotiated with a loan shark, and I can't imagine there's any more alpha posturing that could possibly be necessary. Not that you weren't extraordinary. That's a full night of activity. Even by Las Vegas standards." Oh, thank the gods, he'd left out the part where... "And you jumped through a flaming hoop to entertain a dinner party. We can't forget that."

Damn it.

Of course, I noticed he'd left out the part where I told him I loved him. Apparently he did want us to forget about that.

Fuck it. I could wallow in my rejected misery later on. Right now I had Raven, with no disasters hanging over us and all the danger in the rearview.

"Yeah, let's go home. Come home with me? It's not fancy. You'll hate it."

Raven squeezed my hand again, and it went straight to my stupid, aching heart. "I won't hate it. Yes."

We picked our way through the rubble of the club until we reached Blake and Declan, talking in undervoices by the front door.

"Thank you for showing up and evening the odds," I said, as they looked up at our approach. "What are you doing here, anyway?"

Blake grimaced. "He figured out I was hiding something before I had a chance to confess, and then I had to tell him all of it. We had someone keeping an eye on Audacity. Your exit from the premises was hard to miss. And of course we followed along, because I wasn't about to get left out of this. Oh. I never made it to your apartment to drop off your stuff."

He dug around in his jacket pocket and produced my phone, keys, and wallet. I took them, freshly aware of having no pockets of my own, and of the air currents brushing my free-hanging balls. Good thing shifters didn't have a lot of modesty—our clothes didn't shift with us, after all.

"I know it was Blake who came up with the idea of getting you into Cunningham's little soirée," Declan said with a sigh. "If you're wondering if we're about to have another alpha challenge."

Thank the gods for Declan's common sense. It wasn't usually the most prominent alpha trait—case in point, literally everything I'd done recently.

"He was the brains of the operation," I agreed.

"That's a very kind way of putting it," Declan grumbled. "I'd have said the idiot-in-chief."

Blake turned on him and began to argue, and I chose that moment to pull Raven away.

"Someone's waiting to take you home," Declan called after us, and then immediately, "If you think there's a better description for setting up a friend to go into a rival hotel and pose as a fucking circus tiger, then I'd be glad to—"

The club's door slamming shut behind us cut him off, although Blake's reply, a little higher pitched and a whole lot louder, filtered through.

One of Declan's guys ushered us to a car very much like the one we'd stolen from Cunningham, and he didn't even comment on my naked ass on his leather seats.

Raven and I thanked him, but otherwise sat silently in the back during the fifteen minutes it took to get to my apartment complex. We didn't even touch. My hand that wasn't getting blood all over my wallet and phone rested on the seat near him in the hope that he'd take the bait, but he'd folded his own carefully in his lap. And then turned his head to stare out at the passing lights of Vegas, giving me his rumpled hair and a tantalizing glimpse of his long neck to gaze at.

If Declan's driver thought where I lived was a dump, he was too polite to say so, merely hopping out to open Raven's door while I climbed out the other side.

Raven followed me up the stairs, down the long breezeway, and through my door without comment. Finally, I shut it behind us and flicked on the light. Raven glanced around at the shabby couch and shabbier carpeting, the cheap, chipped fake wood coffee table and TV stand, a couple of dirty coffee mugs here and there.

And then he swayed, put his hands over his face, and burst into tears.

Chapter 20

Raven standing in my own apartment, my *den*, all battered and sobbing, pushed every button I had and a few I hadn't even been aware of.

Maybe I should've expected this, what with his months of playing mind games and being used by a total fucking asshole like Cunningham, plus the stress of sneaking around and trying to escape, plus whatever Cunningham had done to him over the last few days, plus escaping and getting shot at and falling twenty stories, seeing me broken and nearly dead, driving the getaway car and making the deal with Louie and watching me and Cunningham fight...

Yeah, it actually showed his remarkable resilience that he hadn't cracked long before this. But the breaking of tension could be a real bitch, and honestly, I might've been having my own freakout if I hadn't already burned that out healing every single part of my body in the most agonizing possible way.

He might not want mine and Cunningham's blood all over him, but no power on Earth could've kept me from wrapping my arms around him, pressing his head to my chest, and holding him tight.

Raven huddled there, shaking violently enough that I was afraid he might've shattered into pieces all over the floor if I hadn't been keeping him together, enclosing him in my big body, kissing his hair, not saying a damn thing—because the only words that came to mind were *I love you*, and that didn't seem likely to comfort him much.

But at last, as he started to wind down, I felt like I had to break the silence. "I know my apartment's a mess, but I didn't think it was that bad," I tried.

A weak, watery, choking laugh that ended on a sob was probably all I deserved for that joke.

"Come on," I tried again. "Let's get in the shower. I can't match whatever amenities they have at Endless Sky, but there's always lots of hot water in this place, at least."

He stumbled as I started to move, so I slipped an arm under his knees and carried him. When had I last scrubbed the shower? Shit. It got pretty clean from all the hot water and soap running down over it all the time, yeah? Although there might be traces of glitter.

Fuck it, he wouldn't care. I didn't think.

Raven leaned his head on my shoulder in a way that pressed literally every button in the universe that a protective alpha who'd recently realized he was hopelessly in love could have, and then I was setting him down gently in the bathroom, flipping on the shower, and helping him undress.

The massive erection I'd grown in those couple of minutes couldn't possibly have escaped his notice; my breath came fast and shallow, and my hands shook as I gently unbuttoned his shirt, tugged down the zipper on his trousers, knelt to ease one strappy sandal and then the other off of his bruised feet. But he didn't remark on it, and when I set the second shoe aside and knelt up to tug his trousers down off his hips, his cock hadn't stirred. I took a hint and didn't touch it, but I did press a kiss to the mark on his thigh where he'd been grazed by flying concrete in the stairwell.

Steam billowed up around us, the heat of it already starting to soothe the last of my aches.

That was nothing to how deeply it soothed my most instinctive nature to slide Raven's shirt off his shoulders, leaving him bare to me, and help him into the shower's warmth and comfort.

Mine. Really mine, now that I'd disposed of that fucking bastard who'd tried to own him, and had never shown a shred of worthiness of the honor.

Of course, I'd only done the easy part, hadn't I? Made a fool of myself on a stage, taken some severe physical damage, and knocked Cunningham on his bleeding ass. Any dumb beast could've pulled that shit off.

"You were the real MVP tonight," I said, the words coming out softly, mingled with the rush of the shower. I'd put Raven under the hot water, and he'd closed his eyes and tipped his head back to let it pour down through the mess of his hair. The water swirling down the drain was running brownish, mostly from where it hit me around his smaller body. Gross. Hopefully he'd think the shower was gross only because of tonight's shenanigans, and not suspect the preexisting condition. "Getting away from him to come and find me was genius. And getting us out of there when I was incapacitated. And taking care of Louie. You think fast on your feet. Thank you for trusting me."

He opened his eyes and blinked at me.

"You earned it," he said simply, and sucked in a shuddering breath. Psyching himself up for something?

I tried to brace myself for what came next. Letting me down easy, possibly. Except that it wouldn't be easy. If he tried to let me down now, it'd hurt worse than that fall in the stairwell. That, I'd healed from.

"I always assumed my way was the best way," he said after a moment. "My people's way. That everyone fends for himself, takes the consequences of bad decisions alone. We don't—" His chest heaved with another convulsive deep breath. "We don't love." The words came out so quietly I almost didn't understand what I'd heard. "That's not something we do."

Then it sank in.

And the tightening, twisting pain in my chest did, in fact, hurt worse than the fall. Yep. This was the fairy version of "it's not you, it's me."

My arms shook with the need to pull him close and never let him go. I might lose my mind if I never kissed him again.

But Raven had just gotten away from one greedy, possessive alpha who didn't care about what he wanted.

"You don't need to explain," I said, and I sounded like a robot, because if I let the slightest emotion seep into my voice, I'd lose my fragile grip on my self-control. "You don't owe me anything. You own me, actually."

"For the sake of your mortal sensibilities, I'd like to say I don't really own you, but in order for the magic to work, it had to be real." He went all shifty, gazing over my shoulder. "I don't suppose you can feel it?"

"I can feel it. I'm always going to know where you are. Do you feel it too?"

His eyes snapped back to me. "And that doesn't bother you? That you—that we're—you'll never be free of me!"

Maybe I hadn't collapsed in tears, but that didn't mean I was running on a long fuse, either. What I had left of my patience abruptly exploded.

"Okay, your kind doesn't love," I snapped, leaning forward into his space, wishing I could keep all the hurt and heartbreak inside, but knowing I'd lost that battle. "You won't ever feel about me the way I feel about you. Fine. I fucking get it. And it's all right, because I did everything because I love you, not because I expect you to love me. But do you not understand what it even means? In the abstract? Raven. I love you. Of course I don't want to be fucking free of you! I want to mate you, and keep you, and never let you go, and I want you to want that too, except you can't. Okay? It's not complicated!"

He gazed up at me, long lashes glittering with water, lips parted. Like something out of a story, one of those water spirits that were so beautiful actual gods fell on their knees.

"Tony, ah. We don't love, but we—that is, I mean, I—oh—"

One kiss, just one, bending my neck down so I could nip at his lower lip.

"Mmm. It's not that, it's not that I don't know what love is, but I'm trying to—"

I didn't want to hear it. He could toss me the rest of the way off the metaphorical cliff in a few minutes.

Another kiss, and he melted against me, tipped back over the arm that went around him without my conscious volition. When I pushed a thigh between his legs, he moaned, and now his cock had joined the party. Mine hadn't ever gone down, and it stabbed him in the stomach without shame.

Raven pulled his mouth away, thrust against my leg, and bit the side of my neck, teeth sharper than a human's, stinging, fucking perfect.

"That's what you do, isn't it?" he gasped, and nipped me again, and now it was my turn to tip my head back and groan, that bite zinging all the way down to my balls, weakening my knees. "Bite. To mate. To show how you feel. I can't tell you the way you'd want, but I can show you, too, if you let me."

Oh, hell, I'd knot him against the wall of the shower, and then we'd be screwed, still not washed up and exhausted and stumbling around pulling the shower curtain down.

Instead, I gave in to gravity and knelt down in front of him, grabbing him by the hips.

"Oh!" He caught at my shoulders for balance, but I solved that problem by pinning him against the wall. "I was going to do that for you," he said breathlessly, as I nuzzled into his abdomen. "That is, assuming you're intending to—oh, you are," because I couldn't wait one more moment, and I wrapped my mouth around his cock and sucked him down.

His hands flew up to my head, burying in my hair, and I didn't resist him, going where he pushed me more willingly than any tiger owned by a fairy had probably ever gone. The shower beat down on my shoulders, surrounding me in noise and heat, and Raven writhed all slippery and smooth under my hands, only for me.

The cries he let out as I sucked and swallowed echoed off the ceiling and his scent enveloped me, sweet and lemony and suffused with sex, his pleasure filling all my senses.

Gods, I wanted to feel him come. And I did, as he clenched his fingers and nearly tugged my hair out by the roots, thrust into me, and wailed, shooting into my eager mouth and down my throat.

Raven's come tasted like a lemon drop cocktail, lemon sugar on the edge and then the bite of vodka on the back of my palate, only salty, and more intoxicating than any bartender could craft. For a moment, the tether between us went blindingly bright, the magic of Raven's ownership of me strengthening and pulsing. I moaned around his cock, the sensation that washed through me akin to an orgasm, only in some nonphysical part of me I didn't even have a word for.

He gave a full-body shudder too, and then after a few more convulsive twitches of his fingers, he went limp against the wall.

I pulled off and leaned my forehead against his hip, catching my breath and savoring the lingering heat of him on my tongue.

But I wasn't done with him. My cock throbbed painfully, the shower's attenuated spray a horrible tease, but that could wait. I'd been waiting a lot longer than it had for a certain type of satisfaction. Besides, Raven deserved the full service package, now that he wasn't trying talk me out of using my mouth anymore.

And if I wrecked Raven completely, reducing him to a whimpering mess that I'd have to carry to bed and fuck all night, while he cried with pleasure instead of sorrow and fear and strain, I could live with that too.

When I slid a hand under his thigh and put it over my shoulder, he just let out a soft moan. When I lifted the second, forcing him to brace his back against the wall, he yelped. Pushing his pretty balls and softened cock up and out of my way got a, "Tony, what— oh," followed by a drawn-out, filthy moan as I fastened my mouth over his tight, pink hole and sucked as hard as I'd sucked his cock.

Oh, I'd known he'd be even sweeter, here between his legs at the center of him, and I'd been right. I teased my raspy tongue around in a circle, tracing his rim, forcing him to spread himself wider by getting my head between his inner thighs. The angle gave me a crick in my neck, but I wouldn't have cared if it killed me. So soft, so delicate, stretching around my tongue as I fucked it into him, and how the hell had my enormous cock and knot fit in him, much less pounded into him…

Raven's hips juddered as he tried to ride my face, spreading his legs, moaning, grinding his hole against my lapping tongue.

Gods, I was so hard too, hard enough that I might be willing to try knotting the bathtub's overflow drain if I didn't get inside him soon, but he was reaching a crescendo, letting out high-pitched, helpless wails as he bounced up and down and tilted his body to seek out more friction, more of anything I could give him.

When I thought he might explode if I didn't, I pulled back, slipped my hand between his legs, and shoved two fingers into his wet, loosened hole, crooked at just the right angle.

Raven collapsed, red-faced and shaking, his still-limp cock dripping another spurt of come. I licked it off the tip, kissed the side of his shaft, nuzzled his balls.

"Tony," he murmured. "Tony, oh." As if he'd forgotten any other words.

Good.

"I love you," I said, because I'd forgotten any other words, too. The sound he made at that was something I knew I'd replay in my mind late at night for years.

Getting to my feet, keeping him upright, and then turning us around a bit—with him draped against my side half-conscious—so I could finally wash myself off with some soap took a lot of concentration, and some fumbling. But I got us there eventually, managed to rub us both down with a towel, and then swung him up in my arms again, carrying him out of the bathroom and tumbling us both into my bed still dripping but mostly clean.

He sprawled where I'd tossed him, wet hair spread out enough to get both of my pillows all damp. Half-lidded eyes regarded me lazily, gleaming like obsidian. His gaze snagged on my erection, which stood out purplish and rock-hard and eager, finding his direction as unerringly as our magical tie.

I surveyed him too, from the top of his silky, messy head down to his still-perfect-when-bruised toes, pausing in between at small pink nipples and the elegant lines of ribs and the slight jut of his hipbones. Maybe I should kiss his toes and make it better. But there was so much else I wanted to kiss. Paralyzed with indecision, I leaned down over him, breathing him in. Clean, safe, satisfied, and in my bed. This moment could last forever, as far as I was concerned, with or without ever actually having an orgasm of my own.

"Are you going to listen to me now?" Raven asked, voice a little slurred. "Or do you need to fuck me first before you'll be calm enough?"

Oh, he always had the best ideas, one of the biggest reasons why I loved him. I rolled on top, nudging his legs open with my knees, and reached over to dig around in the drawer of my nightstand. I didn't bring people home very often, but I knew I had to have a tube of something back there.

"I can multitask." My cockhead rubbed behind his balls, not quite slippery enough to push inside him, but wet and satiny, and my eyes rolled back in my head. Yeah, I might be lying about the multitasking. I found the lube and popped it open. "I'll listen while I fuck you. Stop telling me why you'll never love me, though. That's not going to put me in the mood."

The ensuing heavy beat of silence reminded me how tough an audience Raven could be when my jokes sucked.

"Fuck me, then," Raven said, and shifted his legs to give me more room. "After today. After, after everything." His voice shook. "I want you inside me, where I can feel you."

Prepping him didn't take long, even though part of me wanted to linger, in case I never got to stroke his hole again, watch him squirm, see the tightness of his rim stretching to accommodate my fingers, all pink and shiny. You never knew with fairies. Fae things tended to up and disappear.

But I needed him too badly to wait any longer, and once I'd slicked him up enough that he wouldn't get hurt I lined up and sank in deep.

As I bottomed out, the thickest part of my cock opening him up, Raven wrapped his arms around me, clutching my back, pulling me down almost frantically.

"I thought I'd watched you die," he said wildly, and his voice hitched. My chest tight, I clutched him close, braced my knee, and thrust into him, so deep I punched the air out of him in a gasp. "Tony, I thought you were, yes, that, please—you were willing to, to sacrifice everything for me, and no one of my own kind would ever have done it—Tony!"

Fucking Christ, so tight, so perfect around me, his nails gouging down my back, his panting breaths echoing in my ear as I buried my face in his hair, his magic lighting me up from the inside the way I was filling him to the limit, the grip of his thighs around my hips, urging me on.

There was that humming in my ears again, the way the coin had sounded, almost. Only this had a higher, more melodic timbre, and I knew it was him, his pleasure, his desire, his inherent magic, soaking through my skin and suffusing me.

I lost myself in him, shaking apart, my climax torn out of me by the whirlwind that was Raven. He cried out as I knotted him, forcing it as deep as it could go and pushing my come into him, and he pulled me even deeper than that, as if he wanted to consume me.

The world came back slowly, in fits and starts: the sweat cooling on my shoulders and legs, his still-damp hair stuck to my face, my breath stuttering as he shifted a bit under me, tugging on my knot—and on that point under my ribs where his magic had burrowed in and taken up residence.

Raven was petting me, soothing, up and down my spine. He sighed, turned his head, nuzzled my ear, kissed the side of my neck and made me shiver.

"Were you listening?" he asked, the words hushed but still startling in the quiet of the bedroom. "We don't love. We don't even trust. We hide our names, we make careful bargains, we form alliances, and we dally with those we find beautiful. But we never sacrifice."

He sighed and kissed me again. Was that all? Would a subtle fairy lover have understood what he meant? I didn't, although if I hadn't been so bone-weary and wrung out, maybe I'd have been able to make sense of it. To me, it mostly sounded like my old college buddy's descriptions of going to law school. He was grateful, I could tell that much. But I'd never wanted his gratitude.

But hang on, there was something tickling the edge of my brain…

I managed to push myself up on my elbows to see his face, and I stole a kiss along the way, lingering, soft and sweet.

When I pulled back, his eyes were troubled, a furrow between his arched brows.

"Tony, I—"

"You sacrificed yourself for me, though," I cut in abruptly.

"Or you tried, anyway. When we were on the stairs. You tried to give yourself up so they'd let me go. And then you helped me get out of there when I couldn't move on my own, even though you could've died if my plan didn't work. Which you didn't think it would."

He laughed a little, shaking his head. "Be honest, if you were me, would you have immediately said, 'Oh, what a well-thought-out idea, I have complete confidence'? You jumped through a flaming hoop on the command of a man with rhinestones on his jacket."

"Speaking of sacrificing for you," I grumbled, and raised my eyebrows at him. "And don't dodge the question."

"I know," he said softly. "Believe me, I know. Also, those were statements, and you didn't ask a quest—oh, very well, there's no need to flash those eyes at me. Yes. I was willing to sacrifice for you. Because you earned my trust. I told you that. No one ever has before. You changed me," he added, sounding not all that pleased about it, "and I think, I think I belong to you as much as you do to me, actually."

Not without a mating bite, but I choked that comment down. Slowly. I needed to think before I acted, for once, and go slowly, because I suddenly realized, with a warm, joyous ballooning of hope, that Raven hadn't been trying to let me down easy—or at all. He'd been trying to understand something that had, for the entirety of his life, been not only totally beyond his comprehension but outside the fabric of his reality. When we'd met, his disregard for anything beyond his need to undo his magical fuck-up had left me baffled and angry and vengeful, beating my head against a brick wall of a completely different way of existing in the world.

But I'd made the effort. I'd pushed, and I'd tried, and I'd worked at it stubbornly (and sometimes suicidally) until I'd helped him to a solution that fit his parameters. Raven was worth it.

He seemed to be trying to do the same. For me. To act like he loved me the human way, even if he couldn't wrap his brain around the idea that he might be capable of feeling it, too.

Fairies. For fuck's sake.

I kissed him again, because I could.

"Answer me this, then," I said, after thinking about it for a second. I had to meet him halfway on this, try to put it in terms that would be common ground. "Would being with me make you happy? You know, the human way. Kind of human. Like me. Sharing a bed, meals, a life. Somewhere that's not Vegas, maybe? Not sleeping with anyone else, I can't do the free and easy, anyone who's beautiful thing."

"Yes," he answered without hesitation. His dawning smile lit him up from the inside, making him even more luminous than usual. "*Yes.*"

Another kiss seemed necessary, and then more kisses, and then I'd started to rock my hips again, lazily feeling out how much I'd stretched and owned him, how much more thoroughly I could do it again.

I took him like that, at my leisure. At our leisure. Free of anyone else, or any expectations. All mine, because I could make him happy in a way no one else in two realms could.

We didn't break my bed like we'd destroyed the ones at those two hotels, mainly because my one investment in decent furniture had been a steel-reinforced, alpha-proof bed frame, but it creaked ominously, and Raven laughed, high and unselfconscious, dissolving into giggles when I nipped at his throat and growled.

Somewhere near the end of the night, as the desert's pink sunrise started to filter through the half-open blinds, I tucked Raven closer against my chest, staring up at the shadowy ceiling. His head fit perfectly on my shoulder, and I only breathed in his hair and started to choke once in a while, something I'd need to get used to.

"There's one thing I want," I said, and Raven stirred and murmured something incoherent, mostly asleep and annoyed that I wouldn't shut up, if I had to guess. I squeezed his waist. "Seriously. One thing. Will you ever trust me enough to tell me your name, do you think?"

He didn't answer me for long enough that I thought he'd probably pretend he hadn't heard me.

And then he said, "I already did. Now will you let me sleep? You may have noticed, but I had a long day."

He already had. That second night, when he'd cried.

"Raven? Really?"

His head popped up, indignation in every line of his expression. "As if you have any room to talk, Tony the Tiger!"

"That wasn't what I—there's nothing wrong with being called Raven—"

"No, there certainly isn't!"

"—but you gave me your real name? When that's something you'd never do. With anyone. Right?"

His ferocious scowl lost some force in the context of his sex-fluffed hair and kiss-swollen lips.

"I already told you," he gritted out, "you're an exception. To everything. I couldn't resist you, and at this moment you're making me regret it. Now will you, please, for the love of all the spirits of earth and air, go. To. Sleep?"

He dropped back down onto my shoulder with more force than necessary, tugged the blanket up, grumbled, and squirmed around, settling himself like an angry cat.

I closed my eyes and held him tightly, safe and warm and— truly mine. Not because I'd claimed him, although I had, and not because I'd fought for him and jumped through hoops and nearly died for him.

Because he loved me, in not so many words. His exception. For a fairy, that had practically been hearts and flowers.

Without a care in the world, and with everything I cared most about in the world snuggled in my arms, I did as he told me, and I went to sleep. It really had been a seriously long fucking day.

Chapter 21

"Yeah?" I tossed the phone into the center console, only listening with half an ear, because an unknown number almost always meant someone trying to sell me solar panels for a roof I didn't own. "Fuck! Sorry, not you. I'm in traffic."

Why did I always end up crossing the Strip? I knew better. Everyone who actually lived here knew better, although hopefully I wouldn't be living here much longer.

A pause that somehow communicated baffled offense echoed down the line.

"Is this Tony Kaplan?" said a prim, faintly accented female voice, sounding as if she hoped I'd say no.

"Yeah, that's me. What?"

"I asked if you were Tony Kaplan, and you already confirmed that," she said, and now she sounded like she hoped I'd jump off a bridge. "So I don't understand why you're requesting clarification."

I spared the phone a disbelieving glance, nearly rear-ended the SUV in front of me, and bit back another curse.

"I was asking you what you want," I said, with as much restraint as I had left in me.

Raven had been gone for three weeks now. He'd spent nearly that long with me first, and then kissed me, promised to return once he'd "wrapped up a few things" in his own realm, and swanned off to Endless Sky. My patience with literally everything had worn tissue-thin in his absence. I missed him. I fucking needed him, and I'd never needed anyone before, except my family. I ached for him, bone-deep, and even though our magical link shone as bright as ever, always orienting me toward a freaking fairy spa in Summerlin, I couldn't shake the fear that this was the one time a fae would break a promise. Maybe he'd left a loophole that I was too not-fae to notice.

She sighed. "I want to confirm your appointment, Mr. Kaplan."

"I don't have an appointment with anyone. You have the wrong number, or something. Look, could you—"

"You're booked for a massage at Endless Sky this afternoon at two," she snapped. "That is in half an hour. If you—"

I slammed on the brakes way too hard, to a chorus of angry honks from behind me. An apologetic wave in the rearview mirror got me flipped off, and I hit the gas again, still not quite breathing.

"Endless Sky? You said Endless Sky?"

"Yes," she said, and that bridge she wanted me to jump off of had gotten a lot higher. "Endless Sky. In half an hour."

"I'll be there. Thank you. I'll be there in—"

"Good. Was that so difficult?" The line went dead, my screen blinking with the end of the call.

Oh, my gods. Fairies. No wonder Raven liked it better on this side of reality.

And he must, right? Since he had to be coming back. Raven, Raven, Raven…my heart beat to the rhythm of his name, and I didn't even care how incredibly lame it was that I'd think something like that.

I'd only been on my way to get coffee and kill some time, so I didn't have anything to cancel. I hung a right to get out of the traffic jam and hit the gas.

Raven would be so pissed to be picked up in this same shitty car, but he'd have to deal with it. The morning he'd left, before he broached the subject of said departure, he'd told me airily, "I put some money in your bank account."

I'd looked up from my laptop, the screen full of job listings in various cities in the Pacific Northwest. My parents and sister would be thrilled to have me closer to them and were champing at the bit to meet Raven, and he'd agreed that the forests and the ocean sounded like more his speed than neon and dusty rocks. So we were making some preliminary plans. Nothing concrete yet. But I had a good feeling about it.

"Money?" I asked. "Wait, how do you have access to my bank account? Not that I mind, but I mean, how much money? Why? Are we talking twenty bucks for gas, half the rent, what?"

"Oh, you know," he said, and fluttered a hand at me, sauntering over to steal my coffee cup and then dodging as I swatted at his ass. If he didn't want me grabbing it, he shouldn't be hanging around the apartment in nothing but a lace thong and one of my undershirts, was all I was saying.

"No, I don't know, Raven, that's why I asked."

He raised an eyebrow at me over the rim of my own damn coffee and took an obnoxiously loud sip. "You should get a better car," he said. "And new clothes. Oh, and a house. The neighbors put another note on the door complaining about the noise. It's time for us to move on."

"A house," I repeated, wondering—not for the first time, almost certainly not for the last—if I'd lost my mind, or if he had. "A car? And a house? How much money, seriously?"

He drained my coffee and handed the empty mug back to me with a smile. Gods help me, I adored him.

"Enough," he called back over his shoulder, disappearing into the bedroom. "Human money doesn't exist, really. So I never run out, now that no one's monitoring my spending. Get a new car while I'm away for a few days, will you? I hate buying cars. That kind of vulgar, imprecise transaction is so unbearable. No one in this realm knows how to write a contract properly."

"You should talk to my lawyer friend, he'd—wait, hang on a minute, while you're where?" I said, and jumped up and followed him into the bedroom.

That had inevitably ended up with him bent over the side of the bed with the torn thong hanging off one of his ankles, with him making a hell of a lot more noise the neighbors would hate. But he'd also filled me in on his intent to go home, see his mother, and make sure his affairs there were in order.

After which had come the kissing, and the swanning, and my black, miserable mood.

It had occurred to me later that day, staring in disbelief at more digits on the screen than my bank account had ever dreamed of, that Raven hadn't been kept by Cunningham in a style he'd been unused to. In fact, reading between the lines, he'd been slumming it with a casino mogul, let alone with me. The only reason he didn't already have a replacement for the luxury car Cunningham had bought for him was his distaste for car dealerships, and it even crossed my mind that he might've gone through the fairy portal for a bit with the specific aim of forcing me to run those errands for him on my own, so he wouldn't have to be bothered.

No, surely not. Not even Raven would travel between freaking worlds to avoid spending an afternoon signing paperwork.

But maybe.

Anyway, I hadn't bought a new car, because I was stubborn like that, although I had bookmarked a few gorgeous, rural real estate listings on the Washington coast that I thought Raven would like.

But now he'd come back, or presumably would at two, and I couldn't get there fast enough.

Aside from my own desperation to see him, hold him, and kiss him senseless, I had a lot to tell him, just not about cars. I'd called Declan to ask his opinion about Cunningham, whether he'd cause us any more trouble. Declan had informed me, with totally unsuppressed glee, that everyone had heard about me wiping the floor with him, and he'd left the country to escape the embarrassment. Declan didn't think he'd be back. Most of Cunningham's valued business contacts were shifters, and they now thought he was a joke.

"Blake's on my ass to put on a tiger show at the Morrigan," Declan added. "I guess that friend of his you conned into getting you into Audacity was upset about his loss of revenue and worried about his rescue tigers going hungry. I think they could just eat him, but no one asked me. Anyway. Any chance you'd perform? He told Blake that before you kidnapped the host's boyfriend, you were the best big cat he'd ever worked with."

Declan had burst into laughter at my stunned, horrified silence, but honestly, I'd been considering it. I did owe Axel a lot. I'd told Declan I'd get back to him.

At least I didn't have to apologize to Sean. After parking the car for me—in a totally different garage than the one attached to the emergency stairs, because he was a fucking stoner—he'd lost his nerve and quit on the spot. Declan, bless him, had followed through on his promise, and I'd gotten a text from Sean with a thumbs-up selfie wearing the Morrigan's much less hideous valet uniform.

And none of that, satisfying as it was, had given me much joy without Raven to immediately share it with.

I couldn't wait in the parking lot of Endless Sky; I was too impatient. So I pushed open its faintly glowing door at a quarter till two, kind of surprised that it even opened for me. The lobby was disappointingly normal, with some plush chairs and a rack of bottles of lotion or shampoo or something. The place stank of magic, though, and I had to fight back a sneeze.

The tallest, most muscularly intimidating and stunningly beautiful woman I'd ever seen sat behind the desk, her coils of shining brown hair piled on top of her head in a gravity-defying way. On another day, in another life, I'd probably have taken my chances with a violent death and asked her out to dinner...but then she spoke and ruined the effect.

"You must be Mr. Kaplan," she said in a tone reminiscent of every disapproving sixth-grade teacher in the world, her voice unmistakably the same as it had been on the phone. "You're early. But so is your appointment, so you can go through to room four. Don't go anywhere else in the building. You might not return."

Without even bothering to thank her, kind of scared of how she might react, I just nodded and shoved open the door to her right and into the hallway beyond. I found room four down a ways on the left, and I sucked in a deep breath, bracing myself for a letdown. Maybe Raven had sent a messenger to tell me he'd changed his mind.

Maybe he'd sent his gods-damned mother to turn me into a diseased frog.

But when I turned the knob and opened the door, there he was. Sitting on the edge of the massage table with his bare feet dangling, his hair up in a knot with the loose part flowing down around his shoulders, wrapped in some kind of tunic toga thing made out of a shimmering black cloth that could've been cut out of the desert sky at night.

And smiling tentatively, eyes shining brighter than the stars—as if he could have any doubt about what reception he'd get from me.

Two steps across the room and I'd swept him into my arms, bending down to claim his mouth all over again, the scent of him drowning out the spa's weird magic and drowning me, too.

I never wanted to come up for air, but at last I had to, pulling back enough to look into his eyes. His smile had blossomed into something bright enough to outshine every star there was.

"Did you miss me?" he asked, and it was probably the only stupid thing he'd ever said to me.

"I love you," I said, and he pulled me down to kiss me again.

We toppled over onto the massage table, my hands already busy finding their way under the toga thing, searching out smooth bare skin and warmth, Raven laughing into my kiss and trying to rip off my pants. I moved down his body, needing my mouth where my hands were.

"Mate me," he gasped, as I kissed my way up his thigh.

My head popped up like he'd electrocuted me, and I felt like it, too. "Here? On this—the massage table's toast if we do that, Raven."

He propped himself on his elbows and looked down his pointy nose at me. "Yes, here. Now. Tony, I didn't tell you before I left, because I didn't want to get your hopes up, but I went home mainly to find out if there would be any magical consequences of your kind of bond. For you, since I—you know."

"Own me?"

"Yes, that. And there aren't, by the way, as far as the experts can tell me. We can mate anytime we want. Such as now, for example," he said pointedly.

We were going to have a chat about keeping me in the loop in future, but I could see why he'd kept his own counsel on this one. If mating had been magically impossible, the disappointment might have crushed me.

But instead—gods, I was the luckiest man alive. He'd been thinking about being my mate, wanting it, trying to make me happy. Not that he needed to try very hard.

"You could've come home for that." My apartment might not be a bower of roses, but it had to be better than a fairy salon. On the other hand, the cart in the corner had a ton of bottles, and some of them looked like that fancy lube he'd had when we met. I'd started to have my doubts about what services this place offered, actually. Better not to explore that in too much depth. "Why here?"

He bit his lip, cheeks going pink. "I didn't want to wait," he said, uncharacteristically shyly. "I wanted you to—I wanted to see you the second I came through the portal. I wanted you."

Like when you got off the plane after being far from home, and you were in the too-bright, too-loud airport all tired and lonely, and then there was the person you loved, familiar and comforting and real.

It caught at my heart, a string only he knew how to pluck. After everything he'd been through, everywhere he'd been, I was his piece of home.

"You have me," I said, and bent down again, pushing aside the fabric to lay him bare for me.

The massage table collapsed halfway through me driving him wild with my mouth between his legs, and we rolled off of the wreckage onto the thick rug that had been next to it, my jeans open in front but still caught around my hips, his fairy garment hanging in loose folds around him like a robe and his body glimmering pale and lovely, tantalizingly half-hidden.

He climbed on top, blushing but intent as he spread his thighs wide around me and worked himself down onto my cock, trembling with the strain, eyes going wide as he took me in for the first time in three weeks.

"Easy," I said. "There's no rush."

Even though there was, because I might not last long enough to get all the way inside him if he didn't hurry up. My heart thundered like I'd been racing, and I could hardly breathe.

At last he took me all the way, riding me slowly, panting, eyes heavy-lidded.

"Lean down, sweetness," I said, and gently eased him onto my chest. It wouldn't be the easiest way to do this, given the angle, but when had anything with Raven ever been easy, exactly? Life was never going to be predictable with him. I couldn't fucking wait.

I rocked up into him, impaling him on my full length and then withdrawing enough to make him moan, pushing his hair aside to bare his slender neck.

There, right there. That soft, irresistible bit of his skin. My mouth watered.

As he cried out, shuddering in my arms and spreading heat over my stomach, I let myself go. My knot punched up into him, harder than I'd meant to, but gods, his body clenched around me like a blood-hot, slippery vise, and I curled down and set my mouth over the curve of his shoulder and neck.

Fangs down, pricking his skin...and I bit, my alpha power surging and the connection he'd formed when he bought me sparking up to meet it, a swirl of color and sensation and pure, perfect, spine-tingling magic.

The bond had formed, pure and strong, and I dropped my head back and roared in triumph, rattling the windows and the bottles on the cart.

Silence fell. The bond shone between and around us, steady and bright, the sum of my love and his loyalty made tangible. Raven lay still on my chest, rising and falling with my heaving breaths, and I put my arms around him, stroked his back, craned my neck to get a good look at my mark. The imprint of my fangs stood out crimson on his white skin.

"Oh," he breathed at last. "I didn't expect to feel it like this." He lifted his head and gazed at me as if he'd never seen me before. "That's you loving me. That—I can't even describe it."

The wonder in his voice mirrored my own.

"You don't need to," I said hoarsely. "I'm the one feeling it."

"It's incredible. I can't possibly tell anyone I know about this, they'll all want one."

"Too bad," I said, laughing, and wondering if I could start making a sideline income selling tickets to Lucky or Knot to over-sexed fairies. No, probably better not. Even Dominic didn't deserve that. "You own me, and there's only one of me."

"Yes," he said, and no one in the history of the world had ever sounded more smug. "I do. And you—" His lips twitched, and his eyes sparkled, and his stomach quivered, vibrating my cock and knot where they were buried inside him. "I can say this now that you're my mate, can't I? You're—ha—you're grr—"

"Don't you dare!" I growled, but it didn't sound all that convincing, not even to me.

Raven collapsed in laughter, howling into my chest, happy and free and absolutely, undeniably mine.

He and my sister were going to love each other, and make my life hell in the process. Forever, at every family gathering, and on the phone to each other while I made dinner, and with Raven teasing me about him being the favorite sibling while I held him in my arms in our bed, in that beautiful house we'd buy in Washington, with the wind in the trees and the stars shining above. My mate. My love. My family, and our beautiful future.

Even under torture, like being forced to watch that fucking online video of my circus performance at the dinner party from hell, I wouldn't admit it out loud...but that actually sounded, well. Great. It sounded great.

The End

Coin

It took Tony and Raven a lot of trouble and danger to find the solution to their problem—and I'm still more than a little miffed that they thought that problem was *me*. Me! When I did everything in my power, such as generously thwarting their original plans, in order to help them find their way to belonging to one another forever. Well, all right, not everything in my power...I could've given them the answer, but what fun would that have been? My abilities range far and wide, from singing to get my point across, to matchmaking unlikely grouches with their sunshiny perfect other halves, to sticking with bebothered secret agents until I turn their luck for the better. And sometimes I simply cause trouble. You'll never know until you read my stories...

The coin's other adventures can be found in the Fortune Favors the Fae series.

***

Thanks for reading *Lucky or Knot*!

To find out if Declan MacKenna really did kidnap another alpha, make him his sex slave, and then stage a shootout in the desert— or if Blake was truly that much of an asshole before Declan mated him—read *The Alpha's Gamble*. It's part of the Mismatched Mates series, but it can be read as a standalone. Happy reading!

Acknowledgments

My biggest thanks go to Amy Pittel, who worked tirelessly with me to make sure this book got out in the world despite having other commitments and, you know, a life.

Great gratitude is also due to Alessandra Hazard for giving an opinion on the first part of the book, and to Cora Rose for reading all the way through and cheerleading like crazy.

In the acknowledgments of *The Alpha's Gamble*, I gave a shout-out to Bobbie, who came up with the name Lucky or Knot. She'd originally suggested it as a name for what became the Morrigan Casino, but I thought it worked amazingly for an all-alpha strip club. I'd be remiss if I didn't thank her again here. What a great name. I hope I've done it justice!

Get in Touch

I love hearing from readers! Find me in the following places, where you can get more info about my books, sign up for my newsletter, or follow along as I post memes and rail at the writing gods.

 eliotgrayson.com

amazon.com/stores/author/B07NL54KNF

facebook.com/groups/eliotgrayson

@eliotgraysonauthor

Also by Eliot Grayson

Mismatched Mates:
The Alpha's Warlock
Captive Mate
A Very Armitage Christmas
The Alpha Experiment
Lost and Bound
Lost Touch
The Alpha Contract
The Alpha's Gamble

Blood Bonds:
First Blood
Twice Bitten

Goddess-Blessed:
The Replacement Husband
The Reluctant Husband
Yuletide Treasure

Portsmouth:
Like a Gentleman
Once a Gentleman

Santa Rafaela:
The One Decent Thing
A Totally Platonic Thing
Need a Hand?

Beautiful Beasts:
Corin and the Courtier
Deven and the Dragon

Twilight Mages:
The Royal Curse
The Captive's Curse

Brought to Light

Undercover

The Wrong Rake

Lucky or Knot